Praise for

HEELS OVER HEAD

"Clay Small does a masterful job in his debut as a novelist. The uncanny twists and turns kept me up well past my bedtime, as I simply could not put the book down. You won't be able to either!"

—**DAVID NOVAK,** CO-FOUNDER AND RETIRED CHAIRMAN, YUM! BRANDS, INC., AUTHOR OF *THE EDUCATION OF AN ACCIDENTAL CEO, TAKING PEOPLE WITH YOU,* AND *O GREAT ONE!*

"This is not a testimonial. It's a standing ovation to Clay and his book, a truly vivid and entertaining piece of literature from start to finish, back and forth. Clay clearly masters many aspects of writing, and his description of my hometown of Buenos Aires—and more importantly, its ambience and the way we *porteños* behave—is simply perfect. It is one of the best books I have read in years."

—**MARCELO BOMBAU,** A *PORTEÑO*

"A raucous ride through the worlds of hoity-toity academia and high-stakes finance with conflicting undercurrents of ruinous revenge, mistaken distrust, and enduring love controlling the flow—a fast-paced read that was hard to put down."

—**HUBERT CROUCH,** AUTHOR OF *CRIED FOR NO ONE* AND *THE WORD*

"A well-spun contemporary yarn thick with threads of characters and situations that are not always what they appear to be. Anyone can relate to and everyone can thoroughly enjoy *Heels over Head*. Prepare for a fun and captivating ride."

—**TOD J. MACKENZIE,** SENIOR VP, COMMUNICATIONS & PUBLIC AFFAIRS, ARAMARK

"*Heels over Head* furiously kicks in from page one and keeps right on kicking throughout the enthralling story of how misinterpretations and grudges can turn into deadly revenge. I found myself in an all-out reading sprint to get to the finish!"

—**RUSTY RUEFF,** APPOINTEE TO THE PRESIDENT'S ADVISORY COMMITTEE FOR THE ARTS

"*Heels over Head* is an adventure, a whodunit, and a road-trip story all in one. It hooked me with its colorful characters whose accents and turns of speech almost audibly jump off the page. Clay Small brings his own decades of business expertise to bear, not just with insights into how executives think, behave, and sometimes misbehave, but also by confronting his characters with modern issues like gender and marriage equality. As we follow his villains, heroes, and everyone in between, Small cleverly gives us a window into the biases that still exist in the business world. That added dimension will leave you thinking—long after you've untangled the tightly woven storylines that make this book so fun to read."

—**JESSICA SHORTALL,** AUTHOR OF *WORK. PUMP. REPEAT.*, SOCIAL ENTREPRENEUR, LGBTQ RIGHTS ADVOCATE

"Clay has written a captivating and intelligent book that uniquely captures the richness of the connectivity among business, academia, and society in the wonderful city of Dallas, Texas. If you've ever lived in Dallas, you will immediately connect to the characters and the locations described in the book. Everyone else will be simply delighted by the twists and turns of revenge stretching from Wichita to Dallas to Buenos Aires."

—**KELLY MAHON TULLIER,** EXECUTIVE VICE PRESIDENT AND GENERAL COUNSEL, VISA, INC.

"Clay Small has populated his novel with a cast of characters who are both imaginative and credible. He has used his intimate firsthand knowledge of the 21st century American university and global corporation to weave these characters through a thoroughly enjoyable and ultimately satisfying tale of intrigue and suspense. *Heels over Head* was for me the proverbial page-turner, and I sincerely hope I have not read the last of Professor Henry Lindon."

—**JACK WILKERSON,** PROFESSOR, WAKE FOREST UNIVERSITY SCHOOL OF BUSINESS

CLAY G. SMALL

GREENLEAF
BOOK GROUP PRESS

This book is a work of fiction. Names, characters, businesses, organizations, places, events, and incidents are either a product of the author's imagination or are used fictitiously. Any resemblance to actual persons, living or dead, events, or locales is entirely coincidental.

Published by Greenleaf Book Group Press
Austin, Texas
www.gbgpress.com

Distributed by Greenleaf Book Group

For ordering information or special discounts for bulk purchases, please contact
Greenleaf Book Group at PO Box 91869, Austin, TX 78709, 512.891.6100.

Design and composition by Greenleaf Book Group
Cover design by Greenleaf Book Group
Cover images: ©iStockphoto.com/lillisphotography; ©Shutterstock.com/BillionPhotos

Cataloging-in-Publication data is available.

Print ISBN: 978-1-62634-343-6

eBook ISBN: 978-1-62634-345-0

Part of the Tree Neutral® program, which offsets the number of trees consumed in the production and printing of this book by taking proactive steps, such as planting trees in direct proportion to the number of trees used: www.treeneutral.com

Printed in the United States of America on acid-free paper

17 18 19 20 21 22 10 9 8 7 6 5 4 3 2 1

First Edition

This book is dedicated to Miss O, M.E., and the six guys.

I’m not sure what they mean by “revenge is a dish best served cold.”
But I do know this—nobody’s ever satisfied with a single helping.

—HEMAN LINDON, MCPHERSON, KANSAS

PART 1

THE TATS

1

"What about academia interests you?" asked Southerland University's president, Phil Thomas. His nonchalant tone bordered on indifference.

What the hell am I doing here? Henry Lindon wondered. He took in the room's somber amalgamation of mahogany walls, drab portraits of past university presidents, and worn Persian rugs. *Is this really for me?*

He was thrust back into the moment when he realized Thomas was waiting for an answer. "I see teaching as . . . a chance to give back, to share what I've learned in business over the last twenty-five years," Henry answered.

Thomas grinned. "I've heard that answer a time or two. Let's be candid, shall we?" He leaned forward as he steepled his fingers in front of his prominent hawk nose. "I'm reluctant to hire long-term players from the corporate world. They tend to see teaching as a cushy retirement option and do just that—retire on the job."

"That's not what I . . . "

With a slight wave of his hand, Thomas cut him off. "I'm curious about your career at Inveress, Ltd. Your brother told me you started in the law department, rose through the ranks, and, at the time your company Inveress was taken over, ascended all the way up to the CEO chair. Pretty impressive."

"Thanks," Henry said, irritated that even in his own interview, his brother Marvin was front and center. Always being the "other" brother was tiresome. He began to fidget, trying to get comfortable in the hard wooden chair.

"Marvin said UNS Partners out of New Jersey took over Inveress," said Thomas.

"Yes, they took over lock, stock, and barrel with a hostile tender offer at a thirty-eight percent premium above the market price," replied Henry.

"Why was UNS willing to pay such a premium?" asked Thomas with a quizzical look. "They're a huge conglomerate, but a thirty-eight percent premium is one fancy price."

"They wanted a specific cookie operation called San Miguel Galletas, based in Argentina. When we were unwilling to sell just the San Miguel operation, their answer was to take over the entire company."

"Marvelous mentioned that San Miguel developed a special technology," Thomas said.

The mention of Marvin's name was bad enough. Now the mention of his nickname "Marvelous" put Henry on edge. His own interview was not about him. It was about Thomas ingratiating himself with Marvin. But he pushed through.

"San Miguel found the Holy Grail of cookies. They patented a technology to produce fat-free, low-calorie, moist cookies. Their product is delicious."

"It's amazing that you got the drop on the opportunity," Thomas said, as he leaned back in his high-backed, tufted burgundy leather chair. "I would think a company of UNS's size would have people all over the globe scouring for breakthrough technologies."

"Sometimes you're lucky," Henry said with a shrug.

"Henry, in my experience, most CEOs are prima donnas. You're a welcome exception. Marvin shared with me the details about how you single-handedly identified San Miguel and wrestled down the acquisition. And, even better, how UNS was forced to pay an exorbitant price for your handiwork. Marvin was real proud of your work and I bet your shareholders loved it."

Henry wondered what other details of his life Marvin had volunteered. As Henry prepared to ask his first question of the interview, Thomas abruptly stood up, came around from behind his desk, and thrust out his hand.

"Henry," Thomas said with a knowing wink and an aggressively firm handshake, "you'll make a great professor. We just need to find the right spot for you. We have one need in the business school you might be able to fill. It plays to a much earlier part of your career."

"What's that?" asked Henry.

"We have an opening in a course called Corporate Legal Affairs. Are you current enough on legal issues to tackle it?" Henry was not particularly current on legal issues. However, his legal background was deep. Besides, Marylou always said he had a knack for explaining thorny legal issues. Thoughts of his wife triggered a twinge of melancholy. "Henry, you with me? Would that course potentially be of interest?"

"Could be," responded Henry. *One class? That was it?* He was accustomed to seventy-hour weeks.

"Tell you what, let's sleep on it and I'll give you a call in the next day or two."

"Great," said Henry, rising and suppressing the urge to sigh. This had not gone at all as he had expected.

"Please forgive me, but I have a meeting of the Development Committee," Thomas said, placing a hand on Henry's shoulder and easing him toward the door. "Running a university requires lots of resources. Nice spending time with you." The office door closed firmly behind Henry and as it did, his shoulders sagged. The interview had lasted less than ten minutes and been nothing more than a rehash of what his brother Marvin had already told President Thomas.

Is this how universities work? Did Thomas offer me a job? Do I even want to be a professor? Leaving the administration building, Henry stopped to admire the view of downtown Dallas rising above the live oak canopy stretching for half a mile down the boulevard. Henry mused that academia had a certain cachet and working in a beautiful place would be fun, but he felt agitated. Was it the fact that Thomas had brought up the UNS acquisition of Inveress? That deal had deprived him of the opportunity to enjoy the fruits of his work in acquiring the San Miguel company. Or was it that his brother Marvin had hijacked the entire interview process?

As he continued across campus, submerged in introspection, his phone buzzed. It was Marvin. Henry considered ignoring it but knew his impetuous brother would simply keep calling until he picked up. "Hey, Marvin."

His brother's familiar, too-loud voice came bursting over the cell. "Yo, how'd it go? I bet Phil Thomas offered you the job on the spot. I can't wait to hear about it—for sure nobody will ever talk to *me* about a professorship. Tell you what—meet me at the pub and give me the play-by-play over a beer. And hey—I got a big surprise to show you!"

Only a little curious about Marvin's surprise, Henry reluctantly agreed, and fifteen minutes later the two sat on high stools at a raised table at the Trinity Hall pub. The table was the one Marvin favored. Its proximity to the mahogany bar, imported from Dublin, made it easy for him to chat up the waitresses and participate in bar chatter at the same time. Henry preferred a quiet table in the back.

"Sounds like the meetin' with ol' President Thomas went real good," Marvin said in the gentle twang he steadfastly clung to from his years growing up on a Kansas wheat farm. Henry had long ago modulated to a neutral California nonaccent. "He's grown pompous over the years, but he's doin' a good job for the university. You know, Henry, you'd make one hell of a good prof. Gonna do it?"

"Nothing's been offered, and if it is, I'll give it some thought," responded Henry.

Marvin grinned. "That's my bro, always givin' everything some thought. Let's get that beer."

Henry waited as Marvin, as always, started up with the waitress. Predictably, she responded, with batting eyelashes and a toss of her hair. Marvin's six-foot-six athletic frame, handsome face, and affable demeanor were magnets that often drew females into conversation. At just over six feet, Henry had spent a lifetime literally looking up to Marvin. Listening to Marvin's banter, Henry couldn't help but smile at his brother's interminable congeniality. It was hard to stay angry with Marvin, but the memory of the interview still irritated him.

"You must have spent one hell of a lot of time working on Thomas," Henry said as the waitress walked away with their order. "Was that really necessary? I can carry my own water."

His brother's brows went up in surprise. "Hell, you and Southerland University are two of my undisputed favorite things in the world. Can you blame me for tryin' to get them together? Hey, aren't you curious about my surprise?"

"Sure," Henry said off-handily.

With a gleam in his eye, Marvin dramatically unbuttoned his shirtsleeve and slowly rolled it up. "Check 'er out!"

Henry was dumbfounded. On the underside of his impetuous brother's left arm was a large royal-blue tattoo whose words were interwoven by a slave chain. The words read, *"I wear the chain I forged in life. I made it link by link."*

"How freakin' cool is that!" Marvin shouted. Heads at the bar turned to the brothers' table. Henry hoped none of the patrons knew him.

"How did you choose . . . that particular phrase?" Henry asked in a calming voice.

"Come on. You gotta remember," Marvin said. "It's what Marley's ghost told Ebenezer Scrooge."

Henry dropped his chin, closed his eyes, and stroked the perpetual cowlick on the back of his head. He recalled the Dickensian darkness from *A Christmas Carol*. "Was there a special reason to get a tattoo?"

"It's been bubblin' in the back of my head for about thirty years. Ever since that a-hole Guy Wheeless Jr. got his tattoo and we chickened out."

Henry rolled his eyes. "Marvin, we didn't chicken out. Getting that tattoo was stupid and we decided not to act like sheep."

"Maybe. But that didn't stop him from flashin' his cherry bomb tattoo all over school and tellin' everyone we were too chicken to get inked."

"It was a bad idea when you were eighteen and living in Wichita . . . now at fifty-six . . ." Henry shook his head.

Marvin took a drink of his beer, smacked his lips, and laughed. "Aw, Henry, loosen up. You been livin' in that uptight corporate world way too long. Out here in the real world, everybody's got a tattoo."

"Whatever," Henry mumbled. "Guy Jr.'s tattoo dredges up some bad memories for me. A lot of crap flowed from that stupid cherry bomb tattoo."

"Yeah, like that practical joke we pulled on Guy Jr. and his date," said Marvin. "To this day, I get a kick thinkin' about that girl goin' heels over head into his back seat flashing her pretty pink panties."

"Some of the other stuff that followed our little stunt wasn't much fun," Henry murmured.

Marvin leaned back in his chair, his brows knitted together. "Man, just the mention of Guy Jr. sets your ass in a tailspin. All that stuff in Wichita was a long time ago." He signaled the waitress with a raised finger and said, "Darlin', can you sprinkle the infield again?"

■■■

Leaving his apartment atop the Wheeless Strategic Fund office building, Guy Wheeless Jr. admired his patrician reflection in his private elevator mirror. He made a minor adjustment to his electric-blue necktie and, with both hands, smoothed back the sides of his gleaming black hair. The one constant irritant in his appearance caught his eye—the missing top half of his left ear. It looked like someone had cut across his ear with serrated scissors at a twenty-degree angle.

It had been nearly a week since he had been out of the apartment. Pushing through the building's glass doors into Wichita's late-afternoon sun, he spotted his gunmetal-grey Bentley Mulsanne parked at the curb. Nothing of import would occur until the evening's meeting in Chicago, but he had community agenda items requiring attention. A man of his standing had obligations. The driver, Larry, came around the car to open the door.

As the rear door opened, Wheeless's eyes tightened at the sight of his driver's ever-growing cauliflower ear. The ear was an unwelcome reminder of Wheeless's own deformity.

"Afternoon, Mr. Wheeless," the man said deferentially.

"Afternoon, Larry. First stop is the hospital for the board meeting, then the airport." He settled into the backseat. "Catch the fight on TV last night?"

"Not much of a fight, boss." Larry spoke with a wide grin, flashing extensive silver crowns and bridges. "That Mex'can boy reminds me of the ol' sayin' of da man."

"What man is that?"

"Why, Iron Mike Tyson is da man, boss. He said, 'Everybody got a plan until they get popped.' And that's what happened last night. Dat boy come out dancin' like Ali, but when he got popped on his nose, he turn into a twelve-year-ol' girl rest of the night." He shut the back door and in seconds was in the driver's seat.

"Larry, is your son still training to follow in your footsteps?"

"Boss, he just like his ol' man," Larry said with a grin. "Feet don't move too good, but can sure take a punch. He need a bit mo' hop in his step."

Wheeless's cell phone rang and he frowned down at the caller ID. It was Jane Birney, general counsel of UNS Partners in New Jersey. The company was one of Wheeless Strategic Fund's largest investments—it was also the worst performing. "Yes," Wheeless answered.

"Good morning, Mr. Wheeless. Glad to reach you." Her lawyer voice was already grating on his nerves. "The UNS board meeting just concluded and I was asked to reach out about your recent letter."

"Yes."

"Mr. Wheeless, the board, of course, values input from all our shareholders and we certainly value your opinion as our largest shareholder. We understand your concern about what you perceive as our lack of progress. I can assure you that we have redoubled our efforts to improve results. The problems are multifaceted and we have put into place a holistic approach."

"And?" *What ridiculous business-speak. Can this woman speak English?*

"The board has reviewed your proposal for a meeting and, unfortunately, the date you chose is inconvenient. Perhaps you and I should meet so I can be in a better position to present your point of view to the board."

"Ms. Birney, I made myself clear the last time you disturbed me. I don't give a rat's ass about the board's convenience and have even less interest in meeting with you. I gave you months to prepare for the meeting. Our team will be at UNS's offices at 10 a.m. sharp on the date I specified. We will lay out our plan to remedy your company's abysmal performance and, if any member of the board is absent, I will consider it a personal affront. Goodbye, Ms. Birney."

As Birney began to reply, Wheeless calmly clicked off his phone, unfolded the *Financial Times*, and began reviewing the currency quotes.

When they reached Via Christi Hospital St. Francis, the hospital's president was waiting in front of the building. She warmly greeted Wheeless and escorted him from his car to the meeting room. With old-school charm, Wheeless made sure to shake hands and exchange a few words with each attendee. At the meeting's end, he gave effusive praise to the staff's efforts on the hospital's behalf and reiterated his support for the new cancer wing.

Walking out of the hospital building, Wheeless smiled to himself. In their small-minded, parochial fashion, the hospital staff probably perceived him as a generous and amicable benefactor. Reality was starkly different.

Larry opened the car door for Wheeless, who then settled into the diamond-quilted seat, picking up a red folder lying on the adjoining seat. "Those meetings have become a pain in the ass," he muttered to himself, and then he addressed Larry. "Let's head for the airport. I see you left me the red folder—you have some good news?"

Larry's dark brown eyes looked back at Wheeless from the rearview mirror. "Boss, you'll see in there some photos an' some info on one fine lady that gives tours at the Wichita Art Museum. She's called a docent or something. She got quite a pair of getaway sticks on 'er and 'er walk-on-by is sweet as honey. Maybe when you get back from ol' Chi-town you might take a peek at the paintings in the museum." He gave a sparkling silver smile.

"That's the first good news all day," replied Wheeless. He carefully reviewed the red folder's contents, tucked one photo into the inside pocket of his dark blue double-breasted suit, and opened the *Financial Times* again to the currency page.

■■■

Henry returned home from the Trinity Hall pub, walked through the back door, and dropped his briefcase on the antique oak desk in his study. From the kitchen, Marylou called out to him. He had always loved the perpetual smile in his wife's voice. Tonight it was grinding. Conflict in their marriage, once rare, had settled in like a cold front.

Since losing his job, Henry felt disorganized and fragmented. Some of his former Inveress colleagues, with more operatic souls, exited the corporate world bound for new conquests. They climbed Kilimanjaro, piloted a private jet around the globe, or joined archaeological digs in Peru. Others, like his close friend and Inveress executive vice president, Ken Maltman, immediately jumped into new corporate positions. Some simply slid into utter boredom and surrendered to the siren of early afternoon cocktails.

Henry yearned for something concrete, something new, something engaging. Being a professor at Southerland had positive pedigree and would bring him some needed focus. But was he really cut out for the sleepy world of academia?

His thoughts spun to his brother's preposterous tattoo. Those thoughts tumbled inexorably into disagreeable recollections of Guy Wheeless Jr. He sat down in the smooth leather chair behind his desk and reached down to the bottom drawer—then quickly closed it as Marylou breezed into the room.

"Hey, you," she said, tucking her shoulder-length blonde hair behind her ear. "You've been on my brain all day. How'd it go with President Thomas?"

"Guess alright," responded Henry flatly. "He may offer me the job, but it will be because Marvin asked him to hire me, not because of my credentials. It's all about Marvin."

"Well, isn't it nice that Marvin's so supportive?" Marylou sat down in one of the study's two suede high-backed chairs facing the desk and folded her hands in her lap. "Southerland's just a few blocks from here. Being a professor there would be most people's dream job."

"You're right. But I could be a drooling idiot and President Thomas would offer me the job to ingratiate himself with Marvin."

"Does it really matter?" asked Marylou, giving a little shoulder shrug that somehow ratcheted up Henry's irritability. "You'd be a great professor—does it matter how you get there? Just go with the flow."

He banged one hand down on the desk and Marylou sucked in a sharp breath. "I don't want to go with the damn flow!" he yelled. "And I'm sick of Marvin sticking his nose in my business, and even sicker of you jumping in on his side!"

"Come on, Henry, you're getting all defensive. We're just interested in helping you find the next chapter in your life." Marylou gave him a hopeful smile that didn't quite reach her eyes.

Henry stood, flushed with frustration. He glared at his wife. "Marylou, of all people, you just don't get it."

"Don't get what?" asked Marylou with outstretched arms.

"Me. What I'm going through. In fact, you don't *want* to get me!"

"Henry, please . . . please stop yelling. I honestly have no idea what you're talking about."

"Of course you don't . . . you're too busy gallivanting around Buenos Aires . . . you don't have a clue what's going on around here. I've had it. I'm going to bed."

■■■

The next morning Henry was alone in the kitchen nursing his second cup of coffee. Marylou had silently escaped the house's chilly atmosphere for the sanctuary of her office. Henry was alone with his thoughts. *Why do I keep picking stupid fights with Marylou? Why don't I just tell her what I know?*

He drew a line down the middle of a legal-size yellow pad and began making a list of the pros and cons of academia. On the con side he wrote and underlined three times: "Will it be too bureaucratic?" The list was about even when his phone rang. It was President Thomas's secretary—was Henry free to speak with President Thomas? Henry said "certainly" and waited nervously for Phil Thomas's voice to come on the line.

"Henry, top of the morning. I slept on it last night and there's no reason to beat around the bush. Southerland needs a man like you on board—what do you say?"

Before he had a chance to think, Henry heard himself say, "Yes, I'm flattered. Yes."

"Great news. The dean of the business school will be in touch about details. You start in three weeks. See you around campus!"

Four months later, Henry sat in his study writing the finishing touches on the morning's lecture. In his second semester at Southerland, he was getting in sync with the rhythms of academia. He still spent countless hours preparing his lectures. An old adage came to mind: A task expands to fill the time allotted to it. Was he doing exactly that with his lectures? Was all the work really necessary? Was the excess attention a bulwark against the prospect of classroom embarrassment? Or was academic life making him slower and less efficient?

Henry's cell phone buzzed. He recognized the 212 area code—New York City. He answered, "Henry Lindon."

"Henry!" A familiar voice blasted into his ear. "How the hell are ya? I'm glad you're finally out of the Federal Witness Protection Program!"

"Ken Maltman, you old reprobate!" Henry answered with a laugh. "Yeah, they let me out on good behavior," he joked. "How's life?"

Maltman and Henry had grown up together at Inveress. They rose together through the ranks and at the time of the UNS takeover, Maltman had served as Inveress's executive vice president, as well as Henry's confidant. In his mind's eye Henry could see his friend's shiny shaved head, toothy grin, and mischievous blue eyes.

"Tell me, Professor Lindon, how's the world of academia?"

"I hope the students are learning as much as I am," replied Henry. "You still making the world safe for capitalism?"

"But of course. My new gig on the board of Wein has been perfect. Generous pay and not too taxing—right up my alley. Did you see this morning's *Wall Street Journal?*"

"Not yet. Why?"

"Check out the Heard on the Street column," said Maltman. "It sheds some light on UNS's takeover of Inveress. Looks like some of your hometown boys were pulling the strings."

Henry frowned. "Interesting. Believe it or not, I've got to finish today's lecture on libel. I'll take a look at the article first chance. Thanks for the call."

"Good luck with all those young minds—stay in touch."

Henry couldn't resist opening the newspaper sitting on the edge of his desk. He paged through to the Heard on the Street column. The article speculated that UNS had been pushed to make the acquisition of Henry's former company Inveress by a loose federation of Midwest hedge funds. A quote from a confidential source named the Wheeless Strategic Fund in Wichita, Kansas, as the likely leader of the federation. Guy Wheeless Jr., Henry's former classmate, headed the Wheeless Strategic Fund.

Henry tried to smooth down the cowlick on the back of his head and took a deep breath. *What the hell? Guy Jr. was behind the takeover of my company?* Since high school, the name Guy Wheeless Jr. had been synonymous with trouble. Learning that his old nemesis had been involved with the event that had landed him in academia unleashed seething resentment.

■ ■ ■

Following his tried-and-true preclass routine, Henry headed to the gym for some preteaching invigoration. Although the fight against middle-age pounds required constant vigilance, his full head of wavy, auburn-silver hair and round, dimpled face gave him a youthful appearance.

He climbed up on one of the gym's running machines and channel surfed the machine's TV to find some mindless ESPN banter. On the machine next to him was a sweaty thirtysomething in training for bathing suit season.

Henry caught sight of a butterfly tattoo on her thigh peeking out from under her running shorts. He recalled reading that twenty-two percent of college students had tattoos. At some point along the line, tattoos had morphed from a rebel badge of honor to a fashion accessory. Maybe he should ask his students if they had tattoos as a kind of icebreaker. He was still learning how to relate to millennials. Would they think he was cool for asking? After thinking it over, he decided that given the potential embarrassment from a ditzy sophomore admitting to an inappropriate something on a far too intimate somewhere, he should shelve the idea.

Thirty minutes later, after a quick shower in the gym, Henry strolled across the Southerland campus, admiring the architecture.

The gold-crowned cupolas of the campus glowed in the sunshine, and the red brick Georgian buildings, bolstered by white Corinthian columns, emitted an optimistic air of higher education. Expansive lawns with dramatic fountains were populated by pods of fresh-faced students preparing for class. The buzz of student conversation, blended with the rhythmic sounds of bicycles and longboards, reverberated an uplifting energy.

Climbing the stairs of Blake Hall, home of the business school, Henry cheerfully greeted students scurrying along to classes. He noticed Nichole Kessler sitting on a hallway bench, chatting animatedly with girlfriends. Nichole had a shapely runner's build and wore her hair in a blonde bob with powder-blue highlights. With a ballerina's posture and a dazzling smile, she stood out in any crowd.

"Morning, Nichole. How are ya?"

Nichole looked up at him and a smile lit up her face as she stood. "Hey, Professor Lindon. Doing fine, but can't believe graduation's just around the corner. Have a few minutes for me Wednesday morning after your class?"

"Of course. See you then."

He entered the theater-style classroom and removed his Canali suit coat. He felt lucky Nichole had been in his class during his first semester of teaching. She was hard-charging and goal-oriented. Her classroom successes had been rewarded with a membership in Beta Gamma Sigma, the national business honor society, and induction into Southerland's Hide Society, which recognized the university's most intellectually gifted students.

Nichole epitomized the ambitious, modern young woman, laser-focused on burnishing her résumé and preparing for a bright future. This new breed of alpha women unabashedly elbowed past their all-too-frequently clueless male counterparts. For young women like Nichole, the days of attending college in search of a "MRS. degree" were incomprehensible. Any lasting romantic relationships were a distant second to lofty career aspirations. Henry wistfully considered the prospect of teaching an entire class of Nichole clones.

Turning his thoughts back to the morning's lesson, Henry plugged his flash drive into the high-tech podium while the students filled the lecture-hall seats. With time on his hands, he labored over each lecture and thought of them as little jewels. The day's lecture on defamation was a favorite. With a few deft strokes on the keyboard, the title of his lecture flashed on the classroom screen:

FROM THE 19TH TO THE 21ST CENTURY—
FROM OSCAR WILDE TO BRITNEY SPEARS—
FROM THE SUBLIME TO THE DIVINE.

The screen lit up with photos of Oscar Wilde and Britney Spears as Henry began the lecture. "Okay," he began, "who can tell me something about the gentleman on the left?"

No hands were raised. Undeterred, he asked, "Who remembers *The Picture of Dorian Gray*? The portrait in the attic aging while its subject, living a dissolute life in London, remained perpetually young?"

The hands of three European students shot up in the air. *So much for the state of classic education in the US,* Henry thought.

"Let me give you a bit of background on Oscar Wilde. Mr. Wilde was a superstar in his day. He was not only a novelist and playwright of worldwide acclaim, but he was also a bon vivant with a unique wit. Perhaps most famously, he was extremely quotable. Here are some of my favorite Wilde quotes that have survived through the years. I'll let you decide whether or not they're true." Quotes flashed on the screen as Henry recited them.

"The truth is rarely pure and never simple."

"A little sincerity is a dangerous thing, and a great deal of it is absolutely fatal."

"A gentleman is one who never hurts anyone's feelings unintentionally."

After a smattering of laughter from his audience, Henry continued. "So, Mr. Wilde was one of the most famous people of his time, and, although he had a wife and children, he was gay. Unfortunately for Mr. Wilde, being gay was a crime in Victorian England. In 1891, he began an affair with Lord Alfred Douglas, who was then a student at the University of Oxford. Douglas's father, the Marquess of Queensberry, was an infamous tough guy. In fact, he was such a tough guy that he was the first person to memorialize the rules of boxing." Henry began pacing back and forth behind the podium.

"The marquess was outraged at Wilde's relationship with his son and he went to Wilde's gentlemen's club to confront him. When Wilde refused to come downstairs to meet him—for pretty obvious reasons—the marquess left a note for Wilde with the doorman." Henry flashed the note on the screen.

"To Oscar Wilde, a posing sodomite."

Believing he had provided sufficient background, Henry asked, "So what's the issue here?" Most of the sorority girls raised their hands, and Henry called on one in the middle of the lecture hall.

"Well, Professor Lindon, I think, you know, that since the marquess—whatever that is—wrote a note that said bad stuff about Mr. Wilde, this is a case of libel."

"That's one side of it," Henry replied. "Anyone see any issues with Mr. Wilde's libel case?"

All the front-row strivers were now anxious to show that they had done their homework. Henry called on a frail student who spent most days hiding behind his Mac laptop.

"In my opinion, there's a solid defense for the dad, the marquess guy. What he said was the truth, and that's a complete defense to libel, right?"

Convinced the class was on the right track, Henry walked out in front of the podium and continued. "Wilde, despite advice of counsel to the contrary, decided to pursue a libel case against the marquess. On the witness stand, Wilde adamantly denied his homosexuality. Unfortunately for Wilde, the marquess produced a parade of witnesses to testify about Wilde's homosexuality and the marquess won the case. Worse yet, Wilde was found guilty of homosexuality and sentenced to a London prison. But for our purposes, the point of this story is simply this: The case of Oscar Wilde stands for the proposition that truth is always, *always*, a one hundred percent effective defense to charges of slander or libel. So, let's move on to the next case. Who recognizes this woman?"

The photo of Britney Spears sparked the entire class to raise their hands.

"Okay," he said with a laugh, "who wants to tell us about the case of Ms. Spears's mother?"

Henry called on one of the three frat boys wearing tattered baseball caps and insouciantly populating the lecture hall's back row.

"Well, Britney hired this manager guy who basically kinda abused her by yelling at her, hiding her phone, and other stuff, and she kinda went off the deep end. So her mom wrote a book about life in the tabloid world and she dissed the manager dude, callin' him a bunch of bad stuff, and he sued her for libel."

"What exactly did Mrs. Spears say about her daughter's manager?" asked Henry.

Flipping through his course book, the student responded, "She called him stuff like a 'Svengali' and a 'predator.' In other words, she libeled him."

"And what do we think Mrs. Spears's defense will be?"

A number of voices responded in unison, "Truth."

Pleased the class was grasping the lecture's theme, Henry asked, "Any other defenses Mrs. Spears is likely to assert?"

Henry waited as heads dropped down, combing books for an answer. A single hand went up, the hand of a true wiseass from somewhere in Central Florida. He had the pumped-up body of a wannabe professional wrestler and wore dark sunglasses perched on top of his long, curly hair. When he wasn't playing with his hair, he spent class time surfing the Internet. With no one else offering to answer, Henry reluctantly pointed to the student.

"Seems to me that both Britney and her mom should sue for bad tattoos." Incipient giggles came from the back rows.

"I'm not sure what that has to do with this case." Annoyed, Henry added, "What's your point?"

"Professor, everyone knows Britney has the world's worst tattoos. She has one on her neck that says God in Hebrew—trouble is, it's misspelled. And she has these crucifixes and stars on her thighs that are the worst." The wave of giggles rose and flowed across the room.

Rattled by the discussion's errant turn, Henry crossed a pedagogical taboo—he said the first thing that popped into his mind. "I read that twenty-two percent of today's college students have tattoos. Anyone care to tell the class about their tattoos?"

Two students eagerly volunteered innocuous stories about the where, what, and whys of their tattoos. The third volunteer was Andrea Lucero, a student from West Texas who had not distinguished herself academically. Her grade had been the lowest on the last class exam.

"Well, you know, my friend and me got them last spring in Mexico. We got the exact same one. It's a bright purple dragonfly . . . let's just say it's kind of . . . below our backs." The wave of knowing giggles crested.

Realizing he had barreled down an ill-conceived path, Henry glanced up at the clock at the back of the room. Relief swept over him as he saw it was only five minutes until the end of the class period.

"Right." He cleared his throat. "All right, good work. I think I'll let you out a few minutes early today. Class dismissed." The students filed out as Henry released a pent-up breath. *What the hell am I doing here?* he asked himself for what seemed like the hundredth time.

■ ■ ■

Doris Delaney, Marvin Lindon's latest love interest, was a television caricature of a Dallas blonde—she knew it and liked it. Divorced for the second time, she had invested a good slug of her alimony in cosmetic surgery. Marvin had dubbed her "Double D" for reasons besides her initials.

Doris was focused on a single goal—to have as much fun as possible while her looks held out. With her fortieth birthday well behind her, she accelerated her efforts. She was sitting at her home computer, researching hotels for a trip to Buenos Aires she hoped to take with Marvin, when her phone rang.

"Double D, darlin', what are you doin' this fine afternoon?"

"Hey there, Marvelous! Just killing time waiting for you to come on by and pay me a visit. By the way, sugar, you been down to Buenos Aires? Sounds wonderfully romantic."

"Sure have. We swing through the airport there on our way to dove hunt. Maybe me and you should make the trip."

"Well, sugar, that's just what I was thinking," she said with a laugh.

"Hey now, don't forget tonight we're havin' dinner with Henry and Marylou. Marylou's got a business in Argentina. Why don't you ask her about Buenos Aires. Should I swing on by 'round six thirty?"

Dinner with Mr. and Mrs. Professor, and the likelihood of a dinner conversation over her head, was not Doris's idea of a good time. However, happy that Marvin had committed—at least in her mind—to a Buenos Aires trip, she opted to be cheerful. "I do, in fact, remember. Why don't you come around six and we'll loosen up a bit."

"Great. I'll pull by then . . . wear somethin' to turn a few eyeballs . . . if you catch my drift."

Doris could imagine Marvin winking at her over the phone and she smiled. "Sugar, I got just the thing!"

■■■

The predictably punctual Henry and Marylou settled into their table at Javier's promptly at seven o'clock. Tuxedoed waiters glided around the tables, past the restaurant's stuffed black bears, giant blue sailfish, and water buffalo. With its Veracruz–style cuisine, Javier's was a Dallas spot to see and be seen.

"Excuse me," Marylou said as she took a waiter lightly by the elbow. "Before you get away, please bring us a couple of Ketel One martinis. Straight up."

The waiter made a shallow bow and moved toward the bar.

"That sounded desperate," Henry said. "Have a bad day?"

"No. In fact, I had a lovely day." Marylou swept two fingers across her forehead and tucked her hair behind her right ear. "Please, don't start with me. Let's try to be on our best behavior tonight, what do you say?"

"Agreed. Let's start over."

"I'm just bracing for that woman," Marylou said. "Her plastic face looks more frog-like by the week. Do you believe how shiny it is? I love seeing Marvin. Who's more fun than Marvin and we haven't seen him since you started teaching. But when he brings that woman along, it's tough to handle."

Yes, indeed, Henry thought, dragging one hand over his cowlick. *Who's more fun than Marvin? Not me these days, that's for sure.*

"I've been gracious to his four ex-wives and endless girlfriends," Marylou went on, "but this woman's too much."

"I know, I know," responded Henry. "Like all the others, she'll be history in a month or two. For better or worse, Lindon-family eccentricities accentuate with age. Remember my crazy Uncle Jerome? Dad's older brother? Probably never ventured out of Kansas, but in his seventies he convinced himself that his lineage came through Ecuador. He started speaking with what he thought was an Ecuadorian accent and took to flying a huge Ecuadorian flag in his front yard. The folks in town pretty much stayed clear of Uncle Jerome after that. Let's hope Marvin didn't get a full dose of that DNA."

"Speaking of eccentricities, I had a nice chat with Susan this afternoon. She's definitely my favorite of Marvin's exes." Marylou slowly sipped her drink. "It's amazing that Marvin can maintain such a good relationship—should I say intimate relationship—with an ex-wife."

"It's remarkable," Henry said. "Who other than Marvin could possibly have an ex-wife who cheerfully comes over to cook dinner and spend the night? Since he was a kid, Marvin's lived one charmed life. Which reminds me, wait 'til you see his latest nod to fashion."

"What is it?"

"Wouldn't think of spoiling his surprise."

By seven forty-five, the martinis were drained and Henry was growing increasingly impatient. He glanced toward the restaurant's entrance and shook his head. "Here comes the circus."

In his yellow-flowered Tommy Bahama shirt, Marvin walked through the restaurant with the studied nonchalance of an accomplished athlete. Holding his left arm slightly in front of him, he displayed his ink like a young secretary flashing her new engagement ring. Despite Marvin's imposing size and presence, most eyes were on Double D and her one-size-too-small metallic-green dress.

"Oh, Christ, look at her," Marylou whispered. "Give me strength."

"Sorry we're a bit delayed," purred Doris through bee-stung lips. "But we kind of got into some stuff at my place." She coyly pinched Marvin's cheek. "You're such a rascal, sugar."

Flashing his best "rascal" grin, Marvin leaned over to give Marylou a warm hug. She took his arm with both hands and exclaimed, "What have we got here?"

"Doesn't the prof tell you anything?" asked Marvin. He grinned like a proud father. "Like my skin art? Double D says it makes me look like a man of style."

"Let's see here," Marylou said still holding Marvin's arm. "I recognize that quote from somewhere. Now, where was that?"

While Marvin enthusiastically detailed the literary cleverness of his tat to an attentive and amused Marylou, Henry signaled the waiter for drink orders. With the waiter at tableside, Marvin leaned across the table and asked Henry in a stage whisper, "How them coeds lookin' these days?"

Henry gave a sarcastic smile and pressed down on his cowlick. The waiter slipped away with their order and Henry leaned low across the table toward Marvin. "Is that necessary?"

"Sorry, Professor Sensitive. Just makin' a joke," said a smiling Marvin. "Bein' politically correct isn't exactly my core competency. But seriously, how they lookin'?"

Henry could see Doris was enjoying the tension, but he was thankful when Marylou jumped in. "Marvin, not sure if Henry told you but President Thomas asked him to join a task force to address sexual misconduct on campus. You can understand why Henry's feeling a bit sensitive about some stuff."

"All the bad press about sexual misconduct sends the wrong signal to prospective parents," Henry added. "We have our next task force meeting Thursday to try and agree on a report to President Thomas. So far, we've made less than zero progress."

"Back in the day at Southerland the great President Thomas and I were classmates and played on the basketball team together," Marvin said to Doris. "For what it's worth, Phil Thomas talked a better game than he played, never saw a shot he didn't take, and couldn't even spell rebound. But he's been great for the university. Henry, whaddaya think ol' Thomas would think about my tat?"

"Probably pretty much the same as what I think," Henry said with one raised eyebrow.

The women laughed nervously while Henry pushed down the irritation he felt toward his brother. With a fresh round of martinis on the table, the conversation veered away from Southerland University to Doris's favorite topic: group exercise classes.

Henry hid a smile as his wife feigned interest in Doris's pitch. From Pilates to isokinetics to rock 'n' roll spin, Doris was a disciple of them all. She excitedly explained the intricacies of the TRX suspension exercises, such as push-ups with her ankles locked into suspension straps hanging from the ceiling.

Henry took a drink of his martini, tuning out the prattle. He turned to find Marvin discreetly surveying the room's "talent." *Typical*, thought Henry, slowly shaking his head.

■ ■ ■

"So, what do you think of Marvin's tattoo?" Marylou asked as Henry drove them home. "He's certainly proud of it."

"Why encourage him? That tattoo is . . . idiotic. The only thing worse than the tattoo is that infantile quote. The way you oohed and aahed about it and held on to his arm, you could have been one of his dates."

"There you go again," said Marylou, slumping in her seat. "Why so defensive? I was trying to have a good time. Marvin is dear and amusing. I don't understand why you seem so resentful of him lately."

"I don't find any of it amusing and you don't have to live with the consequences of his nonsense. Next you'll say I just need to loosen up."

"Not a bad idea."

They drove home in stony silence.

3

Guy Wheeless Jr. liked the playing field before him. The UNS partners' board of directors wore faces as somber as the dark oak table they sat around. *This will be as easy as clubbing baby seals*, he thought to himself.

Wheeless listened unemotionally for an hour and a half to the graph-filled financial presentation by his chief lieutenant, Edward O'Brian. O'Brian, a tall ultramarathon runner, looked skeletal. UNS's business prospects as outlined by O'Brian were, in a word, dismal.

Silence and downcast eyes greeted O'Brian's invitation for questions. There were none. Wheeless stood, smoothed a lapel on his double-breasted Savile Row suit, and walked purposefully to the room's podium. Standing with intimidating erectness, he looked down the rows of seats, trying to bully through eye contact. He began his presentation without notes.

"Thank you, Mr. O'Brian, for your sobering evaluation of the challenges facing UNS. I assume all of you have read the Wheeless Strategic Fund proposals to enhance shareholder value. Speaking of shareholder value, I'm confident that each of you has clearly in mind that the Wheeless Strategic Fund made a 1.6-billion-dollar investment in UNS, an investment that today has dwindled to 1.1 billion dollars.

"As Mr. O'Brian detailed, UNS has grossly underperformed relative to its peers in the food business. If we look at margins, earnings per share, or, for that matter, any financial measurement tool, results have been uninspiring."

Seeing his audience shifting uncomfortably in their seats emboldened Wheeless. "On the acquisition front, twice in the last twelve months this board has approved an acquisition based on projected financial statements. In both cases the actual sales and profits fell forty percent below the projections. In the vernacular, you have flushed down the toilet a fortune in shareholder money and that means my money!"

"Mr. Wheeless, I must interject here," said Sam Ingalls. Wheeless turned a cold eye on the bank executive and longtime member of the UNS board of directors. "One of those acquisitions you are referring to was the UNS purchase of Inveress. As I recall, you suggested we pursue that deal."

"Yes." Wheeless folded his arms over his chest and gazed unflinchingly at the man.

With heat rising in his face, Ingalls continued. "In fact, you were insistent that we pursue a purchase of Inveress in order to secure that cookie company in Argentina. San Miguel Galletas, I believe it's called."

"Yes."

"You even sent this board a note of congratulations when the deal closed."

"Yes." *This fool is making my job too easy*, Wheeless thought.

"Have you changed your mind?" Ingalls extended his hand in a questioning gesture.

"No, Mr. Ingalls, I have not changed my mind." Wheeless stood as still as a statue. "I made it crystal clear to this board that one specific division of Inveress, the San Miguel Galletas operation in Argentina, was imperative to a successful deal. Further, I specifically advised that UNS undertake an exhaustive investigation to assess San Miguel's ongoing vitality." Wheeless's eyes narrowed. "Unfortunately, you failed to uncover the disastrous labor situation at San Miguel. As we all are painfully aware, ever since UNS bought Inveress, the San Miguel operation has been paralyzed with labor strikes. How in God's name did UNS not know about the labor problems before closing? I think we will learn that someone played you."

"Mr. Wheeless, allow me to address that issue," answered Jane Birney, UNS's general counsel. "Not only did we conduct in-depth interviews and document reviews before closing the transaction, but we conducted an exhaustive post-acquisition review." She sat up straighter. "Nowhere did we find a hint of San Miguel's labor issues."

"Exactly," Wheeless said. "Only the incompetent or corrupt could have missed the San Miguel issues."

"I take offense to your characterization, Mr. Wheeless," Birney responded in an even-keeled voice.

"What you do or do not 'take offense' to is not my concern." Wheeless kept his tone dismissive, his face like stone. "The facts speak for themselves. We're finished here. Mr. O'Brian and our legal team will sit down and explain to you, Ms. Birney, how acquisition due diligence is done in the big leagues. I strongly suggest you restart the process from the beginning. I expect to hear about results, not efforts."

As the meeting broke up, Wheeless signaled O'Brian with a tip of his head that he wanted a word in private. They settled into a small adjacent conference room. O'Brian's long, thin limbs reminded Wheeless of a praying mantis.

"Edward, now the real work begins," said Wheeless. "I'll personally take care of hounding them about expenses. UNS is about to go on a financial crash diet. I want you to find out exactly how those bozos punted the due diligence on the San Miguel business in Argentina. The labor problems should have been obvious to the deaf, dumb, and blind, yet they managed to fuck it up. I don't care how long it takes; I want answers. The only thing they did right was to fire the Inveress management team, and then only after I demanded they take action."

"And that group included your old friend, Henry Lindon," O'Brian added.

"Throwing his business career off the rails felt real good." Wheeless smiled for the first time. "That jackass will never figure out that I pulled the levers. He's retreated to some sort of teaching position at Southerland University. I hear his brother Marvin made it happen. And guess who took his pathetic class?"

"Not your niece, Nikkie?"

"Yes, Nikkie. By the way, I'll be in Dallas tomorrow for our annual lunch to discuss her trust. It's a mystery to me what that girl does with her annual allowance. She lives like an impoverished scholarship student.

"Now—on a different front. Has the fund's foundation made any contributions to the Wichita Art Museum?"

"Don't know for sure," replied O'Brian. "But I doubt it. I didn't know you were interested in art."

"Supporting the museum would be good for our hometown image, giving back to the community and all that crap. I'll leave the contribution to your discretion, but I want a gift that will get the attention of anybody in Wichita interested in the arts."

"I'm all over it," answered O'Brian.

■■■

Waiting for his niece, Guy Wheeless Jr. sat in the French Room of Dallas's Adolphus Hotel admiring the classic Louis XV embellishments. He wore a double-breasted black suit—a touch too formal for even the decorous French Room. The ceiling frescoes of pink angels carrying flower wreaths through cumulus clouds were the perfect complements to the crystal chandelier and the pink marble Corinthian columns.

He looked down at the black marble beneath him, which was polished to a mirror sheen, admiring the angels' reflections in the floor. Checking the dining room to ensure no one was watching, he bent over to check his hair in the black marble's reflection. It was like looking into a still pond. He realized why he was so taken by the room—it was an image of himself, classic and elegant.

His niece, Nikkie Kessler, was late, as always. Spinning the sterling silver fork on the table's bright white linen tablecloth, he reflected on the relationship with his only living relative. Her life had not been easy. Her mother had died of a drug overdose in a seedy Kansas City motel when Nikkie was six. Her itinerant musician father had disappeared a year earlier.

With only Wheeless and Nikkie's paternal grandparents as potential guardians, Wheeless did the only thing possible—he sent her to live with her unwelcoming grandparents in Tulsa. His life had no room for adolescent responsibility. She had spent her youth in a series of New England boarding schools, returning to Wichita infrequently. Their little "misunderstanding" on one of her visits had started the deterioration of their relationship.

Since her matriculation at Southerland University, he saw his niece once a year for the annual meeting required by her trust. Her life may have been rocky, but that did not excuse the fact that she was such a little bitch.

Wheeless looked up from twirling his fork and saw Nikkie standing at the hostess station. A smiling woman in a green slit dress pointed her toward his table. Wheeless wondered why a trust-fund kid insisted on dressing down. Her shorts, red Southerland University tee shirt, and sandals clashed with the restaurant's formal decor. *For Christ's sake, she's dyed her hair blue.*

Her questionable clothing choices could not mask her slender, vivacious sexuality. All her pieces were in the right places. Wheeless stood to welcome her. With arms plastered to her sides, she coolly allowed him to kiss her cheek.

"This place is ridiculously ostentatious," she said circling her arm to encompass the entire room. "Why can't we meet in a diner?"

Wheeless smiled; her hostile behavior was nothing new. "So, Nikkie, how have you been?"

"Fine, couldn't be better."

"Like something to drink?"

"No, and I'm not hungry."

"Well, I am." Wheeless signaled the waiter. *This spoiled brat is not going to push me around. Why is she hiding her best assets under that baggy red tee shirt?*

With Wheeless's encouragement, the waiter painstakingly detailed the lunch specials and suggested wine pairings. Wheeless debated the wine choices with the waiter, drawing out the process as long as possible. He—not Nikkie—was in charge. After intentionally dithering further about his choices, he finally ordered and asked, "And you, Nikkie?"

"Water, tap water."

"Suit yourself," Wheeless said, satisfied he had the upper hand. "As you know, I take my responsibility as the trustee of the trust my father set up for you very seriously. When I became the trustee after your mother's untimely death . . . "

"You mean when she overdosed on Mexican black tar."

What a little bitch! "As I was saying, when your mother passed and I became your trustee, in charge of your future welfare . . . "

She interrupted him, her deep-blue eyes flashing disdain. "Why won't you give me an accounting of how much is in the trust and how it's invested?"

"Nikkie, we've been through this before," Wheeless said, smoothing the napkin on his lap. "I have full discretion to invest your trust fund as I see fit and no obligation to report to you or anyone else."

"I'm twenty-two and perfectly able to take care of myself and my money." She folded her arms tightly across her chest.

"As you know, I have a vast reservoir of financial expertise," Wheeless said with a self-satisfied tone. "I have invested your money successfully all these years. How do you think you're able to receive an annual living allowance of $200,000? Nikkie, I'm curious about what you've been doing with all that cash. Do you mind telling me what you're spending your money on?"

"None of your business. Are you going to give me the accounting? I've been asking for two years!"

"Nikkie, keep your voice down." Wheeless steeled himself. "You're getting ready to graduate from Southerland. Do you need a bump in your allowance for a graduation trip? A new apartment? Some . . . new clothes?"

"I want nothing but that accounting. Don't force me to do something you'll regret," she said with a fierce gaze.

He wrinkled his forehead. *Is she threatening me?* "The trust fund will be totally in your hands when you turn thirty. That is, unless I decide to release the fund to you earlier. That's how your grandfather set up the trust when you were born."

"My trust was set up with my mother as the trustee. Grandfather never thought you would be the trustee."

"But I am. Speaking of your grandfather, there's something you need to know about him."

"What's that?"

"You were a toddler when your grandfather passed away. He was a man of unassailable integrity who single-handedly built the biggest bank in Kansas. He took enormous pride in the Wheeless name and the standard of excellence it stands for. I have done my best to carry on the legacy he built around that name."

"I bet you have," she said in a satirical tone.

Don't let her get under your skin. "Your grandfather realized years ago that three men, one of whom you know, intentionally tried to tarnish our name. As he would want, I have tried to resolve the situation. In the case of one of the men, I was successful. Now I need your help to make one of the other two understand the consequences of smearing the Wheeless name, your mother's name."

"Who in the world are you talking about?" she asked, unfolding her arms.

"Henry Lindon."

"Professor Lindon?" she responded with a querulous look.

"That's him. He and two others tried to humiliate the Wheeless family and I need your help to set things straight."

"I really like Professor Lindon. What's this all about?"

"Nikkie, it's best you don't know all the details."

"It's Nichole. What do you want?"

"Pretty simple. A girl . . . I mean a woman who's . . . put together like you . . . can humiliate a man like Henry in any number of ways. Understand where I'm going?"

"No."

"A man like Henry would find you . . . irresistible. He could get into a lot of trouble with a girl like you." *Do I need to spell it out?*

"Are we talking sex here?" Nichole replied, leaning forward with an incredulous look on her face.

"Correct."

"You've got to be kidding," Nichole said with a nervous laugh. "Why in the hell would I do that?"

"I'll tell you exactly why—to right a wrong against your family name. That should be more than enough. But, since that may be insufficient for you, I'll throw this in—if you put Henry Lindon in a compromising position, I'll release your trust fund to you immediately."

"What's your definition of a compromising position?" Nichole refolded her arms across her chest and glared at him.

"Something we can photograph, something that will get him thrown off campus. You know, you and him in bed, something like that. I don't want him just fired, I want him tarred and feathered and ridden off campus on a donkey."

"You're ridiculous. What makes you think he'll go for any of this?"

"He's a man—believe me, he'll go for it."

Nichole carefully folded her napkin, slowly stood, and tossed the napkin on her empty plate. Deliberately sliding her chair in under the table, she came around to Wheeless's side. With steely determination in her eyes she leaned over and whispered into his ear, "You disgust me. Everything about you disgusts me. Don't think for a moment I've forgotten about my seventh birthday when you brought me that huge stuffed dog. I remember what happened when you said you wanted to play with me and the dog in your bedroom. You've always been a pathetic pervert."

"Let's not dredge up ancient history," he said, turning his head to face her. "That was a misunderstanding. Do we have a deal, Nikkie?" Wheeless asked with a sinister smile.

"The only reason I would even consider your obscene proposal is to get you out of my life forever! I'll call you, don't call me." She turned on her heel, and headed for the door.

Wheeless sat smirking. *She's trouble. I can't believe she raised yet again our little misunderstanding with the stuffed dog. If she compromises Henry and demands her money, I'll just tell her I've changed my mind about giving it to her. Just like when she was seven, there's not a damn thing she can do about it.*

■ ■ ■

Nichole Kessler swung open the screen door too hard, banging it loudly against her garage-apartment wall. She walked across the tiny kitchen and collapsed into the apartment's only piece of furniture—a secondhand couch her roommate had bought from the Salvation Army. She was furious about her creepy uncle. Since her mother's death, he had been nothing but a constant and deep source of pain. His absurd request that she put Professor Lindon in a "compromising position" was just the most recent insult.

She closed her eyes and willed herself to calm. She let her thoughts drift back to her days in the string of East Coast boarding schools. She had changed schools annually in search of an elusive happy home. She recalled the lonely nights she lay in bed and willed herself to be like one of the local New England ponds: deep, still, dark, and reflective. It was the last part, the reflective part, that caused problems. When she was reflective she could not avoid the hard, cold truth—she was all alone in a very scary world. Her uncle was a monster and her paternal grandparents were too old and infirm to be able to care about her. There was no one else. She understood early on that she was resolutely alone and learned to draw strength from her reality.

Nichole smiled at the vision in her mind of her gangly, awkward teenage years. Shy and bookish, she kept to herself. Then the six-month miracle unfolded. She turned nineteen, was admitted to Southerland University, and gained seductive weight. It was a metamorphosis—the chrysalis of her awkward youth opened and out stepped a beautiful butterfly. She noticed boys turning their heads for the first time and soon grown men were doing the same. When she flashed her smile, locked doors opened wide. Friends, always in short supply, became magically abundant.

She stepped on Southerland's campus her freshman year supremely confident in herself, her beauty, and her iron will to succeed. Despite the deluge of friends and academic successes, she never lost sight of the poignant and pivotal fact of her life: She was positively alone. From that painful reality, she drew the strength to deal with any obstacle. Her Uncle Guy was a major impediment, but she had a plan to deal with him.

She picked up her cell phone and dialed the number of her investigator. "Hi, it's Nichole. Just checking in—anything new?"

"It's good to hear your voice," answered a deep male voice. "Your timing is perfect. We have news on a couple of fronts."

"Super, what've you got?"

"We've done a lot of digging on your trust fund. And your suspicions look to be correct. Uncle Guy has been systematically draining your trust. But we can't figure out why. He's got more money than he knows what to do with. Why take yours?"

"Pretty simple," replied Nichole. "Because he can. He thinks he's an advanced species, free to do as he pleases. Hear any more about the women?"

"Yes, as a matter of fact. I was in the process of putting down the details in my weekly report. Do you want me to take you through it now?"

"No, I'll wait to enjoy the report. I'll call back in a week. Thanks."

Nichole hung up, satisfied that the case she was building against her uncle was coming together nicely. If he didn't change his mind about her trust, he would deeply regret it. Her thoughts turned to his obscene proposal. She began toying with whether there was a way to accommodate her uncle's request and get him permanently out of her life without doing any harm to Professor Lindon or, more importantly, to herself. The outlines of a plan began to take shape in the back of her mind.

■■■

Spring break had crept up on Henry, and when he entered the lecture hall to the sounds of students talking excitedly about vacation plans, he knew the days had begun running together in his head. Pushing the disturbing thought aside, Henry projected the morning's lecture title on the screen:

SCANDAL BEGETS LEGISLATION

This was his last class before spring break, and Henry knew the students would be attention-challenged. Using the Scandal Begets Legislation theme, he drew parallels between the stock market crash of 1929 leading to the Securities Act of 1933 and the corporate scandals of the late 1990s leading to the Sarbanes-Oxley Act. Predictably, the students were most interested in the corporate scoundrels from the likes of WorldCom, Enron, Tyco, and Adelphia—especially the details of Dennis Kozlowski's Tyco-funded lifestyle, including his eighteen-million-dollar apartment, with its six-thousand-dollar shower curtain, as well as his wife's 2.1-million-dollar Greek island birthday bash.

Henry's final topic was the Foreign Corrupt Practices Act. He explained how the act made it a felony to give anything of value to a foreign official to bolster business. Even doing a favor for a high-placed official could trigger a violation of the act's felony provisions.

As Henry detailed the Foreign Corrupt Practices Act, he felt the students' interest begin to wane. To his annoyance, one of the frat boys in the back row was sound asleep with his tattered baseball cap pulled down over his eyes; his two frat brothers found it thigh-slappingly funny.

Henry dismissed the class after passing out the Supreme Court decision on gay marriage and advising the students that their next class, after spring break, would start with an analysis of that decision. The students fled the room, no doubt anxious to pack their swimsuits and head out for Padre Island or Fort Lauderdale for a week of bacchanalian abandonment. A whisper of envy floated through Henry.

Outside his office, Henry found Nichole Kessler waiting for him. She was dressed in pink running shorts and a small white crop top exposing her belly button.

"Morning, Professor Lindon!" she said with a bright smile. "I hope class went well. Before I leave for spring break, I wanted to check to make sure you got my email."

"Hey, Nichole. Um, didn't see anything, but come on in and I'll take a look."

Nichole followed Henry into his office, closed the office door, and sat down. Henry, wondering why she closed the door, turned on his computer and found a 1:35 a.m. email from her.

> Professor Lindon—hope you are having a great semester so far! I definitely miss starting my Mondays and Wednesdays in your class. I just wanted to email you to see if you would be willing to write me a recommendation for an internship this summer with the office of Senator John Cornyn in D.C. If you are too busy, don't hesitate to tell me. If you are able to, it doesn't need to be addressed to anyone in particular, I just need to pick it up in a sealed envelope. Thanks for your consideration. Have a nice day!

"Sure, Nichole. I'd be happy to write the recommendation. Sounds like an interesting job."

"Super! I appreciate you saying yes." Nichole looked down at her hands in her lap and then up at Henry with a puckish smile. "My friend told me you had a tattoo discussion in class last week. That's amazing!"

Henry laughed uncomfortably. "To tell you the truth, I don't know much about tattoos. I'm not even sure how the discussion got started."

"I'm really into the history of tattoos," Nichole responded, growing more energized. "Did you know that Winston Churchill's mother had a tat on her wrist of a snake eating its tail? I read it's a symbol of eternity. And sailors used to tattoo a chicken on one foot and a pig on the other to protect them against drowning. Have you heard about tattoo roulette at Southerland?"

"Uh, no. Can't say I have." *And not sure I want to know*, he added silently.

"Well, it's super cool. Students who are into tattoos sit in a circle, let's say eight of them, and spin a bottle—like spin the bottle in high school. But for tattoo roulette, the person the bottle points to has to get a tat. Then you spin again and the next person chooses what the tat will be. It can be anything. Then everyone heads down to lower Greenville Avenue to watch the inking!"

Regretting he had raised the topic of tattoos in class, Henry attempted to change topics and asked, "Who's your friend in my class?"

"Andrea Lucero. She told you about the identical dragonfly tats we got in Mexico."

Nichole stood up and, in a pirouette movement, turned her back to Henry. With a slight gyration of her hips and a giggle, she looked at him over her shoulder and yanked down her shorts, exposing a five-inch-long bright purple dragonfly on her right cheek. A gape-jawed Henry sat dazed as she then slowly, and rather provocatively, pulled her shorts up again.

■ ■ ■

Nichole skipped happily down the steps of the business school building. She congratulated herself on her cleverness. The idea to flash her tattoo had jetted into her brain during her daily run. She conceived of it as a foolproof plan to accomplish Uncle Guy's ridiculous demand to put Professor Lindon in a compromising position. Confident that Professor Lindon was not the type to become entangled with a student, she knew her plan made perfect sense.

Using the ruse of showing Professor Lindon her tattoo, she would tell Uncle Guy, with all sincerity, that she had pulled down her shorts in Professor Lindon's office as the prelude to getting him into a compromising position. His lack of interest was not her fault. She had done all she could—it was time for Uncle Guy to keep his promise. Maybe she would not have to resort to using the information from her investigator.

She bit her lower lip, slowing her pace and repressing her excitement. Professor Lindon would never tell anyone about what happened in his office, would he? How could he say anything without implicating himself in inappropriate behavior? After all, it would be her word against his.

Nichole quickly reassured herself that no one at Southerland but she and Professor Lindon would ever know what happened. She was about to graduate and would never see him again. If for some unfathomable reason he raised the issue, she would say it was a joke that went slightly off the rails.

Walking to the center of campus, Nichole looked for a spot where no one was within earshot. It was time to cash in on her ingenious idea. She sat down on the concrete bench that encircled one of the campus's massive fountains. Checking again to ensure she was alone, she took out her cell phone and dialed her uncle.

"Hello, Nikkie. Have news?"

"I did what you asked. Now keep your promise—release my trust fund to me."

"Hold on, not so damn fast. I wasn't expecting a call so soon. That's awfully quick work. Give me the details."

"Simple. I did exactly what you asked. Walked into his office in a skimpy blouse and short shorts, closed the door behind me, and had a pleasant conversation. When he was relaxed, I pulled down my shorts . . . like a five-dollar hooker."

"How badly did he want it?"

Her uncle's words quickened. Some vile kind of excitement over the picture she had painted? Remembering his hand up under her dress when she was seven, she shuddered.

"Actually, not at all. I did what you asked and he was flat-out uninterested. That's not my fault. I did what you asked. I'm done."

"You telling me that prig had no interest?"

"Zero interest. I utterly and absolutely humiliated myself. I want the money, *my* money. I'm done." *And, most of all I want you out of my life!*

"You've given me nothing to use against Henry. You're done when I say you're done."

Nichole took a deep breath and when she spoke again, her voice was hard as steel. "No, Uncle Guy, I'm done. Wire the money or else."

4

The Crescent towers were populated with oil exploration companies, commercial real estate operators, hedge funds, and law firms—all drawn to Dallas's robust economy. The muted office reception areas were adorned in Texas motifs, replete with stuffed oversize leather furniture, cattle-strewn oil paintings, and Remington sculptures commemorating exuberant cowhands waving six-guns. The interior offices combined idyllic photos of smiling families and diplomas from prestigious universities.

But not the MM Enterprises offices.

The chairman of MM Enterprises, "Marvelous" Marvin Lindon, believed an office should reflect a sense of humor. A full-service bar and a thousand-gallon saltwater fish tank dominated the reception room. Each wall was painted a different tropical pastel—pink, yellow, green, and blue. The only things brighter than the walls were the phosphorescent tropical fish chasing each other around the tank's coral and waving seaweed.

The office's "library" had been transformed into a lounge. All books and business tools had been removed and replaced with couches and deep, comfortable chairs. The walls were lined with photographs of Marvin and his many friends on boys-only adventures.

The Library filled with Marvin's friends around five o'clock on Wednesday and Friday afternoons. Sometimes five friends showed up; other times he entertained twenty. Henry always said Marvin maintained the office as more of a social club than as a place of business, and Marvin couldn't fault his observation.

Marvin sat behind his desk, enjoying the quiet of his private office, a safe distance from the Library. He delighted in the fact that his inner sanctum had been christened "Marvin's Garden" by friends because of the many business strategies and shenanigans that had blossomed there. Since the sale of his industrial tape business, the shenanigans predominated and he wasn't ashamed of that fact; nor was he shy about sharing his life's philosophy with anyone willing to listen—get what you want and when you've got it, have the good sense to enjoy it. He had what he wanted and was having one hell of a good time.

Marvin glanced at the framed photos of his three daughters and their families. The only other wall decoration in Marvin's Garden was a photograph of the 1978 Southerland University basketball team with a beaming, dark-haired captain Marvin Lindon in the center, holding a basketball. Although his hair had turned the clean, bright white only the Irish achieve, when people looked at the photo's beaming farm boy with coal-black hair, narrow hips, and broad shoulders, they easily recognized that the energetic and athletically built young man was Marvin.

He smiled at the faces in the team photograph of his best friend and business partner, John O'Souza, known to everyone as John-O, and a skinny Phil Thomas, the Southerland president. The two were trying to look tough and were barely recognizable under their helmets of wavy brown hair and bushy mustaches.

Marvin knew his business might be considered less than glamorous—industrial tape was far from sexy—but he made sure he kept the zest in MM Enterprises in other ways. The key to his success had always been his unwavering attention to client relations. He took obsessive care to inject fun into all his business dealings and budgeted generous funding for "customer relations." Marvin loved entertaining his clients and they, in turn, felt like members of an elite club. MM Enterprises' "business trips" to major sporting events like the

Super Bowl, the Masters, and the NBA championship had become the stuff of legend in the Dallas business community.

Marvin leaned back in his chair, remembering how he'd once thought he was going down for the count—and the day it had all turned around.

MM Enterprises had hit a major impasse. Chinese suppliers began undercutting MM's prices. He and John-O had spent several long days battling, without success, over how to respond to the new competition without slashing the coveted customer-relations budget. Finally, they had retreated to the Trinity Hall pub.

Sitting at his usual high-top table next to the bar, Marvin had all but surrendered to the inevitability that cutting the customer-relations budget was the only feasible response to the Chinese threat. As he and John-O searched for alternative plans to avoid sucking the fun out of the business, John-O ordered his third different pint of beer.

"John-O, why do you keep changin' up your order?" Marvin had asked, honestly perplexed. As far as he was concerned, there was one beer—Pabst Blue Ribbon.

"For one, I enjoy the different hops, but I also like the fact they each come in a different glass with the name of the brewer on it."

At that moment, the lightbulb of invention went on in Marvin's head. He would play the same game as the brewers. For close to nothing, he could imprint unique corporate logos onto his tapes and charge a premium price for the customized product. Best of all, premium pricing for the customized products would eliminate the need to cut prices and allow him to keep the customer-relations budget intact.

His client list soon grew to include FedEx, American Airlines, and Kroger. His payday arrived when 3M decided they had to have his technology. After selling his business, Marvin was a rich man with a lot of free time on his hands.

Now, years later, it was Wednesday afternoon and four regulars had already secured their first drinks and retired to the Library to hash out the day's ridiculously convoluted golf bets. Phyllis, Marvin's assistant for the past nineteen years, played many roles in Marvin's life, including that of office mixologist.

He could hear the sound of muffled conversation down the hall and debated joining his friends. Making a rare decision to put business before pleasure, Marvin hit a "favorite" button on his speakerphone. Ten minutes later, Phyllis walked into his office with a knowing look on her face.

She put one hand on her ample cocked hip as she lectured him. "Marvelous, the guys are settling down in the Library, waiting for you," she said. "Are you listening to a company earnings call?"

"It's the second-quarter call from that Colorado marijuana company I took a position in."

"How's that working out for you?" Phyllis asked, a skeptical look on her face.

"Smokin'! Absolutely smokin'!" He laughed at his own joke and disconnected the call. "Let me ask you somethin', Phyllis. Whaddaya think about all those food trucks all over town? It's like I'd never seen one and now they're everywhere. Last night they were in the parkin' lot at the booze store doing one hell of a business. I grabbed some Mexican from one called the Rip and Roar Taco. Wasn't half bad."

"You're talking to the wrong woman." Phyllis shook her head. "Street food of any kind freaks me out. I mean, do you really think they're washing their hands?" She tipped her head to the side. "Why don't I get you a PBR? You can talk food trucks with the guys."

Marvin got up and sauntered down the hallway toward the Library, softly humming "Here Comes the Sun." To his surprise, Henry was standing at the bar in the office's main reception area.

"Well, bless my soul," Marvin said, putting his arm around Henry's shoulder. "To what do we owe this good fortune? You know I feel kinda like that old *Little Rascals* routine. You know the one, where the geography teacher asks the class if anyone can make up a sentence usin' the word isthmus."

Well accustomed to his role as straight man for his brother's sophomoric humor, Henry deadpanned, "No, can't say I remember that one."

"Oh, c'mon! We watched the show together at least a hundred times. One of the Rascals puts up his hand and tells the teacher he can make a sentence with isthmus and says, 'Ith muth be my lucky day!' Hell, that's how I'm feelin'—ith muth be my lucky day. Come on down to the Library and see what kinda trouble the boys are up to."

As the brothers turned toward the Library, Henry said, "Marvin, something happened today at the university with a student that I'd like your take on."

"Sure. First let's see what's up in the Library."

The golfers and three other regulars, including John-O, lounged comfortably on the Library couches. John-O was Watson to Marvin's Holmes, Ed McMahon to his Carson, and Steve Van Zandt to his Springsteen. The loyal best friend, always ready with a supportive laugh and willing to stand just outside the spotlight. He was always in the action but never the main event.

Their relationship had been unchanged since John-O was the hardwork ing, rebounding power forward, and Marvin was the all-conference shooting guard at Southerland. For decades, the two had been fierce competitors twice a week on the racquetball court and regular teammates on golf course fairways.

As the brothers entered the clamorous Library, a smiling Marvin addressed the group. "I assume you boys are explorin' the benefits of compassion and critical thinkin'."

"Not exactly," John-O answered from his seat. "It was all over the news a while back, Marvelous. This idiot Sanford, you know, ex-governor of South Carolina? He was supposedly presidential material back in 2009, then he goes MIA for a week and his office tells everyone he's hiking the Appalachian Trail without a cell phone. So everybody's wondering if he's dead or what. Well, some reporter busts Sanford's sorry ass when he arrives in Atlanta on a plane from Buenos Aires. Not exactly the Appalachian Trail. Lo and behold, this numbnuts was actually down in Buenos Aires shacked up with some television reporter gal. With genes like that running around South Carolina, it's no wonder the Confederacy went down in flames."

"Please, tell me it's no surprise to you boys that the man's got no pride," Marvin said. "By definition, politicians got no pride. Henry's spent a bunch of time down in Argentina."

"Yeah, sure have," said Henry. "Argentina is a magnificent country and my wife's business partner lives in Buenos Aires. But you and John-O went bird hunting down there last fall, didn't you?"

With Henry's segue, Marvin was off, ruminating on the joys of dove hunting in the grain fields of western Argentina. With John-O providing the laugh track, Marvin regaled the group with his recollections of the morning they managed to shoot nearly five thousand doves.

"Me and John-O each had two gun handlers standin' behind us loadin' shotguns. We'd blast away and when the gun was empty, turn around, and they'd hand us another fully loaded. Hell, by lunchtime, the shotguns were too hot to handle and we were too damn tired to lift 'em!"

■ ■ ■

An hour later, Doris Delaney was sitting in the Avalon Hair Salon with strips of tinfoil in her hair pointing in every direction. Her usual stylist, Shay, a sad-eyed, willowy blonde, used a paintbrush to apply the hair dye and then folded each strand into a square of foil. Doris figured she was about halfway through. She sighed and glanced over at the nail station beside her, where a striking young woman was having her fingernails painted bright green.

"I love that color, sugar. What's it called?" asked Doris.

Looking down at her nails, the young woman replied, "It's called Here Today, Aragon Tomorrow. Kinda wild, isn't it?"

"I swear, names of nail polish these days are as crazy as the colors! Well, it certainly works on you. Wish I was just getting my nails done today. Sugar, when you get to my age this hair thing can rule your life. I'm in here every Wednesday. One week I'm getting it cut and the next, like now, I've got God only knows what kind of chemicals in it. I look like a Martian. And I feel guilty about the time I spend in here. I could be in the gym."

"Well, ma'am, you look like you're in amazing shape."

"Oh Lord, don't call me ma'am! Please, call me Doris." She smiled contentedly at the invited compliment she had reeled in. "I bet you're a student at Southerland. What's new over there? There's always something going on."

The girl smiled back at her. "Well, I'm getting my nails done today because

I love Wednesdays. It's kind of the start of the weekend. Things kick off with the food trucks that park around the huge flagpole. It's the only day they're allowed on campus. I just love the way they're all so brightly painted and the smells are to die for. Some of them have a DJ on board—it's just one big party."

"What fun! Do you have a favorite truck?"

"Different ones show up every week, but I do love Lilly's Lollapalooza. The guy who runs it is jacked and the sushi is the best."

"Absolutely agree," said Shay. "I love the one called Oink 'n' Moo BBQ. The ribs are so tender, and then to top it off with a cookie from the Hummingbird Sweet Shoppe . . . that's about as good as it gets." She peeled off her elbow-length rubber glove, revealing a multicolor paisley, full-sleeve tattoo. "Okay, Doris, time to hit the dryer."

"That's her nice way of saying it's time for more torture!" Doris said as she stood. "Nice chatting with you, and I'll have to give those food trucks a try. Tell me your name again, sugar."

"I'm Nichole. Nichole Kessler."

■■■

Henry watched Phyllis wipe down the bar and prepare to close up shop at Marvin's offices. As the regulars filed out for the night, still debating golf bets, he and his brother headed back to Marvin's Garden.

"Have time *now* to give me some advice?" Henry asked testily. Of course, Marvin had been too busy entertaining his buddies to take ten minutes out for his brother. He felt immediately ashamed of his pettiness. After all, Marvin had gotten him the job at Southerland and now here he was, hat in hand, asking for advice. How pitiful was that? The brothers sat down in the oak rocking chairs in Marvin's Garden.

"What's on your mind, bro?"

"The whole thing seems so ridiculous it's hard to know where to start. My class got into discussing tattoos and the whole conversation went sideways. I . . . well . . . asked a dumb question."

"What kinda question?" Marvin asked, slowly rocking back and forth.

"I asked if any of them had tattoos." Henry closed his eyes and leaned back in his rocker. Why had he ever brought up those stupid tattoos in class? It's Marvin's fault, he thought. He was the one who put the whole idea of tattoos in his head in the first place. He opened his eyes and saw his brother looking down at his own tattooed forearm.

"And the problem is?" Marvin asked.

"A student said she and her friend both got the same purple dragonfly tattoo in Mexico."

Marvin laughed. "So what? Probably half the coeds at Southerland have done that and a whole lot worse. What's your point?"

"The point is . . . well . . . her friend, who was in my class last semester . . . well . . . I've seen that same purple dragonfly tattoo . . . on her butt."

"WELL, FUCK ME TO TEARS!" Marvin yelled, nearly catapulting himself out of his rocking chair. "I never thought you had it in you, Henry! Was it great?"

"No, no, no." Henry got out of the chair and started pacing. "You're not listening. She came to my office to talk about getting a reference for a job, and then pulled down her shorts to show me her tattoo. Nothing more."

"Henry, you tellin' me a girl lookin' for some kind of job reference yanked down her drawers in your office and nothin' happened? What . . . was she moonin' you? What's this girl's name?"

"Her name isn't important. I don't know why the hell she did it. Maybe she thought it was funny. Now the question is, what do I do?"

"Like how to ask her to dinner?"

"Marvin, this isn't a joke." *Why do I ask this maniac for advice?* Henry sighed, debating whether to just say forget it or keep talking.

"Okay, okay," Marvin said. "I just don't get what you're askin' me."

"Should I report the incident to the university? Should I tell your buddy, President Thomas, what happened? Should I talk it over with the student? Should I tell Marylou?"

Marvin launched out of his rocker on to his feet. "Henry, have you lost your bleepin' mind? Some girl drops her drawers in your office and you want to announce it to your wife? Are you kiddin'? Must I remind you that the Code of the West applies here?"

"I understand the Code of the West," Henry replied, dejectedly sitting back down in his chair.

"Sounds like maybe you need a refresher. The Code of the West is sacrosanct." Marvin took on a rare, serious tone. "It's all about how men and women are hardwired different. Women talk about everything, anything, and, lots of times, nothin' at all. All that chatter builds up a cosmic, interconnected spiderweb of information that they use against us. Our only hope is to keep matters secret. Bro, the Code is our only defense."

"You're right, you're right." He did not want to appear weak in front of his brother. "The whole thing has me spooked. The Code of the West applies . . . I won't say a word to Marylou. But should I tell Phil Thomas? What if he finds out what happened? Then won't it look like I was hiding something?"

"Henry, how the hell is he gonna find out? You think this girl wants to tell the world she dropped trou in your office? I've known Phil Thomas forever. Believe me, with all the BS on his plate, he wants nothin' to do with your little dustup. Please, radio silence the whole damn thing."

■ ■ ■

Across town, Marylou Lindon was finishing a telephone conversation with her Argentinian business partner, María José Cifone. "Are you still planning to come to Buenos Aires next week?" asked María José, her voice, as always, filled with excitement.

"Absolutely," Marylou said. "I'll take the overnight American flight on Friday and see you for lunch around one o'clock Saturday after I've had a chance to put myself back together."

Marylou smiled. How many times had she wished that her Argentinian friend lived in the States? She just didn't get to see her often enough these days. During the last four years, Marylou and María José had built a robust business importing Chinese-manufactured home furnishings and selling them to interior designers across Latin America.

Their business had launched with a stroke of good luck. The magnetic and youthful María José smiled her way onto the Susana Giménez morning television show in Buenos Aires to exhibit their new Chinese import—a shiny, twenty-inch-long, red porcelain pig. Susana, or Su, as Buenos Aires's best-known television personality is known to all, loved the red pig and gushed on air about putting it on her home mantel. Overnight the partners had to triple their production orders. In the following months, the red pig became an unlikely icon of international sophistication for Argentina's middle-class homemakers.

During their first two years in business, the partners worked from their homes, but as sales continued to build, they opened offices in Dallas and Buenos Aires. To help them feel closer than the five thousand miles separating them, Marylou suggested they build identical office spaces in each location. The offices had the same number of square feet, the same rugs, the same drapes, the same desks, and the bookshelves were filled with their home-furnishing products. The final touches were the oversize, bright red abstract paintings matching the color of their now famous pigs. When one woman visited the other's office, she felt completely at home.

Their personalities, however, were not identical. María José, ten years Marylou's junior, was wildly creative and affectionate. Anyone meeting María José just once was assured of enthusiastic hugs for life. She had long made her living in interior design, but her passions were painting and sculpture. The fun-loving Marylou was a successful CPA with superior business instincts. María José's artistic creativity and Marylou's organizational skills proved a potent business combination.

"Any chance Henry will come?" María José's tone over the phone was soft, her accent melodious. Marylou loved her voice—her question, not so much. "Marcello and I miss him. Indeed, it seems like everyone misses Henry. I ran into Mikel Jiménez. You know, Mikel who owns that wonderful shop where Henry bought all those shirts? Well, he misses his favorite client. I would imagine his cash flow has suffered as well!"

Marylou's heart sank a little. "Henry certainly loves Mikel's shirts, but he won't be making the trip. He's . . . busy with his new life as a professor." She hesitated for a moment and then rushed on before she changed her mind. "María José . . . can I share something with you?"

"Indeed, of course!"

"It's not just his new job. I don't understand what happened but Henry and I . . . we're just not getting along. It seems like everything I say irritates him and so I end up avoiding talking to him. I'm worried about him . . . about us." Marylou's eyes filled with tears.

"Oh, Marylou, I am so sorry." Her friend's gentle Latina voice wrapped around her like a comforting hug. "You must not worry. Men go insane every seven years; it is in their genes. He will come around. Good men like Henry always do."

Marylou reached into her purse for a tissue as the first tear spilled down her cheek. "It's as though he resents me—but I don't know why! I just don't understand him."

"My dear Marylou! What you need is a good cry, a long talk, and a great big glass of wine! That is exactly what we will do when you get here, it is my promise."

Marylou wiped away her tears and took a deep breath, cheered by her friend's kindness. "That sounds wonderful," she said. "And I'll wear the jacket you sent me from Mikel's store."

"Oh! Do you still like it?" María José asked in delight.

"Oh yes, I love it!" said Marylou. "It goes with anything. You are so dear to be thinking of me all the time."

"Indeed, the pleasure is mine. I hope you enjoyed the little card I enclosed in the box, the one I wrote in Spanish to help you practice."

"*Claro que sí . . . muchísimas gracias, mi querida,*" Marylou replied in halting Spanish. She had no recollection of the card. She remembered Henry had opened the box, mistakenly thinking it was for him. She made a mental note to ask him about the card.

"*Ciao, ciao,* María José."

"*Hasta pronto,* Marylou."

Marylou hung up the phone and sighed, then turned back to her work. But she couldn't focus on compiling the new catalog. She glanced up at the clock. It was past seven. She'd been working long hours lately—was that why Henry was so unhappy with her?

Driving home, Marylou found herself stopped in Northwest Highway's rush-hour traffic. She was tired from a long day behind her desk, and as she thought back over her conversation with María José, a lonesome feeling crept over her. After nearly three decades of happy marriage, why was this emotional distance growing between her and Henry? Her woman's intuition told her Argentina was somehow to blame—he always changed the subject when she brought up Argentina, and he never went with her to visit anymore—but why?

Henry once loved Argentina. He had introduced her to the country and to María José. She was married to Marcello Cifone, Henry's legal counsel in Argentina. For eighteen months, the two men had worked tirelessly on acquiring the San Miguel Galletas cookie company, located in the city of the same name in the northwest part of the country. Henry christened the painfully drawn-out transaction the Deal from Hell.

On Marylou's first trip to Buenos Aires, Marcello knew he and Henry would be locked up in an all-day Deal-from-Hell meeting. He thoughtfully arranged for María José to take Marylou on a tour of Colonia, in Uruguay, the colonial city a quick ferry ride across the Río de la Plata from Buenos Aires. Not only was Marylou fascinated by Colonia's nineteenth-century flavor, but she and María José became fast friends. From that day on, Marylou never missed an opportunity to join one of Henry's frequent business trips to Argentina.

As their friendship grew, the couples vacationed together across Argentina. Marylou often reminisced about the couples' trip to El Calafate near the tip of the continent, just above the South Pole. They drove through Patagonia to the Perito Moreno Glacier, strapped crampons on their hiking boots, and ascended. At the hike's end, their guide unpacked a bottle of scotch and chipped off chunks of million-year-old blue ice into glasses. With a raised glass, Henry offered a touching toast to the glories of Argentina.

But something changed. Henry had lost all interest in Argentina. He now had more time on his hands and, given the financial success of the business she had built with María José, Henry's change of heart made no sense. She had tried talking with him about his attitude change, but, in typical Henry fashion, he shrugged off the discussion and changed the topic.

A sharp car horn jolted Marylou out of her thoughts and she stepped on the gas to close the gap in the line of traffic. If only it were as easy to close the gap between her heart and Henry's.

■ ■ ■

Henry sat in his study rereading a card he kept hidden in his bottom desk drawer. He heard Marylou coming through the back door and the opening and closing of kitchen cabinets. Glancing again at the note, his anxiety morphed to anger. Peeved she hadn't bothered to visit him in his study, he put the note back in its hiding place, got up, and went to the kitchen.

"Hey you!" Marylou cheerfully greeted him. "Sorry I'm late, but I got to chatting with María José. You know how that is. Did class go okay?"

"Class was fine. Went down to Marvin's office to see how all the guys are doing." *I was really there to talk about the dragonfly tattoo. The Code of the West means I can't talk about it with you.*

"That's nice," responded Marylou. "I got the feeling you weren't real interested in that group."

"Why say I'm not interested in those guys?" *She's right. I'm totally uninterested in those lazy hangers-on.*

"Sorry. Just got the vibe you weren't."

"I don't need negativity. Why in the world wouldn't I like Marvin's friends?" *Why can't I bring myself to tell her what's really on my mind?*

"Come on . . . let's not fight. I'm going to make a salmon salad. How about dinner out on the porch, a glass of pinot?"

"No. Can't you see your constant negativity is wearing me down to the bone? Congratulations, another evening ruined. I'm going upstairs."

5

Guy Wheeless Jr. was on a call with a London-based investment banker when he saw his chief lieutenant, Edward O'Brian, sitting in his outer office with a briefcase on his lap. Still listening to the banker, Wheeless put down the antique Swingline stapler he was toying with and waved his hand to signal O'Brian into his office. O'Brian rose and obediently hurried through the door.

Rolling his eyes, Wheeless made the too-much-talking gesture with his fingers. He ended the call saying, "Nigel, if and when you have the information I'm looking for, send me an email. Good day." He stood and led the way to the glass conference table on the other side of the room and took a seat. O'Brian took one across from him.

"The damn Brits are too polite to be of any real use," Wheeless said. "So, how was your time at UNS with the lovely Ms. Jane Birney?"

"It's like pulling teeth with those people," O'Brian said as he removed folders from his briefcase. "Jane paraded out an army of junior geniuses to demonstrate all the effort they had put behind due diligence on the San Miguel operation. The amount of time and money they spent was pretty impressive."

"Yeah, let's not confuse effort with results. Learn anything?"

O'Brian shook his head. "Despite the reams of files they shared with us, we didn't gain any insight on how they missed the labor issues. There was one oddity in the time lines they produced that's could be worth digging into."

"Yes?" Wheeless sat up straight.

"The Argentine attorneys kept a very meticulous negotiation time line," O'Brian said, holding up an Excel spreadsheet. "For each meeting they set out who was present, the issues discussed, and the parties' positions on each issue at the end of the meeting . . ."

"Edward, what's the point—cut to the chase."

"I'm getting there." O'Brian shuffled his papers to find a different spreadsheet and held it up. "The time line shows endless meetings with Henry Lindon, his Argentine attorney named Marcello Cifone, and Argentine government officials. The subject was always the same—the tax breaks Inveress wanted from the government. They could never reach agreement. Then, Lindon was called back to the States. Miraculously, two days later, the government officials granted all the tax breaks Lindon had been requesting.

"Here's the kicker—the time line shows the deal agreed to was under the exact same terms as the government officials expressly rejected two days earlier when Lindon went Stateside. There's zero explanation of why the government officials radically changed their position. Smells like some cash passed under the table; after all, it is Latin America."

"Interesting. Very interesting." Wheeless leaned forward and placed his fingers lightly on the glass table. "Put a microscope on exactly why the officials changed their minds. I especially want to know what role that tight ass Henry Lindon played."

"I thought we might take a fresh look at the pro forma financial statements UNS produced to support the Inveress transaction."

"Fuck the pro formas!" Wheeless slammed both hands on the glass table. "Did you hear what I just said? I want one hundred percent focus on the government officials' change of heart and Henry Lindon's role. In fact, let's get real intimate with Henry."

"You want the whole treatment—tap his phones, hack his computer?"

"Absolutely," said Wheeless. "No detail is too small. I want to know when this prick takes a leak."

"Any preference for the system we use?" O'Brian squeezed his papers back into his briefcase. "Lately we've been working with some ex-FBI guys out of Kansas City. They like to use Kismet or Aircrack-ng."

"Don't be such a bore, Edward." Wheeless rubbed his forehead. "Get the information any way you can."

"I'm on it."

"One more thing. Did the foundation make that contribution to the Wichita Art Museum?"

O'Brian nodded. "Like you said, I spoke with the director, a little French egomaniac named Aubuchon. Told him the foundation was thinking about a possible contribution and the frog threw out a number he thought would intimidate me. I think he shit his pants when I agreed."

"How much?"

"A million."

"Nice work; I would have been happy at double the amount. Now get out of here."

Without waiting to see if O'Brian left, Wheeless walked into his private bathroom and stood in front of the mirror. His hair was perfect.

The ploy with Nikkie fell flat, he thought. *Was it because Henry was such a prude? His brother Marvin would have gone after it like a rabid two-dicked dog. Or had Nikkie really pulled down her shorts at all? That little bitch is certainly not above lying. Maybe she made an effort, but there were no results, no photo, no nothing. I'm not going to release her trust money for a flawed effort. What can she do about it? Nothing, absolutely nothing.*

Wheeless knew it was time to change tactics. It was a long shot, but maybe, just maybe, there was a way to tie Henry Lindon to some wrongdoing—perhaps even tie him to a bribe—in connection with the San Miguel deal. Maybe careful, methodical Henry had finally left himself exposed.

He reached into his inside coat pocket and took out the photograph his driver, Larry, had given him a few days before. He decided that with the foundation contribution in place, it was time for a visit to the Wichita Art Museum to check out this tantalizing new prospect.

■■■

The next morning, Henry climbed the stairs of Hunt Hall, the first building constructed on Southerland's hilltop campus. As he entered the building's rotunda, he was bathed with different shades of light cast by the stained-glass concave ceiling. He committed himself to make the best of the bureaucratic mess known as the Task Force on Sexual Assault.

The task force embodied Henry's main issue with academia—so much of university life was a bureaucracy wrapped in red tape. The smallest of decisions became captive to a system oriented toward delay. He yearned for the corporate world's bias for action.

A dangerously nuanced mandate hindered the task force from the start. The vast majority of sexual assault complaints—over ninety percent—came from freshmen women, a group wrestling with the harsh realities of individual freedom for the first time. The university had aggravated the situation by dismissing a student's accusation of rape that eventually wound up as a criminal indictment at the hands of the publicity-hungry district attorney. Soon, evidence surfaced that the accused had a sexual predator history but was still allowed on campus. The university's predictable answer to the public outcry was the creation of the task force.

The organization of the task force was a classic academic compromise. The appointment of twenty members was a recipe for failure. With representatives from the student body, alumni, staff, and the faculty, even the strongest leader would have difficulty forging a direction, much less a consensus. In a bureaucratic miscue, President Thomas had compounded the problems by naming four co-chairs.

As Henry entered the drab conference room, he saw the four co-chairs seated at the head of the well-worn conference table. He smiled to himself. *They look like the* Star Wars *bar scene*, he thought.

On the far left sat Shaheed Singh Nanak. Nanie, as he was known to his colleagues, was a Sikh from the Punjab. He wore his hair in a canary-yellow turban and had a full black beard that covered a rarely smiling face. He looked every part the ascetic. A professor of Asian religions, he preferred solitary research to the give-and-take of the classroom.

Sitting to Nanie's right was Mildred Underwood, the assistant dean for student life. She was a "lifer." Millie had never left campus for more than a week since the fall of her freshman year. Crowding middle age, she wore her hair in the long, unflattering style of her student days in the late sixties and caked on enough makeup for a Broadway musical.

Ron Areosin, a former offensive lineman at the University of Texas, ran security operations at Southerland. Despite his resolute cheerfulness, time had been unkind to Ron. His huge frame was ideal for packing on pounds and eroding joints. As he nodded in response to something Millie was saying, his large shaved head shone like one of the campus's golden domes.

The final co-chair was Emily Parker, whose unruly head of curls and matching rose-red lipstick resembled those of a circus clown. Belying her appearance, Emily was a law professor who took herself and her position within the university community very, very seriously.

Henry slid quietly into a chair next to a task force member from the student body. He nodded a silent hello. After the group was settled, Emily Parker began the meeting.

"Before turning to our agenda, I'd like to share with you the details of a most unfortunate incident that occurred last night and comes within the prescribed charter of our task force. We should anticipate negative press coverage of a multimedia variety. As head of university security, Mr. Areosin will share the details of last night's regrettable events."

Ron Areosin began, his West Texas drawl filling the room. "Thanks, Emily. Campus was unusually quiet last night until around 11:30. At that time, a Sigma Sigma Sigma pledge, on some sort of dare from his pledge brothers, decided to surf the wave sculpture—that huge sixty-foot-long sculpture with all those square metal poles erected out over the shallow pool . . . with the poles in constant motion like waves in the ocean. Y'all know what I'm talking about? I think the sculptor is named Calatrava, or somethin' like that. One of my guys told me he's famous." Several of the members of the task force nodded assent and Ron continued.

"Well, a group of 'em went to the sculpture and this kid got excited and told his buddies he was going to make it a night for the ages and gets buck nekkid. Well, he jumped up there in his birthday suit, but slipped and got the toes of his left foot caught in the moving poles. He fell over and . . . well, he landed on his stomach and his thing . . . you know, his . . . member . . . oh, hell . . . his penis, got crushed by the moving poles. When my guys arrived on the scene, he was screaming bloody murder and gushin' blood like a fire hydrant while his buddies hopped around like a bunch of wild geese." Ron chuckled, then changed his laugh to a cough as Millie turned baleful eyes on him.

"The student's parents have been informed and the fraternity has been placed on probation," Millie added in an officious tone. "The student, who was obviously in need of medical attention, has voluntarily withdrawn and will not return to campus this semester."

"Why just a semester?" snapped Emily. "This is precisely the type of sexual misconduct that is rampant on this campus and, I would add, the type of behavior this task force is charged with addressing. Expulsion would seem barely adequate."

"Can I jump in here?" asked the student body representative sitting next to Henry. "I hope I'm not out of line, but are we having some issues with definitions? Look at the facts: This sorry dude gets his schlong crushed while trying to surf the wave sculpture. No disrespect intended, but that sure doesn't sound sexual to me. I mean, I've never heard of sex ending with a mashed pecker."

The meeting disintegrated into a multiplicity of arguments. The room was silenced by the booming voice of an alumnus from West Monroe, Louisiana. Henry sighed and crossed his arms over his chest, trying to stay attentive.

"Ladies and gentlemen, please!" the alumnus bellowed. "Take a deep breath, mah friends. We're here to resolve some serious issues, not argue among ourselves. Mr. Areosin, I 'preciate you bringing this mattah to our attention, but we are not here to solve every bit of campus tomfoolery. On this one, I believe we're sniffin' down the wrong rabbit hole. Heck, at some of those snotty-ass schools in the East, a whole class full of them fools run around the campus in nothin' but their damn Nikes. I agree with my young friend here: There was no sexual assault—unless the damned wave sculpture wants to file a complaint!"

The room filled with laughter. Nanie silently raised his arm straight in the air and held it there until quiet returned. "Let's all take a moment," he said softly. "We need to regain our footing as a task force. I suggest we take this opportunity to review our charter and see if we can agree on the best way forward."

As his fingers slowly drummed his cowlick, Henry knew he had to do his best to pretend he was paying attention to the droning discussion that lacked any hope of resolution. He again wondered if he was cut out for the bureaucratic world of academia. Rather than focusing on the committee's work, his thoughts ricocheted back and forth between the tattoo incident in his office, growing anxiety about Guy Wheeless Jr., and how he would tell Marylou he knew what was going on in Buenos Aires.

■ ■ ■

That afternoon, a very different kind of task force was at work in Marvin's offices. Marvin and John-O, self-professed college basketball gurus, were in the Library planning their annual assault on the college basketball summit—a trip to Las Vegas to gamble on the Final Four tournament.

The Library's narrow conference table was strewn with copies of *Basketball Times, Slam*, *College Basketball*, and *Sporting News.* Assorted newspapers from across the country—including *The New York Times,* the *Cleveland Plain Dealer,* and the *Los Angeles Times*—were spread open to the sportswriters' columns rationalizing their picks for the upcoming tournament games.

Marvin, in a demonstrative show of disdain for a *Dallas Morning News* sports columnist, theatrically crumpled the newspaper in both hands and dunked it hard into the wastepaper basket.

"Marvelous, let's take a break. My head's swimming from all these numbers." John-O got up from his chair and fell onto a nearby couch. "We need to talk trip. Think it's time to change things up, maybe stay at one of those new spots on the strip? Me and the wife stayed at The Venetian last time we went to Vegas. With the canals and Italian gondolas, it was pretty sweet."

"Oh, I don't know, John-O," Marvin said. "We've been doin' this trip for what—almost twenty years—and always flop at The Mirage. I love the action in their Race & Sports Book. Wasn't it just last year you scored five grand at their blackjack table?" Marvin reached into the popcorn bowl for an overflowing handful. "I feel like we're askin' for trouble if we change. You know, some kinda jinx. The boys expect to be at The Mirage. Hell, a couple of 'em are already confused enough. And if they tell their wives they're goin' to some fancy-pants new hotel, that'll kick the hornet's nest. Let's stay the course. Are you gonna email the boys about the dates and the hotel?"

"Yeah, I got it," agreed John-O. "Some of 'em want to know if we're going to fly out on a private jet again."

"Sure, we'll go NetJets." Marvin shook his hand and tossed some popcorn kernels into his mouth. "You know for some of 'em it's their favorite part of the trip. You only live once and if you can't spend money havin' a good time with your friends, what's the point of havin' money?"

"Okay, I'll let 'em know," John-O said, doing a full body stretch on the couch. "Planning on any guest appearances this year or just the regulars?"

"I'm tryin' to talk Henry into taggin' along." Marvin paused to throw a piece of popcorn in the air and catch it in his mouth. "We need to loosen up that boy. I thought once he left the corporate world for an ivory tower, he'd start havin' more fun like back in the day. He's been walkin' around with a burr under his saddle for way too long."

"Hell, Marvelous, Henry showed up at the Library last week and had a couple of pops with the boys. That's a step in the right direction," John-O added with a frown. "When you say loosen him up, you mean like we loosened up Phil Thomas a few years back?"

"No, no, no," Marvin said as he brushed the popcorn crumbs out of his hands. "Henry certainly doesn't need that degree of attitude adjustment. I'm sure ol' President Thomas won't forget his big night in Vegas anytime soon. On another front, John-O, I've been thinkin' on my food truck idea. Those food trucks remind me of the good ol' days flyin' Southwest Airlines."

"How so?" John-O said with a laugh. "Both have wheels?"

"Remember when Southwest got started, and those immediate turn 'round trips we used to take to Houston? Fly down there, fly right back?"

"Marvelous, I'll never forget, maybe the best days of my life. With those $19.99 round-trip tickets to Houston and free booze on board, it was the cheapest bar in the Lone Star State. Remember the Saturday night we made back-to-back round trips?"

Marvin chuckled. "The free booze was manna from heaven, no doubt about it. But what about that eye candy!"

"Praise be! You're preaching the gospel, Marvelous." John-O sat up and made prayer hands under his chin. "The hot pants on those stewardesses! My, has our society taken a pathetic turn—when was the last time you saw hot pants? Remember those two stewardesses that took us home to their place over near Rice?"

"Be still my heart. What I'd give for another spin," Marvin said, placing his hand over his heart. "But that's exactly my point. Southwest wasn't sellin' jet travel; they were sellin' sex and free booze. And that's the opportunity for us. The food trucks in Dallas are just sellin' food. We'll get us some lookers to work the truck and sell sex. I asked Henry to find out about the permit process for the trucks. We'll put our heads together with him when we get back from Vegas." He took a drink from the Dr Pepper bottle in front of him and smacked his lips. "Yes sir, I can see some mighty interestin' days ahead."

■ ■ ■

After dinner, Henry sat in his study putting the finishing touches on the next morning's lecture. His cell phone vibrated.

"Henry Lindon," he answered.

"Henry, Jane Birney. Hope I'm not interrupting you."

Crap. Henry nearly said the word out loud. Birney had led UNS's hostile takeover of Inveress. It galled him that UNS had swooped in and deprived him of the benefits of the Deal from Hell he had worked tirelessly to put together. Unfortunately, the lucrative severance deal UNS gave him when the company showed him the door required cooperation with UNS for twenty-four months. He couldn't duck her.

"No, not at all, just . . . reading."

"Good. I'm calling to see if we can get together to discuss a business issue."

So typical, Henry thought. *No small talk, no how's the family. Just a direct launch into business.*

"What's the issue?" Henry asked, rolling his eyes. He was pretty sure that whatever she had in mind would not be good news.

"We're experiencing issues with the San Miguel operation in Argentina. Since you know as much about that operation as anybody, I'd like to pick your brain."

"What type of problems?" Henry asked.

"Operational issues. I'll fill you in when we get together. Can you come up to our offices in New Brunswick? Or if more convenient, I'll be in Mexico City next week and we could meet there."

"Mexico City might work."

"Great. My office will email details in the morning. Good night, Henry."

As Henry reflected on what issue Birney might have in mind that would drag him to Mexico City, his cell phone buzzed again. He recognized the number.

"Ken Maltman, twice in one week! How the hell are you?"

"Damn good. How's the cushy life of a prof? Got your scuffed loafers and cardigan sweater on today?"

"School has its moments. You'll never guess who just called me . . . Jane Birney."

"My sincerest regrets. How's the ice queen?"

"Unchanged and unrepentant—the woman's got just one gear," Henry answered.

"Man oh man, better you than me. But I've got a little something you can maybe help me with. Just might lighten your load."

"Okay, shoot." Henry imagined his friend leaning back in his office chair, rubbing his shaved head as he'd seen him do a hundred times when they worked together at Inveress.

"Remember after UNS kicked us to the curb and we all scattered, I accepted a position on the Wein, Inc. board of directors?"

"Of course. Still working for you?"

"Been great, but we have an issue and I'm hoping you can help me out. Wein's president and CEO announced he'll step down in December. He's done a hell of a job, big shoes to fill. By a strange sequence of events, I was appointed head of the nominating committee to find a replacement. I walked around Manhattan for two weeks with a long list of candidates in my pocket. Now I've cut the list to one, and you're on the top! Can you climb down from that ivory tower of yours?"

"Ken . . . I'm flattered." In truth, Henry was more shocked than flattered.

"Can I take that to mean you'll consider it?"

"You bet . . . absolutely." Henry's heart rate increased at the mere thought of getting back into the game.

"Perfect. Obviously this is all hush-hush. Wein does extensive background checks on all management personnel. I had to go through their vetting process and it's a major-league pain in the arse. But if I can slide through, a man of your rep will have smooth sailing."

"This is great, Ken, thanks. I'll need to talk it over with Marylou."

"Of course. Give that pretty gal a squeeze for me. Think hard on this one, Henry—it's a great opportunity. I'll check back in next week. Sleep well."

Henry's head spun. The elation of the Wein opportunity eclipsed Birney's annoying call. He had a shot—leave academia's impenetrable wall of red tape behind and regain his standing in the corporate world. He wouldn't miss academia. The inertia of the university's bureaucracy was simply too much for him.

Thinking back on the last meeting of the task force on sexual assault solidified the decision for him. He couldn't sit through another aimless meeting—it was time for a change. Opportunities for a CEO position didn't come up every day, especially one with his good friend Ken Maltman heading the nominating committee. And like Ken had said, he had no reason to give the Wein vetting process any thought.

6

Marylou rolled over and stretched out her arm to the empty side of the bed. Henry was gone. For the entirety of their marriage, Marylou was always the first one out of bed. That pattern had reversed after Henry lost his Inveress job. Insomnia was like an unwelcome supplement to Henry's severance package.

Tying her white satin robe as she walked down the stairs, Marylou stopped in front of Henry's study. Still in his pajamas and with a pencil behind his ear, he was busy with Internet research.

"Mornin'. Have you been up a while?"

"More than a while," Henry replied. He pulled his arms over his head, stretching his back. "Sure hope this tossing and turning is a temporary affliction. Coffee's on."

Henry closed the Wein, Inc. website. His ex-colleague Ken Maltman was right; it was a great prospect. But, how could he raise the issue with Marylou at this awkward time? Maybe the Wein opportunity would spark the courage of honesty. Sleep-deprived and without a clear plan on how to talk to his wife, Henry headed for the kitchen.

After a silent breakfast spent watching the morning news, Henry and Marylou cleared the dishes, working in unison. Years of marriage had led to a tacit divvying up of the household chores. Their only child, Laney, was married and living in San Francisco, taking a fruitful opportunity for daily small talk with her. Marylou felt keenly the loss of that daily connection.

"Henry, remember, I'm leaving for Buenos Aires tonight," Marylou said, her tone light, impersonal. "I promised to meet Susan for a drink at the Dallas Country Club before I head to the airport. Susan's always good for a giggle or two."

"Things around here would be a whole lot different if Marvin had just stayed married to Susan." Henry was striving for the same easy tone. "What did it last, six months?"

"Sounds about right." Marylou closed the dishwasher. "But somehow they manage to have a one-of-a-kind relationship that works for them."

Was it his imagination or did Marylou sound wistful?

She held out her empty coffee mug. "Another cup of coffee?"

"Okay."

"Heard your phone ring a couple of times last night. Anything interesting?"

"I guess so," Henry said begrudgingly. "The first call was from Jane Birney, remember her? The general counsel for UNS who directed their hostile tender offer for Inveress."

"I remember. We sat with her at the deal's closing dinner." She pushed her hair behind her ear. "Not exactly Ms. Warm and Fuzzy."

"That's her. Not the type you want to vacation with, but she's effective on the job and has always made good on her commitments to me." Henry placed his coffee mug on the center island of the kitchen. "She has questions about that San Miguel Galletas deal Marcello and I worked on before UNS took over Inveress. Remember we called it the Deal from Hell?"

"I wonder what that robot really wants?" Marylou said, with irritation in her voice. "They didn't need any help from your old Inveress team, but now they're looking to you for answers?"

"Pretty outrageous. But with Guy Wheeless Jr. owning a big chunk of UNS stock, this will give me a chance to check on what he's doing at UNS."

"I hate to see you getting all paranoid about Guy Jr.," Marylou said, nervously twisting her wedding ring around her finger. "All that silly stuff happened way back in Wichita and you told me that he's now richer than King Midas. Surely he's got better things to do than mess with you."

Henry felt the pressure of resentment intensifying inside him. "I'm not paranoid, and I've had it with you saying that! I showed you *The Wall Street Journal* article about how Guy Jr. led the group that pushed UNS to buy Inveress. Why the hell am I paranoid to think he's involved with UNS's ongoing strategy?"

"Sorry," Marylou said quickly. "I'll never mention paranoia again. Please, let's not fight. I'm leaving for Buenos Aires tonight."

"Of course you are," Henry said with a sarcastic tone.

"What is that supposed to mean?" asked Marylou.

"You're spending an awful lot of time in Buenos Aires," he said, fighting to damp down the pressure building inside him. "How long will you be gone this time?"

"Looks like a week, maybe a tad longer." Marylou sat on one of the stools at the Carrara marble-topped kitchen island, toying with a half-eaten bran muffin. "That wonderful, silly red pig has been such a success, but I'm afraid we're out of runway. María José has some ideas on new items to replace those sales." She glanced up at Henry. "She and Marcello keep asking when you'll make the trip. María José told me even that charming shirt guy, Mikel Jiménez, asked about you."

Marylou's mention of "that charming shirt guy" ratcheted up the pressure. Henry's head felt like a food processor blending a toxic mixture of hurt and resentment at an ever-accelerating speed. The pressure built past the point of control and burst out all over Marylou.

"If you spent a little less time on Buenos Aires and more time on your family, maybe we'd have a real family."

Marylou's mouth dropped open. "What the hell is that supposed to mean?"

"You know exactly what I mean."

"No, I don't!"

"Let me spell it out for you. Maybe if you'd spent a little less time running around Buenos Aires and more time being a mother, Laney wouldn't have felt the need to move two thousand miles away."

Marylou's lower lip began to tremble. "You son of a bitch!" she screamed. She stood for a split second, burst into tears, and ran up the stairs.

■■■

Hours later, Marylou returned to an empty house to finish packing for her trip. Henry was gone and for the first time—maybe ever—she didn't want to find him.

She sat alone in the kitchen sadly staring off into space. Feeling lonely in her own house, she wondered how her marriage had deteriorated to this point. Why was her every word with Henry the wrong word? A therapeutic fight was impossible, because she had no idea what to fight about. Why was Henry so antagonistic about Buenos Aires? Lonely and frustrated, she silently began to cry.

That afternoon, Marylou parked her car in front of the new clubhouse at the Dallas Country Club and checked her makeup in the rearview mirror. She lifted her sunglasses, revealing tear-swollen eyes. She knew she would have to keep her sunglasses on. She stared at the clubhouse and shook her head—it looked like a Cotswolds manor house on steroids. The stone-and-brick behemoth, topped with a slate roof and eighteen spiraling chimneys, stood as a fifty-two-million-dollar monument to Dallas's insatiable pursuit of respect and unshakable belief that bigger is unfailingly better.

After locking her car and making her way to the building, she hurried up the steps and through one of the club's monastery-like stone corridors. Moving past walk-in-sized fireplaces and multiple dining rooms with fifty-foot vaulted ceilings and huge Texas-themed oil paintings, she eventually arrived at an enormous stone patio overlooking the golf course. She found Susan propped up on a lounge chair with an ice bucket holding a bottle of white wine at her side. She was sunning her slender legs.

"Girl, you look awful comfy and I like what you've done with your hair!" Marylou leaned over and gave Susan a quick hug.

"Take a load off, Lou. Let me pour you a splash of California's finest," Susan said as she waved to a man walking off the eighteenth green.

Marylou settled into another lounge chair beside her friend, under the shade of a burnt-orange umbrella. She accepted a glass of wine from Susan with a sigh and a forced smile. A glass of wine wasn't going to fix anything, but maybe it would round off the edges of her anxiety.

"How was dinner with Marvin and that bimbo he calls Double D?" Susan asked.

Marylou took a sip from her glass. "Please let's not ruin the day. I'd much rather hear about you. Are you and Marvin getting along these days?"

"Lou, it just tickles me." Susan got up to turn her lounge chair toward Marylou. "It's like the only thing we needed to build a relationship was a divorce. Crazy. From the day I met Marvin to the time the ink was dry on the divorce papers was less than five months. Hell, I've had house orchids last longer than our marriage!

"Our whole marriage was ridiculous," Susan went on. "We weren't ready for it, and once it was over we started taking the time to get to know each other. It's a work in progress. Nothing like you and Henry. You met in high school, right?"

"Yep, and Marvin was responsible for getting us together." A light sheen of sweat caused Marylou's sunglasses to slip. She pushed them back up her nose.

"What were Marvin and Henry like back then?"

"Pretty much the same as now." Marylou felt herself relaxing. "Henry's always been understated and cautious. He likes to carefully weigh every alternative and then weigh them a couple more times."

"No one would use 'understated' to describe Marvin," Susan said, leaning over to pour Marylou more wine.

"No doubt. Marvin has always been impulsive and was born without the shy gene." Marylou recrossed her legs to get more comfortable. "Their mother, Helene, once told me she prayed every Sunday that someday Marvin would find interests beyond basketball and girls."

Susan raised one carefully sculpted brow. "Did Helene have any insights about Henry?"

"I remember her saying that waiting for Henry to make a decision was as painful as watching a cow chew her cud—the process just went on forever." The women shared a laugh at the visual.

"Sorry," said Susan. "But I can just see Henry chewing his cud, that calm look on his face! Sounds like mom knew her boys pretty well. So how was Marvin responsible for getting the two of you together?"

"It's a nice story from a simpler time." With a touch of gloom, Marylou reflected that it had also been a far happier time. "It was the summer of 1975 and we were all in high school in Wichita. I was brought up in the 'big city' of Wichita with three sisters and a brother. Henry and Marvin grew up on the Lindons' wheat farm out in McPherson. It was just the two of them growing up together. Being only eleven months apart, their parents called them their Irish twins."

"It's interesting that despite being Irish twins, they're so different-looking."

"No doubt about that. As I'm sure you've heard before, Marvin was a big-deal basketball player in town." Marylou's fingers made air quotes around the words *big deal*. "That's when he got that silly nickname, 'Marvelous.' A sports reporter from *The Wichita Eagle* called him that and it just stuck for all these years."

"Men sure love silly nicknames," added Susan.

"Yep, good old Marvelous. So he called and asked me out, but, to tell you the truth, he intimidated me—he was incredibly handsome and so popular. He had a huge head of crow-black hair and was as tall back then as he is today. Everybody in town knew who he was. He wasn't just a big deal in his school; he was a celebrity in the city."

"Did you go out with him?" Susan asked, reaching into the ice bucket to check the wine's level.

"Oh, no, are you kidding? I was little seventeen-year-old Marylou Williams from West Wichita and I was scared to death! I made up an excuse." She smiled slightly. "The funny thing is, turning him down just seemed to make him more determined to get me to go out with him."

"Sounds like Marvin. And the pursuit began!" She lifted her wineglass in tribute. Marylou laughed in spite of herself.

"Did it ever! He used to drop by the shoe store at Towne East Square mall every Saturday. I worked there on weekends. He kept asking and asking—" She broke off, remembering how persistent Marvin had gotten.

"You've never told me this!" Susan said, pulling her legs up and wrapping her arms around them. "He must have really liked you."

Marylou shrugged. "Maybe. I think more likely he just couldn't stand that a girl had actually turned him down. Then one Saturday he told me he and his brother Henry were going to a friend's house for a pool party that night. He said I had to come."

"Now the truth comes out," Susan said. "You were interested in Henry. That's why you didn't want to go out with Marvin."

"I guess I was a little interested, yeah," Marylou said with a sad smile. "Henry was so shy back then and he had these big dimples that gave him such a darling smile."

"I bet he was a cutie. Go on, girl, I'm loving this." Susan reclined to a more relaxed position.

Marylou leaned her head back against the lounge chair, thinking about that long-ago Saturday night. "Isn't memory weird?" she finally said. "I couldn't tell you what I had for lunch yesterday but I remember every detail of the day I met Henry. I spent the afternoon with my older sister trying on about every outfit I owned. We finally settled on my tightest bell-bottom jeans, a flowing white gypsy top, and hoop earrings. Remember that look?"

"Absolutely. Loved it!"

"Well, anyway . . ." Marylou felt her body relaxing even more. The wine had done its work and her worries over her marriage began to fade a little as she reminisced. "The boys picked me up in their father's old green Ford pickup from the family farm. They had washed and waxed the truck—it just sparkled. Henry had asked their friend Cindi Greenwood to come along. Cindi was a loud, wonderful lunatic of a girl with an infectious laugh—the type of girl who could make a party out of cafeteria meat loaf. I remember Marvin opening the truck door for me and saying, 'It's gonna be nice and snug in here. Marylou Williams, meet Cindi Greenwood and my favorite brother, Henry.'"

"So he had that same goofy sense of humor as a boy," Susan said with a grin.

"Of course. That'll never change," Marylou said. "Off we drove into a gorgeous, hot summer afternoon, all four of us scrunched together in the truck's cab, pressing against each other, with the AM radio blaring. I still remember how it felt—the wind blowing through the cab's open windows whipping our long hair in every direction, with Cindi helping Janis sing 'Me and Bobby McGee.'" She closed her eyes, remembering. "The highway asphalt was steaming from a quick rain and the summer heat—it was like driving on a cloud. It was the closest I've ever been to a magic carpet ride." She shook her head. "Christ, was I ever that young?"

Marylou stared off into space and fell silent.

"So . . . what happened?"

"Well, the friend's parents were on vacation in Colorado and had foolishly left their son in charge of the house. The minute we arrived at the party, Marvin, as usual, became the center of attention. He got caught up in drinking beer, talking over high school glory days and about the adventures ahead of him at Southerland in the fall. Totally ignored me. And that was fine by me. It gave me the entire evening to get to know Henry."

"Nice."

"It was perfect. Henry was so attentive; we sat together on the pool's edge slowly kicking our feet in the water. I don't think we stopped talking for more than thirty seconds the whole evening." Marylou adjusted her sunglasses. "Unfortunately, the evening ended on a sour note."

"How so?" Susan asked.

"A kid named Guy Wheeless Jr. showed up at the party. He had . . . I guess you'd call it . . . an accident . . . at school earlier that week, and half of his ear was blown off."

"Yikes! What kind of accident?"

"Something about a cherry bomb. Somebody played a misguided prank on him. But enough about my sordid past," she said, forcing a smile. "What's going on with you?"

As Susan detailed her phone call with Marvin that morning, Marylou's thoughts drifted back. Guy Jr. and his creepy posse had shown up drunk at the end of the pool party. He'd been sporting a huge bandage around his injured ear. Marvelous announced to the party that Vincent van Gogh was in the house. Everybody got a good laugh and some of them started catcalling "Vinnie." Guy Jr. took offense. Push came to shove. Guy had made a beeline for Marvin and just missed him with a roundhouse punch. Marvin responded with a right fist to Guy's solar plexus, bringing him to his knees gasping for air.

"Lou, did you hear what I said?" Susan asked. "I'd love to have seen what the three of you looked like back in your Kansas days."

"What? Oh . . ." Marylou took off her sunglasses, put them on the table, and reached for her purse. She found her phone and paged through the photo archive, found the black-and-white photo she was looking for, and then handed the cell to Susan. Her friend smiled down at the picture and Marylou could barely hold back the tears.

On the screen was a beaming Marylou standing between the Lindon brothers, Henry with his arm around her slender waist and Marvin with arms raised in a Nixonesque double peace sign.

"What a great picture, I . . . " Susan looked at Marylou's red-rimmed eyes. "Lou, you look like you've been crying—like you're about to cry now! Is everything all right?"

Marylou awkwardly put her sunglasses back on. After a few silent moments, she sighed. She needed to talk. Of all people, Susan would understand. "No, everything is not all right. Talking about the good old days makes it just that much worse."

"And I thought I was the only one with Lindon brother issues," said Susan. "Now, take a deep breath and tell me everything."

■■■

Henry's day combined the best and worst Dallas had to offer. At Marvin's prodding, he had reluctantly set out to identify the steps necessary to license a food truck. Rattled by his fight with Marylou, he made a series of wrong turns in a city he knew well. Getting lost exacerbated the pressure of the resentments and confusion swirling in his head.

He finally found the vehicle inspection site in the mean streets surrounding the Cotton Bowl. From there he was directed across town to city hall for an audience with a Mr. Brock, Dallas's "Deputy Chief, Department of Code Compliance Services, Restaurant and Bar Inspection Division." Predictably, Mr. Brock was out of the office for "personal reasons." No one knew when he would be back, and sorry, no one else could help.

He crossed the street to the Dallas city attorney's office, housed in a nondescript building more appropriate for a struggling bail bondsman. In a stroke of luck, the office was empty except for a young intern anxious to be helpful.

While explaining to Henry that the thing he was talking about was not a food truck but rather a "Mobile Food Preparation Vehicle," the intern rattled off nine different licenses required for operation of the "MFPV." Henry's mind was on Marylou and he heard little of what the intern was saying. He rationalized his inattention by concluding that if Marvin was truly interested in acquiring a food truck, he would swing back for the details. He had enough information to conclude that the process would be a pain in the ass.

As Henry attempted to disengage, the intern delivered one last bit of advice—if Henry wanted to see some of the MFPVs in action, he should stop by the new Klyde Warren Park that was built over the Woodall Rodgers Freeway. Henry thanked him for his suggestion and, once back in his Tahoe, headed in that direction.

Klyde Warren Park exemplified how the city was willing to take chances. Up until recently, Woodall Rodgers Freeway had been a poorly conceived six-lane highway built in the 1960s that sliced Dallas in half. An ugly gash across the city's midsection, it had separated the growing Uptown area from the city's traditional downtown.

As Dallas's ballyhooed Arts District had exploded, the freeway had become an urban open wound. Undeterred by cost or precedent, the city launched a radical plan to pave over the open highway, transform it into a tunnel, and then top it off with a five-acre public park. The project, as brash as

Dallas itself, was an instant success. A piece of inner-city blight was gone and in its place was a carnival-like urban green space complete with playgrounds, water features, reading areas, board games, hundreds of trees, performance pavilions, a dog park, and of course spaces for food trucks.

Henry parked and approached the area. Rendered indecisive by the array of colorful food trucks, he paced back and forth in front of them for ten minutes. Finally, he settled on the bright purple Guava Tree truck. He took his Cuban sandwich with a side of yucca fries to a bench next to a group of elderly chess players. The meal's highlight was the spicy, coriander-flavored dill pickle that lay across the length of the sandwich. He watched scores of customers line up at the trucks' windows. Some trucks were clearly busier than others, but they were all doing a brisk business.

On his way out of the park, Henry spotted the Craving Cream truck. The truck had a giant plastic sugar cone plastered into the roof with strawberry ice cream dripping down the side panel. Rationalizing that the truck was too clever to pass up, Henry decided to violate his no-dessert rule.

As he stood in line, he overheard a couple at the front of the line giggling over their ice cream choices. The man had shaggy, prematurely grey hair and was teaching pig latin to the woman in a red tee shirt and matching red Texas Rangers baseball cap. The young woman accepted her chocolate cone and apparently found "ocolatechay" wonderfully amusing. She turned away from the truck's counter with her cone, took three steps forward, and stopped, her eyes widening.

"Professor . . . what are you doing here! I mean . . . it's a surprise . . . to . . . uh . . . to see you here," Nichole Kessler said, tripping over her words. "You . . . you come here often?"

"First time I've been in the park. How about you?"

"About once a week; I'm really into food trucks. Sorry, I'm being rude. This is my landlord . . . I mean friend . . . Doc—I mean—Jack Rockwood."

Doc/Jack Rockwood looked to be in his mid-thirties. Henry and the young man shook hands, exchanging obligatory how-ya-doings.

"So," Henry said to fill the awkward silence, "I haven't seen you since . . ."

"Yeah . . . we need to talk."

Before Henry could respond, the man at the Craving Cream truck counter called out to him. "Yo, mister, what's your pleasure?"

Henry stepped up to the counter, ordered a vanilla cone, and turned around to join the couple. He found Nichole standing alone, chocolate cone in her hand, looking young, diminutive, and nervous.

"Where's your friend?"

"I told him I needed a word in private with you. This is so . . . awkward! Professor Lindon, I owe you an apology. What I did . . . in your office . . . just wasn't right. I hope you weren't . . . offended."

"I've got to tell you," Henry said shaking his head. "That was certainly . . . perplexing. What were you thinking?"

"It's . . . complicated." She stepped to the side and tossed her uneaten chocolate cone into a trash basket. With hands grasped nervously together at her waist, and with a pensive look on her face, Nichole said, "Believe it or not, it all goes back to a . . . a terrible relationship with a relative. Can we just say it was a joke that went bad and forget the whole darn thing?"

"Good by me." A part of him wanted to reach out and help the complex young woman standing in front of him. But a voice inside his head urged caution. She had yanked down her shorts in his office; God only knew what might be next. Did he really want to wade into her problems?

"But are you okay? Everything all right?" Henry asked.

"I'm so embarrassed . . . " Nichole looked down at her black Vans. "I'll be okay. Some things aren't right at the moment—like I said, it's pretty complicated." She hesitated for a moment and when she looked back up, Henry was taken aback by the sudden steely determination in her eyes. "I have a plan to get everything back on track."

"Glad to hear it. I'm here if you want to talk." Henry extended his arm to shake hands.

"That's so sweet!" The sun lit up Nichole's dark-blue eyes as she switched on her most effervescent smile. "Can I give you a hug?"

■■■

Henry wearily turned the Tahoe into his driveway, killed the motor, and sat there for a few minutes thinking about his chance encounter with Nichole. Given his sandpapered emotional state after the morning's confrontation with Marylou, having to deal with Nichole in the park felt like piling on after the whistle. Nichole was perplexing. She said the reason she pulled down her shorts was complicated and due to a terrible relationship with a relative. What could a relative possibly have to do with her pulling down her shorts in his office? Nichole would soon graduate and it was unlikely he'd ever see her again. He tried to block her out—he had more pressing matters.

Marylou's car was gone. Likely, she was already in the air, on her way to Buenos Aires. As he finally headed inside, Henry was left with the reality he dreaded—when and how he would tell Marylou he knew the truth about what was going on in Buenos Aires. He had been a coward, yelling at her over nothing, when the truth was on the tip of his tongue.

Once in his study, he sat down in the ergonomically correct chair behind his desk and opened the bottom drawer. With a sigh, he leaned down and picked up the card again, silently cursing the day he first saw it.

When the box had arrived from Mikel Jiménez in Buenos Aires, Henry assumed it held the shirts he had ordered from his favorite shirtmaker. He opened the box only to find a light green, stylish woman's jacket. There was also an unaddressed sealed envelope.

He wished now more than anything that he hadn't opened the envelope that day, but he had. After reading the message, he had looked back at the box's address label and saw, belatedly, that it was addressed to Marylou. He reboxed the coat, sans card. He later gave the box to Marylou and apologized for accidentally opening her package. *Apologized!* The thought of it galled him. She had seemed to think nothing of it, and was delighted with her new jacket. He watched her try on the jacket, while gritting his teeth with the pain of his discovery.

Now, he read the card for what seemed like the hundredth time.

> Mikel Jiménez on Avenida Alvear
> Avenida Alvear, 3133
> Ciudad A. de Buenos Aires
> Argentina
> *Querida Marylou,*
> *¡Déjese envolver por esta muestra de mi afecto para mantener el calor hasta que esté en mis brazos una vez más!*
> *Besos,*
> *MJ*

Henry's chest tightened with anger. Nothing had changed. The card still said the same thing as the first time he read it. He could not escape the clear meaning of the note from his so-called friend, Mikel Jiménez.

> Dearest Marylou,
> Wrap yourself in this token of my affection and stay warm until you are in my arms once again!
> Kisses,
> MJ

As Marylou had painfully reminded him that morning, Mikel was brimming with Latin charm. He didn't want to believe that the woman he had known since she was seventeen, and the woman having an affair with an Argentinian lover, were one and the same. But reality set in again. There it was in black and white on Mikel's personal card.

Henry replaced the card in the drawer, got up from his desk, turned out the light, and surrendered into one of his suede-covered armchairs. He thought about burning the card. He wanted to somehow erase the memory of it from his brain, but he knew he could never forget—and besides, he needed it. Needed it for when he confronted his wife with her betrayal. Drifting into an uneasy sleep, Henry dreamt of the endearing way Marylou tucked her hair behind her ear.

7

With Marylou in Buenos Aires and Southerland University on spring break, Henry left a day early for his meeting in Mexico City with UNS's general counsel, Jane Birney. He always stayed in the same hotel—the Polanco Boutique Hotel across from Lincoln Park's concrete urban ponds. The Polanco neighborhood, with its easy access to museums and restaurants, was an area he knew well. It was also one of the few neighborhoods in the enormous city of over twenty-two million residents where he felt comfortable walking alone at night.

He was delighted that his old compadre, Francisco "Paco" Toledo, was free to spend the day with him. When they had first met, Paco was a young partner in a Mexico City law firm, and Henry was still a member of the Inveress law department. They worked together on a sensitive antitrust investigation, and Henry convinced Paco to come in-house as part of the Inveress law department. Working together over the years had forged an enduring friendship between them.

Paco, a fifth-generation *chilango*, had lived his entire life in Mexico City. He made up for what he perceived as that cultural shortcoming by traveling extensively. During one of his trips to Europe, he met a lovely blonde Brit named Patricia. Patricia was soon living in Mexico City and they married a year later. To Paco's delight, Patricia spoke Spanish with a lilting British accent.

Paco and Patricia picked Henry up at noon, dressed for a day on the town with their old friend. Patricia wore a bright, flowery, basque-cut dress and aviator sunglasses. Paco sported a straw Panama hat and a pale-blue, linen guayabera shirt. Henry felt a bit stodgy in his green polo shirt and khakis. After a round of affectionate hugs, they drove south to the San Ángel neighborhood. Paco pulled the car into a public parking space. He hopped out of the car and handed fifty pesos to a large scowling man who stood with folded arms on the sidewalk.

"Paco, why did you pay that guy for a public parking space?" Henry asked.

"My friend," Paco laughed, "it is the Latin way. I pretend he is protecting my car, and he pretends that he is not a thief threatening to steal it. This way, we're both happy. It's what we call *dando y dando*: We both give and get a little something. It is a way of life south of the border. Now let me show you an example of marital bliss, Mexican style."

Henry enjoyed Patricia playfully taking his arm as they walked down the hill. "How's my friend Marylou?" she asked.

Henry heard the question but didn't answer, came to a stop, and stared at an exquisite white house on a bluff. He tried to steer his friend away from the volatile subject. "Wow, what's that?"

"That's the San Ángel Inn, a beautifully preserved hacienda," Patricia said. "Today you're in for a treat! We are going to enjoy *la merienda* there."

Henry turned to her. "Sounds great, but what's *la merienda*?"

"Patience, amigo," Paco interjected. "All in good time. Now, look down the hill at where we are going."

Henry surveyed the affluent neighborhood, replete with ancient jacaranda trees with brilliant violet blooms calling out for attention. On a corner sat a compound of two separate concrete-block homes surrounded by a picket-like fence of erect columnar cacti—a pragmatic yet charming fence for Mexico.

"All right, I'm game. Where are we going?" he asked dutifully.

"Right there," said Paco, pointing to the concrete-block homes. "The home of Frida Kahlo and Diego Rivera. Wait until you see how these famous Mexican artists lived."

As they walked down the street, Patricia provided background on the star-crossed lovers.

The notoriously left-leaning couple had built their compound of separate homes and studios in the functionalist architecture style. No frills, only functional spaces for their work. The compound consisted of two separate concrete blocks. One block was painted red to symbolize the fiery Rivera, the other blue for the slightly calmer Kahlo. Only a narrow rooftop bridge joined the two separate blocks. Before building the houses in 1933, the artists were already famous, Rivera for his giant murals advocating workers' rights and Kahlo for her self-portraits of a slightly mustached woman with an ever-present unibrow.

They climbed the stairs to Rivera's studio and Henry was struck by its playfulness. It was bathed in natural light streaming through the glass walls and ceiling. Huge black, red, and white papier-mâché puppets, some fourteen feet tall, stood around the room. They all had macabre faces and more than one sported Satan horns. Despite the grisly decor, the house held the promise of lighthearted amusement. Rivera had used the extensive pulleys and ropes around the room to hoist the marionettes into dance for his guests' enjoyment.

"Isn't the light in this room fantastic?" Patricia asked. "Can't you just see that wild man dashing around from one painting project to the next and, I guess, from one woman to the next? Legend has it that the only thing he was more prolific with than his art was women."

They climbed the stairs past Rivera's bedroom, with its cramped bed, to the roof and walked across the narrow bridge to Kahlo's concrete block. Paco pointed to a narrow concrete stairway that descended from the bridge to the studio in Kahlo's house.

"Diego certainly valued his privacy," Paco said. "You can see how difficult it is to get up those thirteen stairs from Frida's studio and then across the narrow bridge to Diego's house. Frida had a terrible trolley-car accident as a young girl. That accident eventually left her tied to a wheelchair. For Frida to see what was going on in Diego's block took Herculean effort, and that is exactly what Diego wanted. It's the Mexican version of living separate lives."

An hour later, they started back up the hill to the San Ángel Inn. Henry thought the artists' separate quarters were a metaphor for the eroding state of his marriage. How had he allowed things to disintegrate to this point? Why was he unable to simply confront Marylou with what he knew?

"When do I find out about *la merienda*?" Henry asked.

"Right now, my old friend," Paco replied. "In Spain, a traditional *merienda* is a light afternoon snack to carry you over to dinner. In Mexico, we have perfected the concept. Prepare yourself for a relaxing afternoon of food, drink, and music. Nothing, and I mean nothing, will be hurried!"

The three friends entered the seventeenth-century hacienda's ornate entry hall, which was filled with carved wood and large plaster shell designs built into the walls. Henry spotted a woman dressed in a festive peasant dress standing to the side of the room holding a well-crafted wooden birdcage topped with a schoolhouse steeple and screen windows on two sides. The cage was painted bright yellow and green and sat on a broomstick stand supported by a wooden tripod base.

"Not sure I've ever seen a birdcage being carried into a restaurant. What's she doing?" asked Henry.

"She is a Mexican fortune-teller. Give it a try?" Patricia answered.

"While you two learn your fate, I'll find a table," Paco said, hurrying off to the dining room.

As Patricia bargained over the price in rapid Spanish, Henry noticed that the cage's hand painting was intricately done in a cosmos motif with planets and stars swirling around all sides. The cage held two yellow finches. Their names, *Alicia* and *Fernando*, were painted below their respective holes. Little baskets fastened to the wood below their names held small pieces of folded paper—pink papers for Alicia, blue for Fernando.

"Henry, the señora wants you to choose which bird will tell your fortune. Alicia or Fernando?"

Henry selected Fernando for the honor, and the fortune-teller sprinkled a bit of birdseed in front of the bird's hole. Then she opened Fernando's tiny door and Fernando quickly hopped out to eat the seed. He looked for more, but realized he would have to work for his meal. Fernando reached into the basket of blue papers, picked one up with his beak, and dropped it into the fortune-teller's hand. The effort was rewarded with a second course of seed.

The fortune-teller handed the folded paper to Henry. Looking over Henry's shoulder as he unfolded the tiny paper, Patricia read out loud, "*En boca cerrada no entran moscas.*"

"What does it mean?" asked Henry.

"It's a Mexican *dicho*, like what we call a proverb," Patricia replied. "Literally it says 'flies do not enter a closed mouth.' What it means is sometimes it's best to keep your mouth shut."

"Oh, I get that. It's what my brother Marvin calls the Code of the West. He uses it every time he thinks silence is his best bet, especially with issues involving women."

Maybe it was Marvin's sophomoric Code of the West that kept me from confiding in Marylou about what I learned? He clenched his fist. *This is ridiculous. I need to have this out with her immediately.*

"Paco told me about your brother." Patricia's words brought Henry back to the moment. "They call him Marvelous, I believe. I understand his personal life has much in common with Señor Rivera's." Patricia smiled.

"That's one way of putting it," Henry said, as he shoved his hands into his trouser pockets and tried not to voice the irritation he felt.

"Ah, a Romeo," she sighed. "Foolish women always go for those types."

Has Marylou been foolishly taken in by a Romeo? Have I been the foolish one to let it go on so long without saying anything?

"Henry?" Patricia asked, concern in her eyes. "Are you all right?"

"I'm fine, just fine. Everything's . . . fine."

"Okay," she said, sounding puzzled.

Henry reached for an excuse. "Hey, pay no attention to me. Just trying to take in all of this, on top of a touch of jet lag."

"Oh, of course! Come on then." She again linked her arm with Henry's. "Paco is probably wondering what has happened to us. Let's see what kind of table he has."

■ ■ ■

Henry was cheered by the inn's huge dining room filled with bright tropical flowers and tables topped with white tablecloths. Paco happily waved to them with his Panama hat. He had a table along the back windows overlooking the inn's carefully manicured rose garden.

The waiter placed thin orange slices, lightly dusted with chili powder, and small shot glasses of mezcal on their table. Demonstrating the tradition, Paco bit into the spiced orange slice and then sipped his mezcal. Soon, Henry was talking enthusiastically about the smoky flavor of the agave-based drink.

"Everyone gets excited about tequila, but if you ask me, mezcal is superior," Paco explained. "Tequila sold its soul in the name of consistency, while every mezcal is different. We will try a few different ones. Henry, sit back and relax. Will you put your trust in me to order for the table?"

Henry's hunger grew with another round of mezcal. A second waiter brought a basket of warm corn tortillas and three salsas. Following Paco's lead, Henry brushed guacamole on his tortilla, scooped on what Paco described as "Mexican caviar," and added some white tubers dusted with cayenne powder. The sweet and savory combination was delicious, and Henry helped himself to another serving.

"This is real Mexican food, no Tex-Mex here," said Paco, holding up his fork. "We had this dish at my *abuela's* house . . . my grandmother's house . . . every Sunday when I was a boy."

"So what exactly are we enjoying?" Henry asked.

"Oh, Henry, I thought you knew," Patricia replied with a giggle. "You filled your tortilla first with escamoles—ant eggs—and then some maguey worms, the same kind of worm that floats in the bottom of mezcal bottles."

In response to Henry's wide eyes and unhinged mouth, the couple burst into laughter. Henry soon joined them and jokingly demanded prior review rights of any new course.

As promised, *la merienda* continued for three happy hours. Paco told Henry about the many changes in Inveress since the UNS takeover. The conversation turned to Henry's meeting with Jane Birney scheduled for the next day.

"I miss you every day, my friend," Paco said. "Our world's a lot less interesting these days. Have you heard that Jane is on the warpath about your San Miguel Galletas deal in Argentina?"

"No." Henry softly dabbed his mouth with the heavily starched napkin. "What's the problem?"

"My old friend, please keep this between us. It's simple yet complex. Simply, UNS is losing their shirts in San Miguel. There have been constant labor issues at the San Miguel Galletas plant and production is down nearly forty percent. It's complex because UNS refuses to admit they may have made a mistake in valuing the business. I hear some hedge funds are hounding them about expenses in general and the San Miguel deal in particular. I bet sweet Jane has some questions about how the deal came together."

"Thanks for the heads-up." Henry nodded to Paco. "You know, of course, Marcello Cifone in Buenos Aires. He's a great lawyer and a better friend. The two of us worked on the San Miguel transaction for eighteen months. It dragged on so long that we christened it the Deal from Hell. UNS can look to their heart's content. There's nothing there. I'm concerned, however, there may be some mischief behind the scenes."

"What kind of mischief?" Paco asked, placing his elbows on the table.

"I bet one of the hedge funds that pressured UNS to buy Inveress is the same one that's now leaning on them about the San Miguel deal." Henry softly drummed his fork on the table. "Someone I knew growing up owns that hedge fund. His name is Guy Wheeless Jr. and, to put it plainly, he has a vendetta against me, my brother Marvin, and a high school friend of ours."

"After all these years?" Patricia asked.

"I know it sounds ridiculous. I'll tell you the story over those Mexican cigars Paco's always talking about."

■ ■ ■

The Te-Amo Robustos were lit, the *tazas* of coffee were poured, and feeling the buzz of mezcal, Henry began. "Marvin and I grew up on a Kansas wheat farm in a little town called McPherson. When it came time for high school, our parents decided to send us to a Catholic school in Wichita called Kapaun Mt. Carmel. I guess they thought the priests would be a good influence on us."

"Well, they were living in a fool's paradise, were they not, my friend?" Paco said with a laugh.

"No kidding. Anyway, they rented a little house close to the school and Dad commuted back to the farm every day."

"Wow, sounds like your parents were determined to give you boys a good education," Patricia said, and then winked. "Despite your naughty natures."

"Oh, we were amateurs compared to Guy Wheeless Jr. He had been in the school since kindergarten and by the time we arrived, he practically had his own gang. Guy Jr.'s group ruled the roost and took a visceral dislike to Marvin and me from day one. Guy's dad was the president of the largest bank in town and his son thought the universe revolved around him," Henry said, thinking back.

"I know the type," Patricia said, rolling her eyes.

"Yeah, Guy Jr. got off on bullying other kids—that started in grade school—and by high school everybody was pretty much afraid of him." He paused, grimacing. "Except Marvin and me, I guess." Henry thought that over for a minute, then took a long draw on his cigar and gently tapped the ash over the ashtray.

"Marvin and I grew up playing basketball together and we played on the Kapaun team. Our best friend, Dan Moore, was a big, rawboned country kid who played center on the team. All three of us were new to the school, played basketball together, and loved practical jokes. We became a tight-knit unit."

"Practical jokes?" Paco asked from behind his cigar.

"Oh yeah," Henry said. "I'll get there in a minute. One night, at a school-sponsored scavenger hunt, one of the items on the list was a picture of a dragon tattoo. A bunch of us, including Marvin and me, ended up in a west

Wichita tattoo parlor looking for a drawing of a dragon tattoo. Everyone on the hunt was full of beer and teenage bravado."

"Boys will be boys." Patricia took a puff on her cigar and smiled at her husband.

"Listen to the woman smoking the big cigar," Paco said, pulling her against him for a kiss.

Henry averted his eyes and kept talking. "Guy Jr. dared everyone to get a tattoo to prove their manhood. When no one stepped up, he jumped in and got a cherry bomb tattooed on his ankle. By the time it was our turn, I had sobered up and convinced Marvin it was a stupid idea. Guy Jr. threw a fit and the next week broadcast to the whole school that we were pure chickenshit. Marvin in particular took offense.

"So we decided Guy Jr. needed a lesson—or maybe it was simply rough justice. Given the trouble that's flowed from our practical joke, I sure wish I could recall more clearly why we did it."

"What did you rascals do?" asked Patricia.

"We executed our plan at the Kapaun prom. The prom was a typical high school dance held in a gym decorated with crepe paper streamers. You can imagine all of us shuffling around in ill-fitting rented tuxedos, hands in our pockets, desperately trying to look cool. Guy Jr., on the other hand, showed up with gin on his breath and paraded around the gym floor like a show pony in his custom-tailored, midnight-blue tuxedo. With his pretty date, in her red chiffon dress, on his arm, he just dripped self-importance."

A waiter interrupted the conversation to pour fresh coffee.

Henry took a sip of the strong Mexican brew and continued. "As the band played Beatles covers, we slipped out the back door to the parking lot. Our friend Dan Moore stood guard at the door while Marvin and I went to Guy Jr.'s car with our tool kit. After some skinned knuckles and a lot of elbow grease, we eventually wrenched off the front bolts from under the passenger seat of Guy's shiny new Camaro convertible.

"When the dance came to an end, all the students and their dates were milling around the gym's entrance sneaking smokes and talking about where to go next. Guy pulled his convertible up to the entrance and opened the car door for his date to get in. As we hoped, he stepped hard on the accelerator to lay rubber and his date went—heels over head—into the backseat. She screamed her head off and tried to pull the waves of chiffon down over her well-exposed pink panties."

"My friend, that was hysterically clever," said a laughing Paco.

"Poor girl! That was awfully mischievous," Patricia admonished him, one hand over her mouth to mask her own amusement.

"I'll admit the stunt was pretty damn good. The other kids loved seeing a bully made to look ridiculous."

"This is an amusing tale of teenage rivalry," Patricia said. "But surely this Guy Jr. must have gotten past it after all these years."

"There's more to the story, Patricia. The week after the prom things got a whole lot worse for Guy Jr."

"How so?" asked Paco.

"Like any Catholic high school, ours had lots of traditions."

"Here in Mexico," said Paco, "the church has difficulty discerning the difference between traditions and bad habits."

"That's a global problem," Henry said.

"Go on with the story," Patricia urged. "I know you two, if you start talking religion, I'll never find out what happened!"

"Okay. Religion officially shelved. Anyway . . . probably the most important school tradition was the Monday morning convocation in the chapel that the entire school was required to attend. During their senior year, students gave a speech about a topic of their choice—it was a rite of passage. The speaker dressed in white clerical robes with gold trim and spoke from the pulpit. Typically, the student's parents came to hear the speech—the whole thing was a big deal."

Henry paused to admire Paco's perfect smoke rings.

"Go on," Patricia prodded, trying to ignore Paco.

"The week after the prom incident it was Guy Jr.'s turn at the pulpit. With his beaming parents in the front row he gave a showboat speech, about half of which he did in Latin to impress the priests. He just went on and on."

"This man, he sounds like a horse's ass," Paco said, shaking his head.

"Pretty much sums him up," replied Henry, as he placed his cigar in the ashtray. "To close the service, the tradition was for the speaker to extinguish the altar candles. Guy Jr. took the four-foot-long candlesnuffer off the rack and paraded up to the chapel's altar.

"When he reached up to put the snuffer over the first candle, there was a quick spark and then a huge explosion. The candlesnuffer was launched into the air and Guy Jr. fell flat on his back. Everyone's ears were ringing from the explosion—a cherry bomb had been wedged into the candlesnuffer."

"What a wonderful twist, a cherry bomb explodes in front of Mr. Cherry Bomb Tattoo," said a delighted Paco.

"It should have been great," Henry said wistfully. "Unfortunately, when the candlesnuffer exploded, a piece shot through the air, hit Guy Jr., and sliced off half of his ear."

"Oops," Paco said. "You and your brother must have been in mucho trouble."

"No . . . Marvin had nothing . . . we had nothing to do with it. But there was no shortage of suspects. Everybody hated him. But, after what happened at the prom, there's no question Guy Jr. held us responsible."

It's regrettable about his ear," Paco offered. "But this is all ancient history. Surely Guy Jr. has moved on."

"You would think so. But given what Guy Jr. recently did to my buddy, Dan Moore, I don't think he ever moved on. But that's way too long a story." Henry realized he had drunk too much, talked too long, and disclosed information better kept to himself. It was time to change the subject. "Patricia," he said, "is politics off the table?"

8

Henry didn't leave his hotel until midday. Still slightly hung over from *la merienda*, he walked across Lincoln Park to a busy intersection. He took care crossing, given the state of traffic in the Polanco neighborhood.

The streets overflowed with cars and pedestrians vying for space, but there were no traffic lights or crossing signs. Pedestrians stepped into traffic, daring cars to hit them. Brakes screeched and fists rose from car windows as the combatants fought a territorial battle for pavement.

Jane Birney had texted him, telling him the lunch reservation was at Casa Hevia, an old-line Polanco restaurant with better ambience than food. The restaurant maître d' escorted Henry to the private room reserved for their meeting. As the maître d' opened the door, Henry was surprised to see Chester Lawrence talking animatedly with Jane Birney. Chester worked in the law department at UNS. He and Henry did not get along.

"Buenas tardes, Jane. Good to see you. And you too . . . um . . . Chester . . . right?"

"Oh, and so nice to see you, Henry," Jane replied. "I'm glad you remember Chester Lawrence. You may recall Chester heads up our litigation department."

"How could I forget?" Henry asked, deadpan. Chester reached out his hand and, after an uncomfortable moment, Henry took it.

Oh yes, Henry remembered Chester—the five-foot-two egomaniac who had made the already difficult acquisition of Inveress by UNS tortuous. Chester wore a constant Donald Trump pout that begged to be slapped off his face. Unable to conceive a good idea about anything, Chester assumed the roles of constant contrarian and cynic.

"Please have a seat," said Jane. "What would you like to drink? And why don't we order?"

As they picked up the oversize leather menus, Henry watched Jane purse her lips in feigned concentration. As always, she was dressed impeccably. Her stylishly long brunette hair was offset by a single piece of jewelry, a double-strand pearl necklace. Other than a hint of mascara and a faint touch of lipstick, she wore no makeup. Undeniably attractive, she was devoid of a most endearing feminine trait—a genuine smile. Henry wondered if the lack of a smile was because of her Botox-fixed facial expression. She never spoke of family, friends, vacations, or hobbies—only business. Could he make it through lunch with the automaton and her attack dog?

Henry sat quietly as Jane described the triumphs and travails of UNS's international business. She rued the day that activist hedge funds had taken aggressive positions in the company and demanded changes.

After the dishes were cleared, she said, "Henry, the reason I asked you here is to get your point of view on what happened during the San Miguel Galletas deal in Argentina."

"Sure," he said, glad to finally find out what all the mystery was about.

"As you well know, the San Miguel operation was the key driver of UNS's decision to acquire Inveress." Jane sat erect in her chair with her fixed facial expression. "We saw the San Miguel operation as our gateway into Latin America. Unfortunately, San Miguel's business performance has come in well short of expectations, and some of our largest investors are demanding a complete investigation of the transaction. I asked Chester to join us because he has been our liaison with some of those investors."

"I read an article in *The Wall Street Journal* about the role hedge funds are playing in UNS's strategies," Henry politely offered.

"They have no 'role' in UNS's strategies," snapped Chester. "They're simply shareholders, nothing more, nothing less. Like any other shareholder, from time to time they have suggestions that we take under consideration."

"Chester, you communicate with activist hedge funds intent on making your life miserable?" asked Henry.

"Don't you think it's important for UNS to understand all of our constituencies?" Chester countered. "I find that some of our least-friendly shareholders are the best sources of information."

"When I ran Inveress, I steered well clear of those constituents."

"But you're not running Inveress anymore, are you?"

"No, I suppose not," Henry conceded.

"Let me tell you what we've found so far and why we asked for this meeting," began Chester, visibly savoring his jab at Henry. "This San Miguel deal has been a mess from the start. From the day we took over Inveress, the plant in San Miguel has been either on strike or threatening to strike. Our inability to produce for our customers has led to multiple product delistings. To make matters worse, our own testing shows the cookies produced in the plant are garbage. It's like the day we closed the deal, everything went down the crapper!"

Henry turned to look at Jane, uneasy with the direction this talk was taking.

Extending his lower lip in his best pout, Chester used a contrived pause to sip his water. Moving in for the kill, he pressed forward. "So we decided to look into this debacle. Know what we found?"

Henry gave a slight shrug, trying to indicate he didn't really give a damn what they'd found, but Chester pressed on, caught up in his own agenda.

"We found that during your negotiation, the government officials had—for no apparent reason—a sudden and 180-degree change in position. Out of the blue, they agreed to give you all the tax breaks you requested. The same tax breaks they had rejected out of hand two days earlier. Sound familiar? Do you know what I'm talking about?"

"I don't like the tone of this conversation," Henry said calmly, his eyes shifting to Jane. "Chester seems to have gotten himself pretty lathered up. I regret you're having problems operating in San Miguel, but what's that got to do with me? If you're having some kind of legal issue in Argentina, I suggest you talk it over with Marcello Cifone, the attorney who represented us in Argentina."

"I'm afraid that won't be possible," replied Jane. Her facial expression remained frozen. "Since we began our investigation of San Miguel Galletas, we have . . . parted ways with Mr. Cifone. If I recall correctly, Mr. Cifone worked for you on the transaction."

"We worked closely together. Can we get to the point here?" Henry raised his hands, palms up. "Is there something you want to ask me? This innuendo about some 'deal' and parting ways with Marcello—I don't think it's getting us anywhere. What's your point?"

Chester began to answer, but Jane cut him off. "Henry, let me be candid. We have completely redone all the due diligence on San Miguel—the process was painful and expensive. I'll tell you what we found. Inveress, at your direction, made a deal with the province officials to reduce the San Miguel plant's tax rate in return for a lucrative package of jobs in the plant. The deal's time line reveals that the government officials consistently rejected the size of the tax breaks you requested and then suddenly reversed themselves."

"So? We're talking about Latin America here," Henry answered, cocking his head. "Tax breaks and commitments on future employment go hand in hand. The officials obviously saw it as a good deal for all parties."

Chester, the bit firmly in his mouth, could no longer be reined in. "I'll tell you the 'so'—*professor*. It sure the hell looks like those officials got something to help them change their minds. And that—*professor*—is a violation of the Foreign Corrupt Practices Act. And, as we both know—*professor*—that means you've put yourself in the bull's-eye for a Department of Justice investigation, which we are prepared to wholeheartedly support."

A heavy silence fell over the three. Henry was certain the posturing clown was wrong about the application of the Foreign Corrupt Practices Act. Without a bribe paid to a foreign official, there could be no violation of the act. Surely Marcello had not authorized a bribe without telling him. The deal was a decrease in taxes in exchange for future employment in the factory, simple and straightforward. No bribe, no violation. Or did Jane know something he didn't?

"Jane, this all comes as more than a bit of a surprise. I came here thinking you wanted my help to address a problem with the San Miguel deal. Instead, you're accusing me of a felony." Henry paused to ensure his words would have effect. "There's nothing more I can or should say. As to your accusations about me committing a felony, I advise you to tread very carefully. I take my reputation seriously. I know a thing or two about libel law and if there's one more word about me being a felon, you'll deeply regret it."

"Truth is a complete defense to libel, correct, *professor*?" Chester asked with a thin-lipped smile that dared Henry to step over the line.

"In this case, that defense obviously has no application." Henry slowly rose from his chair. "Thanks for lunch, Jane. It was a mistake I won't make again."

■ ■ ■

After Henry left the room, Jane got up, closed the door, and sat down in the chair Henry had vacated. "So," she said in an even voice, "what do you think?"

"I think he's a pompous jackass who should be put in his place," Chester replied. "When he has time to reflect, he'll sing a whole different tune."

"I'm uncomfortable with where we're heading," Jane said. "I don't see the viability of your Foreign Corrupt Practices Act theory. I know we're trying to placate that pain in the neck Wheeless, who demanded we dig into every possible part of the San Miguel Galletas transaction, but this is a dead end. There's not a scintilla of evidence of a bribe. Maybe Henry's correct—the government officials saw the trade-off of jobs and tax breaks as a good deal and went for it. I've gone along with your attempt to pressure Henry. You gave it your best shot, and he sure didn't bite. It's time to look at other alternatives."

"Jane, he basically waltzed in here and told us to kiss his ass. Are we just going to take that crap?"

"Why are you making this so personal?" She waved her hand dismissively. "This is business. If there was a bribe paid, either Henry knows nothing about it or he deserves an Oscar. This San Miguel situation is bad enough already. The last thing we need is to trigger a libel lawsuit from Henry. Are we clear?"

"Yeah, I've got it." Chester cocked his head to the side. "So I take it we're not going to the Department of Justice with what we know?"

"Not unless we have some concrete evidence of a bribe. One more thing, Chester." Jane stood and zipped up her briefcase. "There's no reason to talk down to Henry. What good did it do? I spent a lot of time with him during our Inveress acquisition—you underestimate Henry at your own peril."

■■■

Jane gathered her bags and left for the airport. Chester waited a few minutes to ensure he was alone. Then he closed the private dining room door, reached into his briefcase for his cell phone, and dialed.

"Hey, it's Chester. They're both gone . . . no, it didn't go as expected. Henry had nothing to add and without concrete proof of a bribe, Jane's got cold feet and told me to drop the whole thing . . . hey, it's not my fault! I know what the time line shows . . . he's being a hard-ass . . . no, I don't think I can get her to go along. She's afraid he might even sue us for libel . . . when she says no she means no . . . I'm well aware of how much you're paying me, but she's my boss. Fighting with her won't help either of us . . . let me step back and see if there's another way to pursue this . . . yes, I already said it, I'm fully aware of what you've paid me . . ."

■■■

Henry was back in President Thomas's enormous, dark office. The only light sources were the tube-shaped lamps illuminating the dark portraits of the nine past Southerland presidents. Henry liked the way the soft light shimmered on the office's well-oiled mahogany walls. Although he was uncomfortable in the hard wooden chair facing Thomas's huge desk, he tried not to fidget.

"Henry, Henry!" Thomas shouted. "Are you listening to me? Let's take this from the top, shall we? When we first met, you were out to sea—no job, no place to go. Marvin leaned on me to give you a teaching job. He asked after reminding me of his past generosity to Southerland University and, of course, sprinkling in a nice helping of innuendo about future contributions."

"I never asked him to—"

"So I threw you a lifeline," Thomas interrupted. "You'd never taught before, but you had an Ivy League education and I took a chance. I don't make you a dime-a-dozen adjunct. No, I make you a full professor. I know I'll catch holy hell from the faculty, but so what? With a grateful and generous Marvin, it will all work out. I hope you weren't expecting an endowed chair?"

"Phil, of course not, I'm so grate—"

"Don't start with that crap! And Henry, as far as you're concerned, it's President Thomas. So let's review the situation. I gave you a great job and then appointed you to the task force on sexual assault, where I expected you to bring some legal insight and positive influence. There you are with a prestigious position, in a world-class university, with the university's president helping you integrate into the community. And where does that get us?"

Henry froze in the chair. Why was this happening? What had he done wrong? Thomas rose from behind his desk and circled around to loom over Henry. With his hawk nose and hunched posture, he looked like a vulture.

"I'll tell you exactly where it gets us, Henry! It gets us to some blonde coed doing a striptease in your goddamn office! That's where it gets us! And that's just the start. Next, I hear from way too many sources that you can't control your wife from carrying on with some Latin lover. Right, so far? And the topper? The topper! Yesterday the university's attorney informed me that you're under investigation by the Department of Justice for some kind of international bribery. Henry, you are one stinking sack of shit! Do you hear me? YOU'RE FIRED!"

Henry shrank back in his chair. "No!" he cried. "No, no, no, no, no!!"

"Sir? *Sir?* Are you all right?"

Henry jerked forward and opened his eyes. *Where the hell am I?* An American Airlines flight attendant was leaning over him with her hand firmly on his shoulder.

"Sir, you're scaring the other passengers. You were screaming in your sleep."

As Henry ripped off his Bose headphones to better hear the flight attendant, his elbow swung into a glass of cabernet, knocking it into the lap of a young investment banker in the adjoining seat. Fumbling to release his seat belt, the young man shot upright, shouting "What the fuck!"

He vigorously brushed the wine from his pants, splattering Henry and the passengers in the nearby seats. The first-class cabin was in an uproar and Henry began to profusely apologize.

Once on the ground at DFW, Henry yanked his bag out of the overhead compartment and hustled down the corridor to the immigration hall. The hall was packed with college students returning from spring break; harsh sunburns and bad hats abounded. He was relieved not to see any of his students in the line.

Finally reaching the waiting room, he collapsed, exhausted, into a chair.

What the hell's happening to me? Henry thought, feeling flustered and embarrassed. *If UNS goes to the Department of Justice with their Foreign Corrupt Practices allegations, I'm cooked. I need to talk with Marcello immediately. Is there something Marcello didn't tell me? There's no way I'll pass the Wein, Inc. vetting process with an investigation hanging over me like the sword of Damocles. Is it possible Guy Jr. is responsible for any of this? Will my nightmare with President Thomas become a reality in stark daylight? On top of everything, my wife is having an affair in Argentina! And goddamn it, there's red wine all over my shirt!*

PART 2

THE PLAINS

9

When Henry entered the lecture hall, it was filled with the din of high-spirited conversations as the students shared their spring break escapades. He plugged his flash drive into a port on the lectern, and the lecture-hall screen lit up with the day's first topic:

GAY MARRIAGE: IS THE SUPREME COURT ADJUDICATING OR LEGISLATING?

"Welcome back," Henry called loudly, pumping his hands down to quiet the class. "I trust everyone enjoyed the break; now it's time to start preparing for finals. As we discussed last class, today we'll take a quick look at the Supreme Court decision on gay marriage. Then we'll tackle the semester's final topic, intellectual property.

"The controversy surrounding the Court's decision to legalize same-sex marriage boils down to this: Has the Court overstepped its constitutional authority by making, rather than interpreting, law?" Henry stepped from behind the lectern to make his point. "In the seminal Supreme Court case *Marbury v. Madison,* Chief Justice John Marshall succinctly defined the role of the Supreme Court." Henry pushed his clicker to flash the words on the screen:

"The interpretation of the law is the proper and peculiar province of the courts."

"As you can see, the word is *interpretation,* not *legislation*. With the decision on gay marriage, there is a real question whether the Court has crossed a line and usurped Congress's legislative role. Certainly Justice Scalia, in his dissent, thought the Court had strayed from its constitutional role and decided to make law on its own." Henry paused and scanned the faces in the classroom to make sure the students were following his train of thought.

"Justice Scalia described the Court's ruling as a 'judicial Putsch' and a 'naked judicial claim to legislative—indeed, super-legislative—power.' Even for the often acerbic Justice Scalia, those were awfully strong words."

As Henry was reaching his stride, a hand in the air interrupted him. In the front row, one of Henry's brightest students had a question. Sabben Saad, with skin the color of cappuccino and eyes a lustrous grey, was a very modern Muslim woman. She always wore a silk hijab to cover her head. However, rather than concealing her, the hijab served as a perfect frame for her expertly made-up face, accented by chiseled eyebrows.

"Yes, Sabben."

"Professor, is this case about the split among Supreme Court members on constitutional interpretation? The group of justices who are called . . . ah . . . I think you said 'textualists,' who believe the Constitution means what it says, and the other justices, who think the Constitution is a living document that should reflect changes in our society?"

"Great question. Some of the Court's members believe that constitutional interpretation should change as society evolves . . ."

Another hand shot up before Henry could finish. Jake Locke had spent the semester in silence. He never missed a class and was always dressed in well-pressed chinos and a heavily starched button-down Oxford shirt. Pleased that Jake was finally participating, Henry pointed at him to speak.

"Professor . . . we're missing the big picture here. Why talk just about constitutional law? There's a much more important source of law."

"There's always lots of questions with Supreme Court cases. What do you have in mind?" As Henry watched the student's eyes light up with intensity, he feared he might not like the answer.

"You're missing the single most important law of all—God's law. The Bible is absolutely clear on homosexuals. The Book of Leviticus says, 'If a man has sexual relations with a man as one does with a woman, both have done what is detestable. They are to be put to death.'"

"Jake, this course is about the laws of men." Henry tried to mask his animosity—he wanted to throttle the student. "A discussion of biblical passages is better left for a religion or philosophy class."

Annoyed and ready to move on, Henry looked down at his notes, but Jake's hand was up again. He reluctantly acknowledged him.

"Professor, we have already talked about biblical passages in this class, why not talk about them again in this context?"

"I'm not sure what you're referring to." Unconsciously, Henry's hand moved to his cowlick.

"A few weeks back, you taught us about the Good Samaritan statutes and how those laws protect someone who stops to help an injured person." Jake appeared to be enjoying himself. "The story of the Good Samaritan comes straight out of the Gospel of Luke. I'm just saying I think the Good Book applies to this issue as well."

The discomfort in the class grew palpable. Henry felt the students watching and judging how he would handle the challenge. He wanted to call Jake an idiot, but knew he couldn't. As he weighed his response, Sabben raised her hand again. "Yes, Sabben."

"Professor, if the class is going to consider religious laws, what about the Qur'an? Or, for that matter, the Torah, or the Bhagavad Gita?"

"Fair point. Actually, we aren't going to discuss any of them today," he said, forcing a smile. "We really need to move on or we won't have time to talk about intellectual property." He flashed past his prepared slides on gay marriage to his intellectual property lecture.

When the class ended, Henry was at the lectern sliding lecture notes into his briefcase as Sabben approached.

"Professor, have a moment?" she asked.

"Of course. What's on your mind?"

"Professor," she said slowly with concerned eyes, "haven't you heard about Jake Locke?"

Henry replied, "I know nothing about Jake."

"Well, Jake's bonkers. He's like . . . always looking for an excuse to let everyone know the so-called biblical foundation for his rudeness. I have friends who change sections if they see he's in the class. He's interrupted all kinds of classes. Professor, I don't understand why the university allows him to get away with it."

"Sabben, I wonder too . . . there's a lot about the university that I don't understand."

■■■

Andrea Lucero left Henry's class and began her trek across campus to her apartment. The campus popped with late spring colors, but Andrea shuffled along in her private fog. Her thoughts focused on Professor Lindon. Why had he allowed that idiot, Jake, to go on like that? She had heard from friends about Jake's antics, but she'd failed to connect the dots—the kid with all the starch in his clothes was the same guy. The Jake incident, on top of a difficult spring break with her Baptist parents, left her feeling severely conflicted.

She walked up the driveway to her garage apartment, passing the white clapboard main house—itself merely a cramped, two-bedroom cottage. It belonged to Doctor Jack Rockwood, a laid-back emergency room physician in his final year of residency. One of his two bedrooms was furnished with a single piece of furniture—a baby grand piano.

As she walked by the house, the piano's energetic sounds told Andrea that her landlord was home. The doctor had long, riotous, prematurely grey hair and a love of boogie-woogie music. Andrea's roommate had affectionately christened him Doc Rock.

Andrea crossed the short spread of unkempt lawn to the garage apartment. The moment she put her key in the door, it swung open. In a fluid motion, her roommate pulled her inside and shut the door. They embraced but when her roommate leaned in for a kiss, Andrea turned her face.

"Having a tough day?"

"More like a rough month," Andrea said. "The trip home was awful. Mom must have asked me a hundred times about boys I'm seeing and I must have told a hundred different lies. I told so many lies, I'll never be able to keep them straight . . . crap, and there's that stupid word again, straight."

Nichole Kessler hugged her closer. "Let's sit down. It's hard work pretending to be something you're not."

"Nichole, we're so different," Andrea said as she fell into the cramped apartment's only sofa. "You see a future for yourself and a way to get there. I'm flat-out lost—I feel like my whole life is one big, fat fraud. Even my Facebook life is phony . . . all those photos with drunken-fool frat boys. I feel like I'm losing my mind. And today's class with that chicken-shit Professor Lindon was the worst."

"What do you mean?" asked Nichole, as she sat down cross-legged on the ragged corduroy sofa.

"That creepy Jake Locke used the Supreme Court case on gay marriage to rant about the Bible's stance on gays. Professor Lindon just let that moron go on and on. Finally, Sabben—you know, that gorgeous Muslim girl—well, she jumped in and shut him down. She said if we're going to talk about what the Bible says about gays, then we should include scriptures from other religions. That idiot Jake had no idea what to say. Sabben is awesome!"

"How did gay marriage come up in a business law class? Want a bottle of water?" Nichole got up and stepped to the kitchen refrigerator, which was three steps from the living room couch.

Andrea shook her head. "You know how Professor Chicken-Shit likes to throw in little stories about what's happening in the Supreme Court? He probably thinks it makes him look smart," she said, feeling the anger well up inside of her again. "He opened the door real wide for that little creep."

Nichole sat back down, opening her Aquafina bottle. "Jake isn't worth your breath, and honestly, I really like Professor Lindon, he's the best professor I've had. He wrote me a great recommendation for that job in DC."

Andrea's fingers tightened into the couch cushion. "Are you going to take the job with Senator Cornyn?"

Nichole shrugged. "Haven't decided. With all the work on the student graduation committee, I can't think of much else. This will be the last summer before I have to get a real job. Maybe I'll just chill. And hey—I've got good news—want some?"

"You bet."

"Remember a week or two back I went to that Avalon hair place to get my nails done? Remember that great green color called Here Today, Aragon Tomorrow?"

"Yeah," said Andrea, looking at Nichole's nails. "It must be tomorrow because it's sure gone."

"Ha ha. Yeah, didn't last long," Nichole said, stretching her fingers apart, displaying the chipped polish. "Well, anyway, I started chatting up this woman with foils in her hair. She's had a ton of work done on her face and she's kind of old . . . but still a hottie. Somehow we started talking about the food trucks that come to campus. Anyway, her name is Doris Delaney, and she called during spring break and offered us a job."

Andrea felt uncomfortable and shifted, pulling her legs up under her. Her toes were almost touching Nichole's legs. "How can she offer me a job? I've never met her."

"I'm getting there." Nichole sipped her water and then tightly screwed the top back on. "She called and said this guy named Marvin—sounds like maybe her boyfriend—is buying a food truck and is going to call it Twenty-First-Century Foxes. He's looking for a couple of foxes," she said, wiggling her eyebrows up and down, "to wear tight tees and skimpy shorts and serve the food. Here's the best part—he'll pay thirty dollars an hour!"

"Wow! And you think this is for real?"

Nichole shrugged again. "We'll see. This Doris woman said she remembered me from the salon and called to ask if I'm interested and, by the way, did I have a friend who would also fit the bill. And I said, 'I am, and I sure do!'"

Andrea felt her spirits rise a notch. "Cool! Living and working together, this will be an awesome summer. Can you talk to Doc Rock about extending our lease?"

"Let's wait until we're sure about the job, okay?" Nichole suggested, draping her arm on the back of the couch. "Speaking of Doc Rock, he asked us over for a drink. Up for it?"

"I'm not up for another night of pot and boogie-woogie piano. I have a better idea." Andrea reached for Nichole's hand. "What do you say we stay in tonight, get under the covers, and watch a movie or two?"

■■■

An hour later, Andrea, fresh from her bubble bath, posed in front of the full-length mirror clothed only in a rolled bath towel around her neck. She watched herself in the mirror, slowly brushing her wavy damp hair. After a few minutes she turned and looked back over one shoulder to see Nichole in bed, leaning back on her elbows, smiling, with half-closed but admiring eyes.

"Hmm. Nice show," Nichole murmured, then she sat up suddenly.

Andrea's heart beat a little faster. "What's wrong?" she whispered. She was always waiting for Nichole to dump her. After all, why would such a special girl want to be with someone like her?

"Nothing. Just . . . all this talk about Professor Lindon reminds me of something."

"What?" She stopped brushing her hair, her throat tightening.

"Come to bed. It's kind of funny . . . it's about our dragonfly tattoos."

Andrea put the brush down, relief flooding through her as she hurried over to the bed and slid beneath the sheets.

■■■

Guy Wheeless Jr. stepped into his private elevator, smoothed his gleaming hair in the mirror, and pushed the basement button. The basement housed the Wheeless Strategic Fund's trading floor. An hour earlier, Larry, his driver, had taken Wheeless's date home. The blonde physician's assistant had been vigorously obstinate—especially about putting on the ensemble he had scrupulously selected for her. The physical exertion required to address his needs left him exhausted but wired. Typically, after one of his special evenings, he was unable to sleep for days.

He stopped at the trading-room door, steadied himself, and then pushed through. In front of him were legions of young men scanning throbbing computer screens and barking into telephone headsets. The enormous room sparked with the electricity generated by the men trolling global markets for any edge.

The room was devoid of investors. Only traders searching for lightning-quick profits worked this terrain. Wheeless liked to think of the men as hellhounds rapaciously braying in pursuit of their prey. He loved his trading floor; he loved his hounds.

He stopped to talk with two young traders sitting back to back. To avoid revealing his exhaustion, he asked simple questions using the fewest words possible. The young traders were anxious to impress the boss. One was working to manipulate the thin translation spread between the Czech Republic crown and the euro. The other was buying pecan futures on a Chinese commodity exchange.

After thirty minutes of quizzing the traders about their strategies, Wheeless saw Edward O'Brian approaching. *I wonder what that skinny bastard wants? He looks like Ichabod Crane.*

"Good morning, I guess," O'Brian said with a yawn. "Four o'clock a.m. Money never sleeps, eh, Guy?"

Wheeless glowered. "What is it, Edward?"

"Can we talk in your office?"

Wheeless nodded and, as the two men walked to the elevator, he overheard the trader working on Chinese pecans whisper to the trader beside him, "What's with Wheeless's ear?"

When the elevator doors closed, Wheeless turned to O'Brian. "Tell that clown trading pecans to clear out his desk—this morning."

"I take it you don't like the Chinese pecan trade," O'Brian said.

"Edward, just do what I say," Wheeless growled. "I'll do the thinking for both of us."

Wheeless led the way into his stark modern office. The men took seats across from each other at the chrome-and-glass side table. "Got some preliminary results from the Henry Lindon phone taps. Might be of interest," O'Brian said, holding out a folder.

"Edward, it's been a long night." Wheeless put up his hand, rejecting the folder. "I'm in no mood, just give me the highlights."

"Of course." O'Brian placed the folder on the tabletop. "Henry's life is not all that interesting. But he had two calls Thursday night that caught our attention. One was from Jane Birney, setting up a meeting with him at UNS headquarters."

"I already know about their meeting and it was held in Mexico City, not UNS headquarters," Wheeless said dismissively. He was growing impatient—he knew more about what was going on than O'Brian did. "Birney again demonstrated her incompetence. She was supposed to be getting information from Henry to help her initiate a Department of Justice investigation of him. So far, there's been a lot of effort, no results."

"How do you know about the meeting? O'Brian asked. "You have a mole in UNS?"

"Yeah, a mean-spirited little bastard in the law department," Wheeless said in an offhand manner. "He came out here to interview me about shareholder issues and ended up offering his services for hire. He's the reason I know what's happening in UNS, even in the boardroom. What was the other call?"

"I should have guessed you'd be all over it," O'Brian said in an obsequious tone. "The second call was from Ken Maltman. He's on the Wein, Inc. board."

"I remember that asshole," said Wheeless with a nod. "We fired him along with Henry when UNS took over Inveress."

"That's him. Well, Maltman offered Henry the CEO job at Wein." O'Brian lifted one eyebrow. "That would be quite the comeback for Henry."

"If that fool Henry thinks he's going to get the job as Wein's new CEO, he's going to be sadly disappointed." Wheeless rubbed his eyes with both hands, then he looked at O'Brian again. "Once you get Birney off her skinny butt and she triggers the Department of Justice investigation, he'll be lucky to even hold on to his half-assed teaching job."

"Do you want to continue the surveillance?"

"Absolutely—keep me current."

O'Brian nodded obediently and left, quietly closing the door behind him. Once alone in his office, Wheeless closed the heavy blinds to keep the sunrise from intruding on his thoughts. He touched the top of his shattered ear and drifted back to that day in the chapel.

From the moment of the explosion, he knew the Lindon brothers had put the cherry bomb in the candlesnuffer. It was undoubtedly Henry's idea. Marvin lacked even a hint of the creativity necessary for such a prank. After that stunt with that silly girl flipping heels over head, it had to be them. No one else had the sheer chutzpah.

He got up from the glass conference table and moved to his ultramodern desk, a seven-by-four-foot rectangle of thick glass on a chrome pedestal. The desktop was spotless and empty, except for six antique chrome Swingline staplers lined up on the front of the desk.

He picked up one of the staplers and began slowly working it up and down. His gaze fell on the framed black-and-white photograph of his father on the glass-and-chrome credenza across the room. Dressed in his favorite pin-striped, three-piece suit, the austere elder Wheeless stared severely into the camera. The expression was a familiar one for his father. In fact, Wheeless couldn't remember his father ever smiling except in derision.

He closed his eyes and leaned his head back, drawn into an unwelcome memory from long ago, in his parents' colonial home.

His father had insisted that the family eat dinner together every weeknight. In Guy Jr.'s younger days, the dinners provided instruction on how to psychologically dismantle a human being. With his older sister the sole target of their father's nightly dissection, Guy could simply observe and learn. In fact, Guy Sr.'s treatment of his daughter was similar to what his son enjoyed doing with houseflies. He would pull off their wings and watch them helplessly carom around his windowsill, grounded, and—without their wings—unable to even buzz.

That was what it was like with his sister. His father would take aim at her current point of vulnerability—her weight, lack of boyfriends, or inadequate scholastic performance—and then drill down relentlessly. His sister would grow mute and agitated, just like the flies on Guy Jr.'s windowsill. Eventually, emotionally dismantled and awash with silent tears, she would retreat upstairs to her bedroom. Some nights Guy Sr. would go to her room to comfort her. It was after one of those late-night comfort sessions that she disappeared from the house to the world of drugs that eventually killed her. His parents neither attended her funeral nor spoke her name again.

With his sister gone, the nightly ritual of criticism and dissection focused on the old man's son. The decisive evening was like any other when they sat down in the dining room to pork chops and sweet potato pie, prepared by the housekeeper. At the elder Wheeless's direction, Guy Jr. had been recounting the day's events at school, when his mother interrupted.

"I saw in this morning's paper that one of your schoolmates, a boy named Marvin Lindon, is going to Southerland University in Dallas on a basketball scholarship. Isn't that lovely? Such a fine school. Do you know the Lindon boy?"

He scowled down at his plate, no longer hungry. "Yeah, I know him and his brother, Henry. They hang out with that hillbilly, Dan Moore. Can't stand those jackasses."

"Honey, that's inappropriate language for the dinner table," his mother scolded.

"Well, I've got my reasons," he muttered. "They pulled that stupid stunt at the prom that embarrassed me and my date. And I know damn well they're the ones who put the cherry bomb in the candlesnuffer that could have killed me." His parents' eyes darted involuntarily to the bandage covering his ear.

As his father's facial features tightened, his mother changed topics. "Let's talk about what we want to do on our Thanksgiving trip to New York City."

Guy Jr. sat hearing, but not listening, as his mother droned on about her insipid little plans for shows and museums. It was no secret that his father hadn't married her for her brains.

While the housekeeper cleared the dishes, his father stood up from the table, looked over his collection of brandies, and poured himself a neat Hennessy. He took a pull on his drink and, with a tip of his head, gave his son the signal to join him in his study.

Settling into his black leather wing-backed chair, his father flipped open his silver monogrammed cigarette case and selected one of the unfiltered Camels for his one daily cigarette. His father had been a man of discipline. After carefully tapping both ends on the cigarette case, he lit it with the matching silver table lighter. As a billow of smoke escaped his mouth and nostrils, he finally got to the point.

"So, you think those Lindon boys and their friend put the cherry bomb in the candlesnuffer that humiliated our whole family?"

"Whole family?" Guy Jr. grimaced. "I was the one who lost half my ear."

"You rolling around on the chapel floor screaming like a three-year-old was not exactly a proud moment for me." The old man's expression turned a shade darker. "Remember the last time we sat in here? Right after the prom incident? What did I tell you?"

Guy Jr. hung his head. "You told me Wheelesses never, ever, allow riffraff like the Lindons and their white trash friend Dan Moore to disrespect us. Never. You told me to get even, to shake those boys to their bones so that they'll never disrespect the Wheeless name again."

"Did you do what I said?" His father's face had turned a feverish red.

"I didn't have the opportunity," he said without conviction. He was wary of what might come next.

His father nodded, stubbed out his cigarette, and stood, extending his hand. Guy Jr. was hesitant, but with the naïveté of youth, he reached his hand out too. His father's fingers tightened around his son's in a vise grip as he pulled back his left fist and slammed Guy Jr. in the eye.

He would have fallen to the floor, but his father's punishing grip held him upright. He would never forget what his father said, teeth clenched, eyes narrowed.

"You remember this moment, boy. There's plenty more like it coming if you keep acting like such a pussy! Your pathetic mother ruined your sister. That's not going to happen to you. Wheelesses don't allow anyone to disrespect us. You failed me the first time and look what happened—another humiliation. Take care of it!"

The next morning, Guy Jr. got up early and sat alone at the breakfast table, intent on controlling his emotions, while cultivating the rage burning within. His swollen eye ached.

The Lindon brothers and their redneck friend had not only humiliated him in front of the whole damn school but had unleashed his father's scorn. Guy Jr. tightened his fists. No matter how long it took, his enemies would pay a hefty price for causing his father to treat him with such loathing and disdain, a price he alone would dictate.

His mother quietly entered the room in her bathrobe and, keeping her back to her son, poured a cup of coffee from the sideboard. When she sat down at the table, he saw her heavy makeup. He had never before seen her with makeup on at breakfast. And, there was something wrong with the makeup above her left eye. It was too dark. A small cut on her lower lip peeked through her dark red lipstick.

She looked up, and her gaze settled on his blackened eye. "Did your father do that?" she asked.

Head down, he mumbled his answer. "Yeah, and it looks like he saved some for you."

After a minute of reflection, his mother said, "Your father is a great man and he loves us both. Sometimes he just loves us too much, wanting things so badly for us that it gets the best of him. Just do as he says and we'll be fine. Someday, when you're older, you'll understand."

No, Guy Jr. didn't understand. He would never understand . . .

Wheeless's left hand was throbbing and the pain brought him back to the present. He looked down and realized he was clenching the vintage Swingline stapler so tightly the bottom of it was cutting into his palm. He put the stapler down carefully and folded his hands together on top of his desk, still trembling from the memory's potency.

He had done as his father commanded. He had taken care of the Lindon brothers' trailer-trash friend, Dan Moore. He had orchestrated his disbarment and rendered him a pariah in the community. Henry was next and then, someday soon, he would take down that buffoon Marvin.

His plan to use his niece, Nikkie, as a honeypot had fizzled. Nikkie, Nichole, or whatever she was calling herself, had probably lied about pulling down her shorts. She wasn't worthy of any trust. A juicy Department of Justice investigation of Henry was a better idea. Henry would be unemployable and ostracized. The long-awaited opportunity to right the wrong to the Wheeless name had arrived—it was the time to act.

10

"Hey, Marvin. How's it going?" Henry spoke into his Bluetooth system as he drove home.

His brother's voice came booming back. "Hey, Bro! Getting a call from you means it couldn't be better. Hell, if it was any better it would be illegal or immoral, probably both. I'm hopin' you're callin' to report a new Tattoogate chapter."

"Thankfully, no." Henry visualized Marvin sprawled out on a lounge chair on his penthouse rooftop with a longneck bottle of Pabst Blue Ribbon in his hand. "I'm calling to see if you want to ride with me to McPherson in the morning to check out the farm's wheat crop. It's been a long time since you made the trip."

"Is there a problem with the guy managin' things? Steve Dixon, right?"

"No, no problem. His name is Steve Dutton. I just think a little interest from distant ownership is good for productivity. It'll also give us a chance to catch up with Dan Moore."

"Great! Sounds like fun," said Marvin. "There's nothin' goin' on I can't kick down the road. Ol' Danny Moore has had a tough run."

"No doubt about it . . . uh, Marvin, Marylou's calling from Buenos Aires and I need to speak with her. I'll swing by your place at seven."

"Best to Marylou."

Henry disconnected from his brother and answered Marylou's call. His wife's lilting voice came over the line, making his throat tighten.

"Henry, I miss you!" she said. "I'm with María José in her office. We finally have things wrapped up for next season. I'll fly back to Dallas the day after tomorrow."

Apparently she had forgiven him for the intentionally hurtful thing he'd said about their daughter's move to San Francisco. He almost wished she hadn't; it would make things easier. *I wonder if she's really even in María José's office.*

"Hey, you know what?" he said, trying to sound casual. "I have an idea. How about you stay put and I'll join you in four days? Exams will be over, so I'll be free. How's that sound?"

The relief and excitement in her voice made Henry grip the steering wheel more tightly. It was awful, not knowing what was real in their marriage and what was just a facade. "What a wonderful surprise!" she said. "I'll make plans with Marcello and María José. Maybe we can catch a performance at Rojo Tango. I love that place."

"Great. Do me a favor? Tell Marcello I'd like to get together for lunch, just the two of us. I have a legal issue I need to discuss with him."

"Sure! This will be such fun. Don't forget a warm coat and a scarf. It's winter in Buenos Aires. Love you, Henry."

"Uh . . . me too. See you soon." He disconnected and then pulled over to the side of the road, suddenly shaking so hard he couldn't drive, as the truth washed over him. *The time has come to tell Marylou I know she's cheating on me.*

■■■

Marylou switched off her phone, spread her arms wide, and smiled at her business partner sitting across the desk.

"I hope you got some of that conversation. What a day! We've finally locked in with our new item for next season and now Henry's making the trip south. Good luck always comes in threes—I wonder what other good news is coming my way?"

"What great timing for Henry's return to Buenos Aires." María José rose from behind her desk and gave Marylou a warm hug. "Marylou, I know things have not been perfect. But I have a very, very strong feeling about his trip. It is destiny—this visit will set things right!"

"I hope so," Marylou replied. "Maybe the friction has been about his job. Most men have their self-worth entangled with their jobs, and Henry most assuredly does. He says he likes being a professor, but I'm not so sure."

"In my kinder moments, I feel sorry for men," María José said as she sat back down in her chair. "We go through life with defining connections to our children, our friends, and our spiritual searches. Men stumble through without giving those things much thought."

"Henry hasn't taken step one in his spiritual journey," Marylou said, twirling her reading glasses. "My latest effort was bringing him to yoga with me."

"I know how much you love yoga," María José said as she pulled her lustrous, long black hair into a ponytail. "Did Henry enjoy it?"

"He did," Marylou said pensively. "Until some of that man stuff got in the way."

"What man stuff?" María José fastened her ponytail with a cylindrical silver clip.

"At the beginning of each class, the teacher says if we get tired and start running on negative energy, listen to your body and take the child's pose to regenerate," Marylou explained. "About halfway through each session, the pace picks up with ten straight sun salutations . . . you know, arms to the sky, bend in half, hands to the floor, throw your feet back, hover just off the floor, up dog, down dog, leap forward . . . María José, you know what I'm talking about?"

In response to María José's quizzical look, Marylou stood. With mock drama, she kicked off her heels, tucked her hair behind her right ear, and dramatically reached for the sky. In her business suit and stockings, she gracefully flowed through a complete sun salutation on the office rug.

"Brava, brava!" María José shouted at the impromptu performance. "Can Henry do that ten times in a row?"

"That's the point of my man story," replied Marylou as she sat back down. "He was content to take the child's pose about halfway through the sun salutations. I was proud of him. It showed he was buying into the whole yoga concept. But then, Henry told his brother Marvin about the class . . . have I told you about Marvin?"

"Indeed. Marvin the much-married one, right? He's walked down the aisle four times?"

"Only three times, according to him," said Marylou. "He claims the first one was just a starter marriage so it doesn't count. Anyway, Marvin decided to come to yoga class, undoubtedly because Henry told him he'd be surrounded by fit, glistening women."

"Did Marvin behave himself in class?" María José pulled her ponytail tighter.

"Let's just say, he was Marvin," said Marylou.

"What does that mean?" asked María José.

"For instance, the instructor always asks new students whether they have any injuries. When the teacher did one of those yogi prayer squats next to Marvin and asked him that question, he hesitated, and then put on his puppy dog face and little boy smile and said, 'We talkin' physical or emotional?' Pure Marvin."

"Got it," said María José.

"Anyway, Marvin is in incredible shape and when the class got into the series of sun salutations, rather than resting, Henry tried to keep pace with Marvin. Very un-yogi. He plowed through and on about the seventh or eighth, he hurt his knee. He couldn't walk right for a week and has begged off yoga ever since."

"Poor Henry. Man's worst enemy is men. And I bet he did not want to talk about it, yes?"

"Absolutely," Marylou agreed. "I tried to talk it over but I guess I hurt his feelings, and you know what that means."

"Indeed, the silent treatment," María Jose said raising one finger in the air for emphasis. "When I hurt my Marcello's man feelings, he acts just like my big, fat, worthless housecat."

"It's hard to picture Marcello as a fat housecat," said Marylou.

"Oh, but my Marcello acts just like the cat. When I hurt his feelings, he silently creeps around our apartment as if on cat paws, wears a superior feline look on his face, and refuses to give me so much as a glance. But just like that worthless cat, he still expects dinner!"

"Too funny, María José!" Marylou laughed. "Listen, what do you say—let's put things to bed here, head to the café, talk over plans for Henry's visit, and work our way through a bottle of Malbec."

■■■

The gunmetal-grey Bentley slow-rolled to a stop in front of the Wichita Art Museum. Guy Wheeless Jr. put down the red folder on the seat next to him and straightened his charcoal tie in the backseat mirror. He directed his driver, "Don't wander. If this takes more than thirty minutes, I've lost my touch."

Wheeless was greeted by Mr. Aubuchon, the museum's director. As the pair entered the museum, Aubuchon launched into a lengthy recitation of how he had been persuaded to leave a prestigious post in New York City to launch his selfless crusade to bring art to the plains of Kansas. When he finally got around to thanking Wheeless for his million-dollar gift, in his imperious French accent, Wheeless was confused as to who had done a favor for whom.

After politely declining Aubuchon's invitation for coffee, Wheeless was annoyed by the man's insistence that he personally show him the museum's collection. Earlier in the day, Wheeless had made certain that the woman described in Larry's red folder was the tour guide that afternoon. Aubuchon's persistence was an unwelcome complication.

As the two started into the museum, Wheeless saw an opportunity to take advantage of the museum director's healthy ego. Taking Aubuchon by the elbow, he managed to feign a humble tone.

"Mr. Aubuchon, I'm uncomfortable. I can only imagine how busy you are with your important work here. The community is grateful for your efforts and it's hard to imagine the state of the arts in Wichita without you. To burden you with a simple tour, given your exacting responsibilities, is . . . well, just not right. I insist that I take the tour with one of your guides."

When Aubuchon returned with the guide, Wheeless was delighted that Larry's photos had not done her justice. With flowing brunette hair and wonderful legs, she had the stride of a younger woman. She reminded Wheeless of someone he knew, but could not quite place.

"Mr. Wheeless," Aubuchon said, "it is my pleasure to introduce Ms. Jennifer Sessel, who will be your tour guide. Ms. Sessel, meet Mr. Guy Wheeless Jr."

"Ms. Sessel, I appreciate you taking the time to show me around."

"Please, call me Jennifer and the pleasure is mine. We are all so grateful for your generous support of our museum. Shall we start in the nineteenth-century gallery?"

Wheeless had researched the museum's collection to score a winning first impression with his tour guide. Entering the nineteenth-century gallery, he pointed out appreciatively the John Singleton Copley portraits of an overfed magistrate and his sour-faced wife.

As they slowly moved around the room, Sessel competently described the paintings. With Wheeless's attentive encouragement, she shared the fact that she had divorced three years earlier, the names of her two children, and some details of her early years in rural Kansas.

Wheeless saved his best material for the twentieth-century gallery. Entering the room, he stopped and asked, "Isn't that Edward Hopper's *Conference at Night*? What an impactful work. To me, Hopper's paintings speak to the American spirit running through all of us. He gives the ordinary moments and people in American life the respect they deserve."

"I could not agree more," Sessel said, clasping her hands together, her soft brown eyes sparkling with excitement. "The *Conference at Night* is my favorite work in the museum! It has a sense of quiet confidence that speaks to my core. You'll be pleased to know we have two other Hoppers in our collection."

A half an hour later, as they exited the twentieth-century gallery, Sessel turned to him. "I hope you have time to see our modern sculpture exhibit. Critics say it is one of the finest in the Midwest."

Wheeless glanced at his watch. "Unfortunately, I'm already late for an appointment I now regret making," he lied. "I have so enjoyed our time together, and the depth of your knowledge about the collection is most impressive. Jennifer, can I ask a favor of you?"

"Why of course, Mr. Wheeless."

"Please, call me Guy. Would it be acceptable if I called you later in the week? The tour was so detailed. I'm sure I'll have questions about the collection when I have some time for quiet reflection."

"Certainly, Guy, I look forward to it."

Shaking hands, Wheeless gently enclosed hers between both of his, holding it for an extra beat. As they turned in opposite directions, Wheeless stole a glance over his shoulder to watch Sessel walk and suddenly realized who she looked like. She could be the younger sister of that stone bitch attorney Jane Birney. His mood soared at the prospects of a special night with a Birney clone.

Comfortably seated in the back of his car, Wheeless checked his email and returned three calls. When he finished the calls, his driver turned his head. "Everything work out for ya in da museum, boss?" he asked. "You were in there for ova' an hour."

"Must be losing my touch," Wheeless chuckled. "But make no mistake, the hook's set—it's game on. And this one will be very special."

■ ■ ■

Promptly at 7:00 a.m., Henry pulled his white Tahoe up to Marvin's McKinney Avenue apartment building. Marvin had purchased the building's penthouse apartment following his fourth divorce, the one that ended his short-term marriage to Susan. Vowing to remain single, he had set out to re-create a bachelor lifestyle.

Marvin had selected the McKinney Avenue location with an interesting logic. He could catch the antique McKinney Avenue trolley outside his building and hop off a block from his office in the Crescent towers. He reasoned that the evening's return trip on the antique trolley would be a perfect venue to meet women. His logic proved to be flawed and he hadn't taken the trolley in years, but he kept his three-thousand-square-foot penthouse.

After being buzzed in, Henry stepped into the apartment and smiled at its meticulous order. Marvin's life was messy in any number of ways, but his apartment was always pristine. Arranged around the huge living room were eleven white couches of different shapes and lengths. Scattered among the couches was Marvin's collection of abstract, clear-glass sculptures on white marble pedestals. The sculptures were carefully chosen for their different-colored interior stripes. The largest was a nine-foot-tall Chihuly sculpture depicting green stalks bursting into golden grains of wheat.

The huge room opened into a restaurant-quality kitchen of spotless stainless steel appliances and countertops. Although he never cooked, Marvin owned every kitchen gadget on the market. He told Henry that the more plentiful his gadgets, the more likely lady friends were to demonstrate their culinary chops.

Henry walked through the living room to glass doors opening onto a terrace, where he admired the unobstructed view of downtown Dallas. On the terrace's edge was a staircase leading to Marvin's rooftop retreat. The expansive rooftop space was carpeted with artificial grass and large planters of carefully cultivated flowers outlining the perimeter. On one end stood an Austin-stone fireplace and on the other an eighteen-foot-long bar constructed of matching stone.

The roof was shaded by two giant pergolas dripping with wisteria vines growing from huge ceramic pots at the structures' corners. The tops of the pergolas were rigged with industrial-power misters to relieve overheated summer partygoers. Over the years, Marvin had graciously hosted every imaginable variety of party on the rooftop.

Marvin came out of the apartment's master bedroom with sunglasses in one hand and his backpack in the other. The brothers looked at each other and laughed. Both were wearing faded blue work shirts, Wrangler jeans, and scuffed cowboy boots.

"I see you haven't forgotten how to dress Kansas!" Henry said. "Ready for a road trip? I'll drive."

"Sure, you can drive, all the way to Addison Airport," Marvin replied. "I called NetJets last night and they're fuelin' up as we speak. Life's too damn short to drive seven hours to McPherson."

"It just seems like a waste of money."

"Henry, pick 'er up! You're drivin' through life with the emergency brake on. Stop and smell the roses and all that." Marvin put his arm around his brother's shoulder. "Besides, if we fly, we'll have time to stop at Neighbors Café in McPherson for some Fancy Browns."

"Those Fancy Browns are just plain nasty."

"Did you hear what I just said?" Marvin playfully squeezed Henry's shoulder. "Relax, Bro! Did you get hold of Danny Moore?"

"I did. He'll meet us for dinner. He wants to go to a new restaurant in the old Ambassador Hotel. Dan paid the place his ultimate compliment—it makes him feel like he's not in Wichita."

▪▪▪

As the brothers drove to the airport, Henry reflected on the numerous trips they had made together to McPherson. The straight shot north on I-35 from Dallas to Wichita and on to McPherson was a trip the brothers had driven countless times to visit their parents. After selling his industrial tape business and making his fortune, Marvin's life had changed very little. His one new indulgence was a NetJets membership. Henry was confident that Marvin took secret pleasure in flying back to Kansas on a private jet.

When Heman, their father, passed away in 2006, their mother, Helene, moved from the McPherson farm to a managed-care facility in Wichita. After her move, the Lindon farm and its hard red winter wheat crop were managed by Steve Dutton, a Kansas State agricultural school graduate. Steve and his young bride, Greta, made the Lindon farmhouse their home. The years of excellent yields and steady wheat prices proved the arrangement to be a modest success.

Greta, with her wild, cotton-candy, light orange hair, had taken a warm interest in Helene Lindon and drove to Wichita twice a month to bring her back to the farm for Sunday supper. For hours at a time, one head of white and the other of light orange rocked slowly back and forth on the farmhouse's front porch. Henry knew Greta had loved Helene's stories about life on the Lindon Farm and the antics of her beloved Irish twins.

As familiar Dallas landmarks flew past the car window, Henry thought back on their mother's death in 2009, and his agreement with Marvin to sell the farm. After receiving a bid above their asking price, Henry was forced to face reality—he could not make up his mind whether or not to sell the family farm. His lack of decisiveness came with a price when an unusually irritated Marvin charged him with taking over the responsibility for the farm's oversight. Henry made quarterly visits to the farm; Marvin hadn't returned to Kansas in years.

At the airport, they climbed the jetway stairs, took seats across the aisle from each other, secured cups of coffee, and buckled their seat belts in the Challenger jet's beige leather seats.

"Whaddaya hear about this year's crop?" Marvin asked.

"The Chicago Board of Trade's annual crop tour came through the county last week." Henry sipped his coffee. "With the drought, they're predicting an average of thirty-eight bushels statewide. Steve Dutton says we'll do a bit better, around forty-five bushels. With 640 acres of the farm planted in wheat, that's 28,800 bushels. Not bad."

"Any guess on price?" Marvin asked.

"You never know with all the manipulations of the commodities markets these days." Henry added. "But I'm betting the price will drift down again, around six dollars."

"So 'round $170,000 before expenses and taxes." Marvin shook his head. "Is this a business we really want to be in? Aren't you tired of havin' to drag your ass all the way up to McPherson?"

"We've been through this before," said Henry. "I'm good with it."

"Before I get all caught up in the farmin' business, or should I say farmin' hobby, tell me the whole Dan Moore story. All I know is that big lug got disbarred and somehow dickface Wheeless was involved."

"Do you want the details, or the condensed version?" Henry was confident he knew the answer.

"Just give me the *Reader's Digest* version."

"In short, Dan got caught up in sex, drugs, and country music," Henry said. "He took on a client he shouldn't have, ended up missing a statute of limitation, and embezzled money from his firm to pay off the client for his mistake. Wheeless got wind of it, did his own investigation, and made sure Dan got disbarred."

"Whatever happened to that cute wife of his?" Marvin asked. "If I'm recallin' right, you took a run at that little filly back in the day."

"No, Marvin, that was you, that was you that took the run. She's long gone."

"Well, sounds like a rough road for Danny Boy," said Marvin.

"No doubt about it. Told me that in a matter of months he got the Four Big Ds—Dishonored, Divorced, Disbarred, and Detoxed."

"Nice to know he kept his sense of humor," Marvin said. He reached into his backpack and pulled out the *Sports Illustrated* swimsuit edition.

Left alone with his thoughts, Henry stared out the jet's window and thought about the mess his friend Dan had made. It had begun when Dan started running around with Suzy, a secretary in his law office. A tornado of a girl, she was a secretary by day and a country music DJ at night, with Sister Suzy as her radio handle.

She and Dan started hanging around with the country music acts that played live on her station. Before long, Dan developed an unhealthy taste for cocaine, his lucrative law practice crumpled, and his life spun out of control. He went from living in a beautiful Mediterranean house on the country club's fourteenth fairway to a Motel 6 room on the interstate.

"Henry," Marvin interrupted his thoughts. "How about one of those nice cheese Danishes the crew got us?" Henry shrugged and his brother got up and retrieved a tray of pastries from the plane's tiny galley. He held the tray out to Henry, who shook his head.

"I'd love one, but I better pass."

"Watchin' that girlish figure of yours?" Marvin teased as he selected two for himself, sat down, and went back to his *Sports Illustrated*. "When you gonna learn to live a little, Bro?"

"Yeah, whatever," Henry muttered. Thoughts about Dan's problems tumbled into thoughts about Guy Wheeless Jr. Why had Wheeless felt the need to jump in and pull Dan down? And now, he was possibly behind the UNS inquiry by Jane Birney. Could it possibly be because of the cherry bomb incident all those years ago?

Henry shifted in his seat. Surely after decades Wheeless didn't still blame him for that? He hadn't even been involved and it was ancient history anyway. Did he need to keep a closer eye on Wheeless, or was he being paranoid, like Marylou had said?

"Henry, there's Wichita," Marvin said, looking out the jet window. "Hot damn! Neighbors Café, here we come!"

11

Henry had warm memories of McPherson's Neighbors Café on the corner of Main and Elizabeth. It was a Lindon family favorite. His father, Heman, had started most mornings there with a cup of coffee, eggs sunny-side up, and country sausage. In those days, the name on the sign said the White Swan, but everyone in town called it the Dirty Duck.

When the current proprietor–the round, cherub-faced Teresa–took over, she decided the place needed a new name and a new attitude. At Neighbors Café there would be no customers, only "neighbors." The walls were lined with photographs of broad, smiling faces. No celebrity photos—only those of customers from McPherson. The waitresses wore tie-dyed shirts to complement Teresa's bright floral apron and matching headband.

The brothers parked their rental car across the street from the café. As Marvin led the way through the door, Henry saw that nothing had changed since their last visit. Teresa greeted them loudly from behind the cash register.

"As I live and breathe," she said. "If it ain't the Lindons' Irish twins. Welcome home, city boys! To what do I owe this honor? Marvin, I know you'll be tuckin' into a Fancy Brown, how's 'bout you, Henry?"

"Nice to be home," Henry answered. "I'll start with coffee." Seeing Marvin stop to compliment Teresa on her latest hair color, Henry deliberately cut past him and slid into one of the tired red Naugahyde booths as far as possible from the counter stools Marvin preferred. He smiled when his brother begrudgingly followed him into the booth.

"I hope you're all right back here," Henry said insincerely. "The counter's too close to that grill. It's not only hot, but it reminds me why this place was called the Dirty Duck."

"Mornin', gents," the young waitress interrupted. She had a mouth full of braces. "What can I get you this morning?"

"First, we need some introductions here," Marvin said. "We can see from your name tag that you're Latisha. This here is Henry and I'm Marvin. You from around here, Latisha?"

"Sure am. Born and raised in McPherson. When I was a little girl, Mama used to bring me in here when she waitressed. This here's like a second home. I'll be a sophomore at McPherson High School in the fall."

"So you're a McPherson Bullpup," Marvin said, giving Henry a wink. "I love the way the students in the high school are called Bullpups and at McPherson College they're called Bulldogs."

Latisha put a hand on her slender hip and said, "If you know that, you must be from 'round these parts."

"We're proud to call McPherson home. We live in Dallas these days. My brother Henry here is a professor at Southerland University."

"What's Southerland University?" she asked.

"Oh, bless your heart," Marvin said, smiling broadly at the waitress. "Don't you worry yourself none about that. I'll have your famous Fancy Browns with a double side of crispy bacon. Henry, what's your pleasure?"

"I'll have some oatmeal," Henry answered, putting down his menu. "Do you have some fresh fruit to go with that?"

"All the fruit we got is orange juice," the waitress apologized.

As she left with their order, Marvin leaned back against the booth and raised both hands in exasperation.

"Really? You're in the Neighbors Café in McPherson, Kansas, and you're havin' oatmeal? Really? This is McPherson, not one of your la-di-da organic places in Dallas."

"Back off," Henry said rolling his eyes. "If I ate like you, I'd tip the scales at about three hundred. Your metabolism has got to be double of mine. Hell, the four cornerstones of your ridiculous food pyramid are donuts, Mexican, barbecue, and Frito pie."

Returning to their table, the waitress slid the Fancy Browns in front of Marvin. Henry watched Marvin close his eyes, bend forward, and blissfully inhale the vapors. The dish covered every inch of the oversize plate—it was a concoction of nearly burnt hash browns, diced ham, green peppers, onions, and eggs, all smothered with melted cheddar cheese.

Henry thought Fancy Browns looked like cow patties. As they ate in silence, Henry watched cinnamon rolls the size of hubcaps being carried by waitresses to large "neighbors" with appetites to match. He turned his head away as a man at the next table slurped down country biscuits drowning in white sausage gravy.

As Henry paid the bill, he watched Marvin inconspicuously slip a fifty-dollar bill into a plastic canister that sat next to the cash register. The canister had a handwritten note, attached to it with two rubber bands, that read "New Booth Fund." *Marvelous to the rescue*, he thought, and then he pushed away the guilt that inevitably followed.

■ ■ ■

The brothers' rental car with Marvin behind the wheel pulled up to the wooden farm gate. They both got out of the car, and Henry stepped over the steel cattle guard to unlatch the gate.

"Is that the same Lindon Farm sign that's been here all these years?" Marvin asked while surveying the area.

"No. That one's about a year old. Greta, Steve Dutton's wife, painted it. She's real intent on keeping some things around here the way Mom liked them. Mom told her it was important to have a hand-painted sign to let folks know there's a woman's touch on the farm. Mom and Greta had a special relationship. By the way, Greta has a surprise for you."

"I love a good surprise!" Marvin stuck his hands into his jeans' back pockets and shook his head as he gazed at the land. "Lookin' at the flat horizon out here still amazes me. Hell, it's like an endless airport tarmac. God created Kansas to grow wheat and not much else."

Henry found the farm warmly familiar, yet disquieting. He knew he should leave it in the past, but for some reason he didn't understand, he was unable to do so. "Can you imagine what our lives would be like if we had stayed here and lived the farm life?"

As they got back in the car, Marvin said, "Livin' the farm life sounds appealin'. Dirt crunchin' under your boots, workin' in the sunshine, helpin' feed the country, and all that happy horseshit." Marvin stopped talking as the yellow farmhouse came into view.

"But if I stayed," Marvin continued, "I would have wasted my days dreamin' about what coulda been. Life's too damn short for wouldas and shouldas. But I do love Kansas when the sun bleaches the green out of the wheat stalks and the wind blows it around like ripples on a pond."

"Agreed," Henry said. "For the two weeks before the July harvest it's the prettiest place in America. The other fifty weeks of moonscape are the problem. I told Steve we'd meet him up at the cow barn." He gave his brother a cheeky half smile. "Maybe you can give him some pointers on shoveling manure. That was always your specialty around here."

"Knowing how to shovel shit has sure come in mighty handy!" Marvin cheerfully replied.

As the brothers parked their car in front of the barn, two old dogs lying in the dirt in front of the barn door struggled up to their feet to greet the visitors with their best barks. They were immediately silenced by Steve Dutton slapping his well-worn DeKalb seed hat against his thigh. Dutton shook hands with the brothers and said, "I've been lookin' forward to showing you what we've been up to 'round here."

The three men toured the wheat fields and talked easily about rain levels, fools moving their wheat crop to corn, and the falling water levels in the

Ogallala Aquifer in western Kansas. They walked back to the yellow frame farmhouse for lunch, and Greta met them on the large front porch with iced tea in glasses with a sunflower motif. She set down the tray and gave Henry a warm hug.

"How you doing, Greta?" Henry said, hugging her back, remembering the kindness Greta had shown their mother. "Having a good day?"

"Henry, any day you visit is a special day. Steve talks about it for a week beforehand. And Marvin! It has been way too long. Welcome home."

"Good to see ya, sweetie," Marvin said, pulling her into a hug so tight it made her giggle.

"My goodness!" she said. "Let's sit down. You boys look thirsty."

The group settled into the rocking chairs, sipping their iced tea. Steve described the latest crop rumors, including the possible onset of the dreaded stripe rust, then the sound of a baby's cry brought conversation to a standstill.

"Is that a baby?" Marvin asked, coming up out of his chair, looking incredulous. "Y'all have a baby?"

"We were blessed seven months ago," Greta said. "Wait right here, and I'll make the introductions after a quick diaper change."

"Why didn't you tell me they have a baby?" Marvin asked Henry.

"If I had, what would your first question have been?"

"Hell if I know . . . suppose, 'what's the baby's name?'"

"Exactly. Give it a minute."

Ten minutes later, Steve opened the screen door for a beaming Greta. In her left arm, she held a bundle of blue, and in her right, a bundle of pink. The sleepy-eyed infants sucked their pacifiers faster as they examined the strangers. Both had their mother's bright orange hair.

"Marvin," Greta said softly, "your mom loved to talk about her Irish twins, and now Lindon Farm has new twins."

"They're the cutest little things I've ever laid eyes on. What're their names?"

Henry waited for the new mother to respond, but to his surprise, she turned to him. "Henry, why don't you introduce the twins?"

He smiled broadly at Greta, honored by her request, and silently mouthed "Thank you." He turned to Marvin. "It's my pleasure to introduce this little guy—he's Heman Dutton, and this blue-eyed beauty is Helene Dutton."

Marvin looked from the adults to the babies and back to the adults. He reached for Helene. Greta handed Heman to Henry.

"Heman and Helene are back on the farm," Marvin announced. "Sweet! This is the best news I've had in weeks. No, make that years! Thank you *so* much."

As the brothers swayed gently back and forth with the new Lindon Farm twins in their arms, Henry felt a tear roll down his cheek. He was too happy to wipe it off.

It was no surprise to Henry that Marvin took center stage at lunch. He held the babies in his lap and was effusive in his praise of Greta's buttermilk fried chicken and waffles. He got laughs from the group when he teased Greta about using the same hair dye on the babies that she used on her own hair. For once, Henry didn't mind so much.

After lunch, the men returned to the fields for more inspection and shop-talk. After discussing the cost of irrigation and the potential difference in crop yield, they walked back to the farmhouse to say good-bye to Greta.

Standing on the porch with his wife and their twins, Steve said, "You know, Greta and me, well now Heman and Helene too, we see living our lives here forever. I know you've been hesitant to talk about it, but can we discuss me some day buyin' the farm? Not pushin', mind you, just askin'."

Marvin looked to Henry for a response. Henry ran one hand over his cow-lick and cleared his throat.

"Our dad always said this land made him proud because special people were born and raised here. You and Greta are exactly the type of folks he had in mind—it's a place that needs a family. I had hoped against hope that someday one of us, or one of our kids, would head back here. I don't think that's happening."

Henry glanced over and saw Marvin slowly nodding his head in agreement; no one from the Lindon family would be returning to live on the farm.

"Steve," Henry said, "I've got a number of things weighing on me. Let us think on it."

"Sure, Henry, you and Marvin think about it," Steve said, drawing his wife closer as she gazed down at the twins in her arms. "Just take your time."

■■■

The rental car pulled away from the hand-painted Lindon Farm sign with an irritated Marvin in the driver's seat. He tightened his jaw. Why hadn't Henry gone ahead and agreed to sell the property? How long was he going to hang on to it? As soon as the farm began to fade in the distance, he turned to his brother, his words coming in rapid fire.

"Why the hell didn't you give the man an answer? We both know sellin' Steve and Greta the farm's the right thing . . . It's what Dad would want . . . and damn, it sure as hell is not a great investment. And what's this stuff about somethin' weighin' on you? Bro, you've been draggin' ass around like an old barnyard hound for way too long. You're not still worryin' about that little tramp stamp episode are you?"

"No. That student is set to graduate. The issue's in the rearview mirror," Henry said in a defensive tone. "But I've got a business issue and a tough personal issue to deal with."

"You've had business issues for twenty-five years and you'll have 'em for the rest of your days. It comes with the territory. As far as personal problems—are you kiddin' me? You've got a great wife, money in the bank, and, I would add, a cool job. What the hell do you have to complain about?"

"This business problem is different." Henry paused and looked out the window at the unending wheat fields. "Remember that San Miguel cookie company we acquired while I was running Inveress?"

"Sure," said Marvin. "You had a great idea, an idea that ended up makin' everybody and their brother real good money when UNS bought your outfit." He shifted uneasily in his seat as he turned from the narrow road onto a broader one.

"A lot of people made money," agreed Henry. "But I had a meeting with folks from UNS. They're real unhappy with how things are going with the San Miguel operation in Argentina."

"So?" Marvin hit a pothole and his hands clenched around the steering wheel. Where was Henry going with this? Could he possibly know about what John-O did in the Bahamas?

"They made accusations that we were able to close the deal as a result of some illegal payments." Henry adjusted his seat belt. "They seem to think I had some role in violating the Foreign Corrupt Practices Act."

"Did you?" asked Marvin, glancing at Henry.

"Not as far as I know."

"Then screw 'em." Marvin raised his middle finger.

"That's easy for you to say," Henry said, his irritation evident.

"Hell, Bro, this isn't your first rodeo. I'm sure you'll figure 'er out." Marvin tried to soften his tone. "What kinda personal issue you dealin' with?"

"Look, this is close to impossible to talk about." Henry turned to look out the window.

"Let me guess." Marvin tapped his chin with one finger. "Got it—you've finally decided to go for that sex-change operation?"

"Bite me."

"C'mon, tell me."

Henry sighed, and the sound of defeat, plus the sudden slump of his brother's shoulders, made Marvin turn serious for a change.

"There's a guy who owns a clothing store in Buenos Aires," Henry replied in a low voice. "I've bought a dozen expensive shirts from him over the years. I thought of him as a friend. His name is Mikel Jiménez."

"And?"

Henry dragged one hand over his cowlick. "You know how Marylou's been spending way too much time in Buenos Aires over the last two years?"

"Yeah?" *Where is this going?*

"Marylou's having an affair with this shirt guy."

"WHAT?" Marvin jerked the steering wheel to get back across the centerline.

"Watch the damn road!" Henry yelled, one hand gripping the dashboard.

"Henry, you gotta be kidding me."

His brother shook his head. "I found a card written from him to Marylou that spelled it out."

"You sure? What'd the note say?" *The world must be coming to an end if Marylou is cheating on Henry*, Marvin thought, keeping his eyes on the road.

"Basically, that he couldn't wait to have her back in his arms," Henry said sadly. "The point is, I know it's going on and I've already waited too long to do something about it."

"When you say 'do somethin' about it,' whaddaya got in mind?"

"Marylou's in Buenos Aires, yet again, supposedly working on that red porcelain pig business with her friend, María José. I'll fly down there and be up front with her."

They drove on in silence. Uninterrupted wheat fields, silhouetted against the enormous barren sky, flew hypnotically past the car windows. The landscape's relentless repetition reminded Marvin of why he had not returned to live on the family farm.

"Henry, you know I love you," Marvin said, breaking the silence. "Somewhere along the line, women can't survive without attention. All of 'em have this insatiable need to connect. You've been orbitin' in your own little universe for way too long—"

"Wait a second," Henry interrupted, his face flushed, his brows furrowing. "Are you saying Marylou's cheating is my fault?"

"That's not what I'm sayin' . . . exactly."

After five minutes of uncomfortable silence, Marvin decided to wade back in. "Do me a favor, just one favor. You're a careful guy who's always thinkin' things through—maybe thinkin' too much. Let's assume you don't have your facts quite right. By some cruel twist of fate, you somehow got it wrong."

"I don't have it wrong."

"You say you're gonna confront Marylou in Buenos—"

"Yes." Henry cut him off and Marvin knew he had to tread lightly.

"Okay, so let's see if we can figure out a better plan." He rubbed the side of his face with one hand.

"Nothing to figure out. I'm going to tell her I know."

"But what if you're wrong? Maybe there's an explanation you haven't thought about? Why not talk to Señor Shirts first?"

"You really think he's going to admit to screwing my wife?" Henry shot back, turning toward Marvin.

Marvin shook his head. "What I think is that you could be makin' a very serious mistake here. Accuse Marylou of cheatin' and she's not, you'll ruin a great thing, and for what? Take it from me," he tapped his hand on his chest. "I've had far more than my fair share of unfortunate mileage around the marriage track. If three failed marriages taught me anything . . . "

"Four—for Christ's sake!" Henry yelled, slapping one hand against the dashboard. "You've been married four times!"

"Big deal. My point's the same." Marvin gave him a wary glance. "You need to calm down, Bro, or you're headed for an overload."

"What do you suggest?" asked Henry. "Stroll into the shirt store and say 'Hey! Afternoon, Mikel. I'll take two white shirts, a blue one, and by the by . . . you enjoy bonking my wife?'"

"No. I'm suggestin' you go the extra mile," said Marvin. "Find the right moment, show Señor Shirts the card, and ask for an explanation. If he has one, great. You've dodged a potential disaster with Marylou. Then ask him man-to-man to keep your little misunderstandin' to himself. He's a man. He'll understand how the Code of the West works, even if he is from Buenos Aires."

"And if I happen to be right?"

"He gives you a crock, you kick his ass on the spot."

"I'll give it some thought."

"Damn it, Henry!" Marvin banged the steering wheel. "You're always givin' somethin' some thought. You can mull shit over like nobody's business. This is a Code of the West issue. Keep your powder dry and your mouth shut until you're absolutely, one hundred percent positive!"

As the miles flew by, Henry silently fumed in the passenger seat. Why did he keep asking his impetuous brother for advice? He was sick and tired of Marvin's Code of the West psychobabble.

But what if Marvin was right?

Should I talk to Mikel before confronting Marylou? Was my experience with the fortune-telling bird in Mexico City some kind of transcendental omen? After all, my fortune said, En boca cerrada no entran moscas—*flies do not enter a closed mouth. Was it a confirmation of Marvin's advice? Or was it simply coincidental?*

Henry contemplated telling Marvin what had happened with the bird, but decided to keep the *dicho* to himself. Any reinforcement of Marvin's Code of the West theory would only rekindle his sermon.

■■■

As the brothers entered the improbably named Siena Tuscan Steakhouse in Wichita's Ambassador Hotel, the flood of late-afternoon light ignited the silverware and multiple crystal wineglasses elegantly laid out on the tables. Brightly colored pieces of modern art and dark wood paneling gave the restaurant an air of sophistication unique in Wichita.

Henry carried the sting of friction from the car ride into the restaurant. Marvin quietly took a seat facing the windows with his back to the room. As Henry sat down across from him, he saw Dan Moore enter the dining room. They made eye contact and before Henry could acknowledge him, Dan put his index figure to his mouth to signal silence.

Dan wore an expensive light grey suit and an open-collared shirt of a darker grey. His suit complemented his fashionably long pewter-colored hair, which he parted down the middle and tucked behind his ears. He playfully tiptoed across the restaurant toward the brothers' table. Henry saw the other patrons smiling in amusement at the large man's dancing bear act.

Henry kept his face expressionless as Dan tiptoed up to Marvin's back, clapped his hands on the man's shoulders, and bellowed "Marvelous! The prodigal son returns!"

Marvin jerked out of his chair in surprise, but was soon laughing as the three exchanged warm hugs and loud backslaps. Henry watched as the two men smiled, clasped each other's shoulders, and gave each other a playful shake. Their hefty sizes had always been a bond.

"Marvelous, been way too long," Dan said, looking him up and down. "You look fit enough to strap on the old high-tops and jump for the rim."

"Thanks, Danny Boy," Marvin replied. "As you can see, bein' here with you puts a big ol' grin on my face. And I'm likin' that soul patch you're sportin'. Sit 'er down and take a load off."

The three gave the waiter drink orders and Henry was surprised when Dan ordered a bourbon Manhattan on the rocks. He concluded that detox had left out alcohol. After small talk about the weather, Marvin said, "On the way up here, Henry filled me in some on your troubles . . . sorry that all came down on you."

"Thanks. I made my own bed, but I sure didn't enjoy lying in it," Dan said, pulling on the triangle of beard below his lower lip. "But, hey, it's sure good to see you boys, reminds me of easier times."

"Tell me," said Marvin, after draining half his beer. "How's the new gig goin'?"

"Knock on wood, it's taken off!" Dan rapped the table with his knuckles. "After the dust settled, I was broke and had to find a way to make a living. Obviously I couldn't practice law, but from all those years at the law firm I knew how corporations worked and, more important, how they hide their secrets. I started a small investigation office and one thing led to another. Now we have three lawyers, seven accountants, and half a dozen investigators. It's a hell of a lot more fun than practicing law."

"Sounds like a nice business, Danny Boy," Marvin said, giving the thumbs-up sign.

"That's not all of it, though," Henry added.

"That's right," Dan said, nodding. "The most exciting thing we've got going is in Mumbai. I hired a computer whiz named Jaya out of KU. We moved him over to Mumbai where his family's from. For the last two years, he and his team have been conducting a data-mining and analytics operation on some of the world's largest corporations. Every piece of publicly filed information is in our database. Even better, we learned how to harvest some very interesting social media stuff. People are willing to share information on social media they would never dream of giving to their employers."

"Is that minin' legal?" Marvin asked, circling his finger at the waiter for another round of drinks.

"We think so." Dan rapped the table again. "Everything's collected in India, and we don't alter data, change settings, or transfer money. We only want information. We look at when an exec tells friends he is going to a different job, when a line of credit has been refused, what hedge funds are thinking about taking positions in what companies. Hell, we even know when execs are having hall sex."

"Hall sex?" Marvin perked up.

"You know," said Henry. "Hall sex is when things get so bad in corporate America that execs passing each other in the corridor spit 'fuck you' at each other."

"Well, I'll be dipped," said Marvin. "Learn somethin' real important every day. Dan, whaddaya hear about the gang from high school?"

"After my very public whipping, I pretty much stay clear of that crowd." Dan popped the maraschino cherry from his fresh Manhattan into his mouth. "Believe me, there are no invitations for Sunday supper. I do keep real close track of one of them, though."

"Who's that?" asked Henry.

Dan sipped his Manhattan. "Our old 'buddy' Wheeless. I track everything he does."

"How is Mr. Cherry Bomb?" Marvin asked. "Henry tells me he's quite the swingin' dick these days."

"Mom told me that by the time a man reaches fifty, life gives him the face he deserves." Dan swirled the ice in his cocktail with his index finger. "If that were true, Wheeless would be the ugliest cuss in town—bald as a vulture with a bumpy head like a walnut shell."

After a day on the farm, Henry couldn't help reflecting about his own mother. She loved to leave her Irish twins with lyrical warnings. When she caught them in some mischief, which was frequent, she always admonished them (with a wag of her finger), "The morning has no idea what the afternoon knows."

Henry was brought back to the moment by Dan's laugh. "Unfortunately, Mom was wrong about that one. Giving the devil his due," Dan said as he gave a tip of his glass, "he's aged remarkably well. Remember how back in the day he wore his hair slicked back, kind of greasy? Well, he's got that style down pat and it gives him a British air that he plays to the hilt with all his Savile Row, double-breasted suits and Jermyn Street shirts. He's on about every civic board in town and spreads nicely publicized donations around to all the right charities. Quite the respected man about town."

"Did he ever get his ear fixed?" Marvin asked.

"No." Dan shook his head. "Like you said once upon a time, he still looks like old Vincent van Gogh."

"So he's still at the bank his father founded?" Henry asked.

"That's right. Followed Guy Sr. into the chairman's seat and immediately made drastic changes," Dan told the brothers. "He created a hedge fund with depositors' money. Didn't bother securing anyone's consent, but that's a whole different story. Using other people's money, he made some wild bets on Japan's currency and Brazilian commodities. *The Wichita Eagle* ran a flattering article describing Guy as the city's newest billionaire."

"Has that success continued?" Henry asked with a frown.

"It's a mixed track record," replied Dan. "After that first remarkable run, he left most of the bank business to professional managers. He fancies himself part of the new breed of activist investors—spends his time making life miserable for companies he's taken a position in."

"Considering your unpleasant history with Guy Jr.," Henry said, "why have you made it your business to know so much about what he's up to?"

"That's easy. About eighteen months ago, out of the blue, we got a wonderful client who pays whatever it takes to get dirt on Wheeless." Dan looked from one brother to the other. "This client pays in full and fast. All we do is tail Wheeless day and night and report back."

"Learn anything interesting?" asked Henry.

"We signed a confidentiality agreement—can't disclose specifics about Wheeless or our client." Dan gave an apologetic shrug. "It's too bad because some of it is prime-time nasty."

"Any specifics? Let's say, public information you can share?" asked Henry, leaning on his days as an attorney.

"Okay," said Dan, nodding. "This much is public record—he moved his office out of the bank building and into a huge old warehouse on First Street over near Old Town. Gutted the whole building down to the studs and reinforced it with steel I-beams. People around here call it the Bunker. He built a world-class, 24/7 trading operation in the basement and the fund's offices are on the main floor. He converted the top floor into a soundproof living quarters. Doesn't leave the building for days at a time. He's like Howard Hughes except . . ."

"Except what?" Henry asked. He began to see the faint shadows of a plan to solve his issues with UNS. Dan just might hold the key to his success.

"Let's leave 'er there," said Dan. "Man, it's good to see you derelicts."

As Marvin took care of the check and told the waitress he'd been watching all evening how good her dangling earrings looked, Dan turned to Henry. "How's Marylou doing? I have great memories of her from back in the day."

"Doing fine," said Henry. "I'll be with her in a few days down in Buenos Aires." *And I'm certainly not looking forward to the trip,* he thought.

"Give her my best. She's everything a man could wish for. Smart as hell, loves a good time, and she's been beautiful at every stage of life. Henry, you're one lucky dog."

Henry saw Marvin staring at him with a broad told-ya-so smirk on his face.

Henry ignored his brother's antics. "Before you go, Dan, I've got some very weird crap happening to me I want to talk to you about. It's about UNS, the group that took over my old company, Inveress. I think Wheeless is behind the scenes at UNS trying to make trouble for me. With all the info you have on Wheeless, you might be in a position to be of enormous assistance to me."

Dan pulled at his soul patch. The center part in his hair lined up with his soul patch, giving him a devilish look.

"Okay . . . maybe. I'll see if we can find a way to work around that confidentiality agreement," said Dan, grinning like the Cheshire Cat. "No one wants to drop the hammer on Wheeless more than me. And believe you me, he's provided one big-ass hammer."

■■■

After buckling their seat belts for the return flight, Henry paged through the day's newspapers, while Marvin absently sampled a tray of cheese and crackers that had replaced the morning's Danish plate. Twenty minutes passed in silence. Finally, Marvin could no longer resist taking a final stab at Henry's Buenos Aires plan.

"Don't want to be a pain in the ass," Marvin began. "But I hope you took to heart what I said about your game plan with Marylou. You got nothin' to lose and everything to gain by talkin' first with Señor Shirts."

"I told you I'd think about it," Henry said. "Since you seem intent on playing the advice game, I've got a question for you."

"Shoot."

"Why the hell, at this point in your life, did you decide to freaking brand yourself and how in God's name did you choose that ridiculous quote for your tattoo?"

"Well, slap my ass silly!" Marvin said feigning shock with wide-open eyes. "I thought it was cool—something no one else would think of usin' as a tattoo. What would you suggest? A flaming basketball hoop? Some wheat stalks? A double roll of MM Enterprises tape? There's nothin' that says tattoos have to make sense. Hell, just gettin' a tattoo doesn't make much sense." As the words left his mouth, Marvin knew he had left himself exposed.

"My point exactly." Henry dropped his head, closed his eyes, and pressed firmly on his cowlick.

"Henry, if we're stayin' with true confessions, here's one back at ya,"

Marvin said, trying to change topics. "Don't want to kick Danny Moore after all he's been through, but what he's doin' is nothin' but tragic. He says he's followin' Wheeless for some client. But you know as well as me what he's really up to."

"What do you think he's up to?"

"It's as clear as the nose on my face. He's lookin' for ammunition to take revenge for Wheeless's role in his disbarment. You remember what Dad said about revenge?"

"Yes, Marvin." Henry rolled his eyes.

"Well it's worth repeatin'." Marvin felt he was back on top. "Dad said he didn't understand the phrase 'revenge is a dish best served cold,' but he knew that no one's ever satisfied with a single helpin'. Dad was right. No one playin' the revenge game is ever satisfied. It just goes on and on. All that talk about Wheeless," he said, as he shook his head, "it's got me jumpy. Please, don't get sucked down the sewer with those two."

"Just being vigilant," Henry said, with one hand raised to cut Marvin off as he started to speak. "Given what we know Wheeless did to Dan, please don't tell me you agree with Marylou that I'm paranoid for thinking he may have it in for me, and for that matter, you as well?"

"Henry, those boys have lived cheek by jowl in the same small town all these years. We got no idea what nonsense has gone down between 'em. Wheeless is a hot shot runnin' around the world doin' deals. Is he really gonna take the time to reach out and do us harm? Other than the great pink panty incident, we never did a damn thing to him."

"That girl going heels over head in his car is not the issue," Henry said, shaking his head. "Wheeless undoubtedly blames us for getting his ear blown off."

"He can blame us 'til the cows come home," Marvin said with a dismissive wave of his hand. "You just need to stay clear of him. If you and Dan poke that snake, he's gonna bite ya."

"You're awful free with advice today," Henry said.

"Only tryin' to be helpful."

"You've been crowding me all day. One more word of helpful advice and we're headed for hall sex."

"Sorry, ya know my intentions are good." Marvin laughed. "Let's change the subject. I've got news on the food truck front."

"What news?"

"I've decided to call my first food truck Twenty-First-Century Foxes. The business model follows the early Southwest Airlines blueprint—you know, pretend to be sellin' food, but really sell good-lookin' girls in hot clothes. So job one is to find some great-lookin' foxes to work the truck. Double D says she found the perfect candidates, a couple of Southerland coeds."

"You know their names?" asked Henry.

"No, haven't met 'em. Double D met one of them in a hair place and she's bringin' them by the office in the mornin' so me and John-O can check 'em out. John-O has a friend doin' some mock-ups on what the truck will look like. By the time you get back from Buenos Aires, we'll be ready to roll."

"What kind of food are you going to sell?"

"I had no idea . . . until today," Marvin said with a self-satisfied smile.

Henry rolled his eyes. "Let me guess—Fancy Browns?"

■■■

Henry dropped Marvin at his apartment and drove toward home with a headful of irritants. *Am I asking for trouble by joining forces with Dan Moore against Wheeless? What will happen if UNS gets the Justice Department interested in a Foreign Corrupt Practices Act investigation against me?*

The potential ramifications of a Department of Justice investigation of the San Miguel transaction were dire. The DOJ would be relentless. Losing his opportunity to become CEO at Wein would only be the beginning of his problems.

As he ruminated on the potential issues he could face, something Marvin had said drifted into his mind. "Everybody and their brother" had made money on the San Miguel deal.

Henry pulled his white Tahoe off onto a side street. Shifting the car into park, he placed both hands on the steering wheel and leaned his forehead into his hands.

Exactly what did Marvin mean by everybody and their brother making good money when UNS bought Inveress? Exactly who did Marvin mean by "everybody"?

After a long few minutes, Henry put the truck into gear, made a U-turn, and headed back to Marvin's apartment.

Marvin opened the door, a bowl of cereal in his hand. "Well, I'll be; wasn't expectin' to see you again tonight. Somethin' on your mind? C'mon in."

The brothers settled across from each other on two of Marvin's white couches. Henry took a deep breath and then took the plunge. "I can't get something you said out of my head."

"That just tickles me!" Marvin said with a self-satisfied chuckle. "You've already come around to some sound thinkin'. Talkin' first with Señor Shirts before you talk with Marylou is the smart move, guarantee it."

Henry shook his head. "No, Marvin, that's not what I'm here to talk about."

"All right . . . so you see the problem you're makin' for yourself teamin' up with Dan to poke that snake Wheeless," Marvin said as he waved his cereal spoon like a baton. "That's good thinkin', Henry."

Wrong again. "No." Henry shook his head. "You said 'everybody and their brother' made money when UNS took over Inveress." He averted his gaze and stared down at the floor before looking up again. "Marvin, please tell me you weren't including yourself."

"Hell, Henry," Marvin said, folding his arms over his chest. "You were the one who told me to buy Inveress stock."

"I absolutely never, ever, told you to buy Inveress stock," Henry insisted, his hands clasped together, his knuckles white.

"You sure as hell did!" Marvin exploded, coming to his feet.

"Marvin, what are you winding up to tell me?"

Marvin put his cereal bowl down on a table. "Remember we were havin' dinner and you were doin' a bit o' celebratin' about closin' on that deal in Argentina—the one you always called the Deal from Hell?"

"Vaguely."

"And you said that company had some kinda secret technology that would change the cookie business." Henry noticed Marvin was having trouble making eye contact. "And since no one else understood the opportunity, you bought the company on the cheap?"

"Again, I vaguely remember the conversation."

Marvin extended his arms toward his brother. "Well damn, Henry, if that's not an invite to invest in a great opportunity, I don't know what is." He broke eye contact and shrugged, staring somewhere over Henry's shoulder. "But relax . . .I didn't buy a single share."

Henry hesitated, trying to read his brother. He was hiding something. "Marvin, did someone you know buy the stock?"

"Well . . . yeah." He looked back at Henry and the frantic expression was gone. He smiled his familiar Marvin smile. "John-O bought a pretty good lick of it. But don't worry, he bought it through our Bahamas account. No one will know."

"Goddamn it, Marvin!" Henry erupted. "Can you hear yourself? What you described is plain-vanilla, old-fashioned insider trading and you've managed to implicate me! Remember what I said about a possible Department of Justice investigation? If the Department of Justice decides to investigate they will undoubtedly look at trading patterns. When they look, we're cooked!" As he glared at his brother, he saw Marvin falter.

"Well . . . " He dragged one hand through his thick white hair, his gaze on the floor. "I guess it's simple." He shrugged and glanced back up. "You'll need to . . .you'll need to make sure there's no Department of Justice investigation."

Henry stared at him, his mouth dry, his heart pounding. "Marvin, you . . . are . . . a . . . FUCKING MORON!"

12

"Andrea!" Nichole shouted over the noise of a hair dryer in the bathroom. "We're going to be late!" With no reply, she impatiently yelled, "Andrea, do you hear me?"

"I heard you. Moving as fast as I can."

Nichole was tempted to go to the food truck interview by herself. As a general rule, Andrea wasn't good with people. At a minimum, she'd be a distraction and potentially a hindrance. While Nichole spent hours researching the food truck business online in preparation for the interview, Andrea said she was too tired to help and had sprawled on the couch watching reality TV shows.

Nichole, dressed in her demure, dark blue business suit, had been ready for thirty minutes. Waiting for Andrea, she grew more irritated by the minute. She told herself to relax—for this meeting she'd have to play the soft, dutiful schoolgirl.

When Andrea finally emerged fully dressed, Nichole rolled her eyes. Andrea's "business suit" displayed more cleavage than was appropriate for a homecoming dance. But there was no time for a change of clothes. They hurried out of the garage apartment to Nichole's car and soon were speeding toward downtown on the Central Expressway.

Staring straight ahead, Andrea said, "You got in awful late last night. What were you doing?"

"I told you," Nichole said, working hard to keep annoyance out of her voice. "I was over at Doc Rock's. You could have come along if you wanted to."

"What's so interesting about Doc Rock? Smoking pot and listening to his boogie-woogie piano gets old real fast."

Nichole knew Andrea was jealous of their landlord, Doc Rock, and sometimes enjoyed torturing her about him. But Andrea had trouble acting normal when she was nervous and Nichole needed her to be calm for the interview.

"Andrea, it's time to get our game faces on. Let's just focus on food trucks for now."

■ ■ ■

Doris Delaney greeted the roommates in the MM Enterprises reception area. Looking around the room, Nichole said to Doris, "I love these offices—the crazy colors, the huge bar, and that amazing fish tank. What does MM stand for?"

"It's named after my friend Marvin," Doris replied. "Lots of people call him Marvelous. It's from his days as a basketball player, quite the star. It's one of those guy things. MM stands for Marvelous Marvin."

"Cool," said Nichole. "What does Marvin do?"

"He invests and travels, but mostly hangs out with his friends," Doris said. "He sold his business a few years back and has . . . excuse my French, sugar, fuck-you money. I'm betting you've never met anyone quite like Marvin."

Fifteen minutes later, Marvin burst into the reception area humming "Ob-La-Di, Ob-La-Da." Under his right arm was a box of Krispy Kreme glazed raspberry doughnuts.

In a house-waking voice he shouted, "Top of the mornin', ladies! Double D, you gorgeous creature! Sorry I'm a bit late, I was up into the wee hours cussin 'n' discussin with my brother Henry."

The girls' eyes were immediately drawn to Marvin's tattooed arm. Nichole wanted to get a closer look at the words. Both nervously stood to shake Marvin's hand.

"Good to meet you, ladies! I'm Marvin. Double D's been ravin' about you. What a great way to start the day! Come on back to the Library where we can chat."

As the group moved toward the Library, Doris hesitated. "I'm going to excuse myself. I've got a spin class calling my name. Maybe I'll see you later, Marvin." Her mouth turned up but a smile never came. "Nice visiting with you girls."

Nichole sat down on one of the couches and Andrea quickly sat down beside her. Marvin took a seat on the couch opposite the two and passed around the box of doughnuts.

A few moments later, a middle-aged woman appeared holding a tray with three blue mugs with red embossed MM logos on them.

Nichole knew the smell of excellent coffee and appreciatively accepted the mug. A pitcher of cream, a bowl of sugar, Sweet'N Low packets, napkins, and several spoons crowded the tray, which the woman set on the coffee table between the couches.

"Thank you," Nichole said, adding cream to her mug. Andrea did the same and then made a mess opening sugar packets and dumping them into her mug. It was all Nichole could do not to elbow her.

"Marvelous, let me know if you need anything else," the woman said, turning to leave. "John-O just called and said he's three minutes away with the truck drawings."

"Thanks, Phyllis." Marvin turned to them and Nichole sat up a bit straighter, using one of the napkins Phyllis had provided to make sure no doughnut crumbs lingered. "Ladies, I understand that the two of you are familiar with the food truck business."

"I hope it's fair to say we're 'familiar' by being frequent customers," Nichole answered enthusiastically. She had done her homework and was ready. "To prepare for this meeting, we did some Web research on the food truck business model in some of the more mature markets like LA and Austin. We see interesting trends in those markets and we put together some regression charts to share with you."

"I understand the two of you are in the business school over at Southerland. You must know my . . ."

Before Marvin could ask whether they knew Henry, a man entered the room tenuously cradling eight cardboard cylinders. As he bent down to deposit them on the coffee table, one tube slid out of balance, causing the rest to cascade onto the table like pick-up sticks. The tubes bounced off the table, knocked over Andrea's coffee cup, and rolled under couches and chairs. Nichole scrambled to help retrieve them. Andrea didn't move.

"Well, hell, I'm sure proud of that entrance," the man said, kneeling to pick up the tubes and smiling at Nichole on her knees beside him. "Hey, I'm John O'Souza. Everyone calls me John-O. Those damn tubes rolling around are the mock-ups for the food truck."

"It's times like this I wish I still had a real library," said Marvin, placing napkins on the spilled coffee. "Let's take the drawin's down to my office where we can spread 'em out."

The group walked down the hallway to Marvin's Garden, and John-O spread the mock-ups out around the room. The group slowly moved around the office, examining the drawings. Standing next to Nichole, Marvin asked her, "Whaddaya think?"

"The drawing of the fox with long eyelashes, pearls, and hoop earrings on the truck's side is spot-on," Nichole said, her index finger tapping her lower lip. "It puts the word 'fox' in context. It might be fun to make more of the fox's tail—maybe extend up over the side to the truck's top. The font for the Twenty-First-Century Foxes logo is great, but it would pop more if it was a different color, maybe yellow."

"Actually, the yellow on your shorts, Marvin, might be just the ticket," Andrea offered in a coy voice and leaned forward, not so subtly flourishing her décolletage.

Nichole had seen Andrea's nervous act before. She wished Andrea would knock it off and stay quiet.

To get back on track, Nichole said, "If we incorporate part of the fox's nose into the truck's grille, it would add a fun three-dimensional touch. Also, somewhere on the truck, we need to call out the food we're selling."

"Ladies, I'm likin' the way you think," said an enthusiastic Marvin. "Tell you what. John-O, what do you say to turnin' the design work over to these young businesswomen and let them take a run at it. You can concentrate on the kitchen equipment."

"Terrific idea, Marvelous," said John-O. "Design work's not exactly my forte. Here's the graphic artist's business card. She'll love working with you."

"Ladies, welcome to the MM Enterprises team," said Marvin. "You're officially on the payroll. While you're at it, maybe you can come up with some ideas on the uniforms you'll be wearin'. It would be nice if they matched the truck. Can you get back to us with your preliminary thoughts in, say, a week?"

Nichole was thrilled. She began rolling up the drawings and fitting them back in the cardboard tubes. She glanced over at Andrea standing in front of the Southerland University basketball team photo on Marvin's wall. She had one hand provocatively on her hip and a fingernail between her teeth.

Spotting Andrea next to the photograph, Marvin went to stand beside her. "That handsome devil in the middle, holdin' the ball, that's a better-lookin' me; that dashin' young prince on my left is none other than John-O. And do you recognize this guy?"

As both girls moved closer to the photograph, Marvin pointed at a bushy-haired boy with a droopy mustache. "That's not President Thomas, is it?" asked Nichole.

"Most certainly is," said Marvin. "See his name there in the small print?"

The girls leaned in closer to examine the photograph. Nichole felt Andrea give off a slight shiver as she dropped her hand from her hip. Sensing her anxiety, Nichole started toward the door. "There's all sorts of surprises at MM Enterprises!" she said with a wave of her hand. "Thanks so much for your time, and we look forward to seeing you in a week."

As the elevator doors closed behind them, Nichole, with clenched fists, squealed with delight, "Yes, yes! Do you believe our good luck? In a matter of minutes, we went from food truck waitresses to 'Design Team Co-heads, MM Enterprises.' What an incredibly lucky day! This will look fantastic on our résumés."

Andrea's expression didn't mirror Nichole's. With a wan smile she said, "It's been quite a day."

Nichole, attuned to Andrea's mercurial ways, ratcheted down her celebratory mood. "Did I miss something in there?" she asked. "When we were looking at the photograph I felt your mood sink."

"I may have done something stupid," said Andrea. "Can it wait 'til we get back to the apartment?"

■ ■ ■

Marvin and John-O walked back to the Library and closed the door. John-O fell onto a couch. "Well, what did you think?" he asked. "They sure look right out of central casting for the starring roles as Twenty-First-Century Foxes. Doris is a good casting director."

"Henry is one lucky cowboy gettin' to scope out that talent on a daily basis," Marvin said. "That Nichole is exactly what we need to work the truck, and smart to boot. Damn, I was about to ask if she knew Henry when you made that inspirational entrance."

"Man, did I look like the house fool. So, what do you see as next steps?" asked John-O.

"First, we need to get rid of that other girl, Andrea, I think," said Marvin. "Every time I looked her way, she was posin' like some kind of fashion model. And that suggestion about the color of my shorts was just weird. She needs a T for trouble tattooed on her forehead."

"Do you want me to call Doris to give some more direction to Nichole?" asked John-O.

"No," responded Marvin. "Let's leave Doris out of this."

"Really? She's been a lot of help."

Marvin nodded. "Double D has been great fun and I'll sure miss her crawfish étouffée, but last week the dreaded M-word floated out there for a second time."

"Marriage?" John-O sat up.

"'Fraid so," said Marvin. "As soon as that word slides out there a second time, that's my cue to hightail it for greener pastures."

"You still want to go after this food truck idea?" asked John-O.

"Yeah, that Nichole strikes me as a smart little go-getter. I'm thinkin' we just wind 'er up and let 'er rip."

"Is this idea about a food truck or the girl?" asked John-O with a knowing smile.

"Don't much matter," Marvin said with a shrug. "Like 'em both."

■ ■ ■

The roommates returned to a steaming hot apartment. Nichole turned the apartment's only air-conditioner unit on full blast and gave it a shake. As it rattled to life, she stood in front of the unit, savoring the cool air.

"I can't wait to get out of these clothes," Andrea grumbled.

Nichole followed her into the bedroom and started shedding her suit. They carefully hung up their clothes in the tiny single closet they shared and changed into shorts, tees, and running shoes. Nichole wore her neon orange Nike Free shoes; Andrea wore her neon green pair.

Sitting on their living room couch, Nichole rehashed the day's events. The foot crossed over her leg bounced with nervous energy. Andrea sat quietly.

"It's hard to get a line on Marvin," Nichole said. "He jumps around like a Labrador puppy and has the body of a dude half his age. Makes decisions awful fast, but looking at his digs, he must have done a whole lot of something right. What do you think that tat on his arm says?"

"What? You got the hots for the guy or something?" asked Andrea. "Christ, he's old enough to be your father."

"I'm not going to lie, I think he's hot, but this is just business," said Nichole. "We threw him a couple of decent ideas on truck mock-ups, and he's willing to give us a shot. We hit the lottery!"

"My suggestion on using the same yellow from his shorts on the truck was a direct hit in the heart of male vanity," Andrea said smugly. "He ate it up with a spoon."

"Maybe. Andrea . . . no offense, but you're not real tuned in to the male psyche. Male vanity is real knotty—the same words that flatter one guy can drive another one bonkers. Maybe Marvin liked your suggestion, maybe not."

"How old do you think Doris is?" Andrea asked. "I wonder if those swollen lips of hers hurt? It's hard to figure how she fits in with MM Enterprises."

Irritated that Andrea had basically ignored her comments, Nichole responded coolly. "She's somewhere between forty and pissed off and she's obviously doing Marvin. Who cares about Doris? What's with you? Ever since we left the office, I could feel your mood sliding downhill. You should be pumped about our incredible break. Why are you being such a Debbie Downer?"

"I don't know." She hesitated. "Like I said, I may have done something stupid."

Nichole inwardly groaned. *Great*. "I'm sure it's nothing terrible," she said aloud, hopefully.

"Did you get a close look at the photograph of the Southerland University basketball team and the players' names?" Andrea kept her eyes downcast and fiddled with the edge of her shorts. "Did you see Marvin's last name?"

"No. What is it?"

"It's Lindon. Remember Marvin said he was up late last night 'cussin 'n' discussin' with his brother Henry? Nichole, Marvin is Professor Lindon's brother."

"Whoa!" Nichole said, blinking in surprise. "Now that you say it, they look a lot alike in the eyes and the chin. Professor Lindon is rounder, shorter, and they sure have different accents. But I can see the family resemblance." She smiled broadly. "Maybe we'll get a chance to work with Professor Lindon too. After my little episode in his office, it might be a tad awkward, but I'm pretty sure he's over it. It'll be cool." Nichole saw no reason to tell Andrea about her chance meeting with Professor Lindon in the park. Too much information confused Andrea.

Andrea's expression grew glummer.

"Now what's wrong?" asked Nichole.

"I know you like Professor Lindon, so I kept something to myself," said Andrea. "When I got to his final exam, we had assigned seating and my seat was right next to Jake Locke, that starched-shirt little weirdo. He kept looking at me and making these clicking sounds like he was trying to gallop a horse." Andrea tried to mimic the clicking sound. "Totally creeped me out! I couldn't think. Nichole, I got an F on the final and a D for the semester. After all the crap that happened in class, I think Professor Lindon put that wacko next to me on purpose."

Nichole sighed. "That's crazy talk. I'm pretty sure Southerland tells the professors to put students in alphabetical order for finals. It makes it easier to track attendance. So, Andrea Lucero and Jake Locke are going to be seated pretty close. Get it?"

"Oh . . . that never occurred to me." Andrea started to twist a strand of her hair.

Nichole narrowed her eyes. "Andrea, what did you do?"

"You know my friend Jena," Andrea said. "The girl who works at the Apple store? Well, she showed me how to send an email that is one hundred percent untraceable. It's a way to ensure what you say is totally anonymous."

"Should I assume you sent a stupid email?" Nichole stood and paced away from her roommate.

"I guess so." Andrea twirled her hair faster. "I sent an email to President Thomas telling him about Professor Lindon's failure to control that idiot Jake Locke and his gay-bashing. I said it was a form of sexual harassment that Professor Lindon let slide."

Nichole turned, her hands clenched at her sides. "That wasn't smart. You got unhinged by an innocent seating chart. You didn't say anything about the seating at the exam, did you?"

"No, nothing."

"Good," Nichole said with a sigh of relief. "If you had mentioned the seating, it would be pretty obvious you sent the email. There's no way President Thomas or Professor Lindon will know who sent the email. So there's no way Marvin will ever know you took a shot at his brother. We're fine. But you need to get a grip on yourself, girl." Nichole sat back down on the couch.

"There was one other little bit of information in the email," Andrea said hesitantly.

"What?"

"Um . . . I said that President Thomas might be interested to know that I showed my dragonfly tattoo to Professor Lindon in his office."

Nichole catapulted off the couch faster than a cat escaping a bathtub. "Andrea! Why did you say that?"

"I don't know! Jeez! I've been out of sorts about everything . . . my parents, my screwed-up life, that asshole Jake Locke, my grades . . . everything. I can't think. It all fell apart for me that day in Professor Lindon's class. I wanted to let that stiff jerk feel some of what I felt. Since you dropped your shorts to show him your tattoo and mine's exactly the same, I figured . . . what the hell . . . it was true . . . kinda."

"ANDREA, YOU TWIT!"

Nichole stood with her fists pressed against the sides of her head. "When President Thomas shows that email to Professor Lindon, and he will, Professor Lindon is going to think I sent the damn email! Can't you see that?"

A wave of nausea almost buckled Nichole's knees. Her brilliant plan to get her trust fund released and Uncle Guy out of her life was already dead in the water. Now, her effort to patch up her relationship with Professor Lindon was at risk because of Andrea's idiocy. Even worse, Nichole had been sure no one would ever learn what happened in Professor Lindon's office but now this twit had informed the university president!

"Don't get all pissy with me," Andrea said, looking up at Nichole towering over her. "Gosh, you were the one who dropped your shorts in his office. And you're ready to graduate. You've got nothing to worry about."

"You better pull yourself together!" Nichole stamped her foot. "I made a mistake flashing my tat. It was supposed to be funny. What you did is a whole different thing. You have no freaking idea how much stuff you've screwed up!" She headed for the door, so furious she was afraid what she might do or say if she stayed. "I'm going out for a run. By myself!"

■■■

Nichole was grateful for the June heat and the cleansing sweat it triggered. With sure strides, she ran across campus to the Katy Trail, the popular running trail leading to the downtown American Airlines Center. She forced her mind to stay blank until the trail's two-mile marker. At full pace, with endorphins pumping through her body, she focused on her problems—starting with Andrea.

Their arrangement had worked because it took so little effort or commitment, allowing Nichole to focus on her studies and school activities. But now, Andrea had become a liability. She had absolutely nothing in common with her roommate beyond casual sex.

Nichole had countless classmates who thought nothing of nearly anonymous hookups with male students. Among Nichole's circle of friends, casual sex with "hookup buddies" was in; romance was out. She was sure, however, that Andrea yearned for a deeper relationship.

As she reached the three-mile marker, Nichole thought back on her first two years at Southerland. She had hooked up repeatedly with a directionless boy from Los Angeles who played on the tennis team. They never went on a date and, other than sex, they had zero in common. Nichole assured herself that Andrea was really no different than the tennis player—it was simply the modern arrangement with different equipment.

It hadn't been about sex in the beginning. When she returned from her fall semester abroad at the London School of Economics, she had needed a place to live for the spring semester. She answered an electronic bulletin board advertisement for a nonsmoking roommate to share a two-bedroom, one-bath garage apartment near campus. Andrea was quiet and welcoming and Nichole moved in.

At first, with an overflowing schedule of classes and extracurricular activities, Nichole rarely saw Andrea for more than five minutes at a time. As spring break neared, Nichole, too busy with school activities to make plans, accepted Andrea's last-minute invitation to accompany her to Acapulco. The combination of sun, boredom, and tequila led to the tattoo parlor where, on a lark, they decided to get identical dragonfly tattoos.

The edgy excitement of their naughty tattoos brought them closer. Comparisons of the artwork in the mirror built a sense of intimacy that eventually led Andrea to shyly confide about her sexuality. One night, again after too much tequila, the confided secret led to experimentation.

Now, running hard, Nichole made her final decision. Andrea had to go. Today. It was irrevocably over and delay was pointless. Their time together would not be a regret, nor would it be a treasured memory. Besides, Doc Rock was proving to be awfully good company.

Nichole stopped at a water fountain and filled a paper cup with water. As she walked and sipped, she admitted to herself that the tattoo stunt in Professor Lindon's office had completely backfired. What she thought was a remarkably clever idea had morphed into an unmitigated disaster. She had been sure the incident would never see the light of day. Now, the university president—of all people—knew.

Professor Lindon was a good man, but there was no way he would take the heat for a half-naked girl in his office. What a disaster! She had heard nothing more from Uncle Guy, but she knew he had no intention of keeping his word. In fact, the whole mess was his fault. She tightened her jaw. No problem. She would deal with Andrea *and* Uncle Guy.

She wanted to outrun the troubles in her head. But she couldn't. She was exhausted and felt a wave of nausea and panic. Taking several deep breaths, she decided to walk home and try to calm down.

Forty minutes later, Nichole arrived back at her empty apartment. She showered, dressed in her red Southerland University tee shirt and jeans, and sat down with her laptop. She immediately saw an email from Andrea:

> Nichole—
> I'm sorry about the email to President Thomas. I'm driving home to Abilene. I won't be back. Let's face it, I needed a relationship and you were just looking for another experience. I hope you find what you're looking for. Andrea.

For a fleeting moment, Nichole felt a mixture of relief and remorse. She knew she was on her own—like always. She had been alone since her mother's death. Once more, there was nothing for her to do but stiffen her backbone and move forward.

With Andrea gone, her next order of business was to erase Uncle Guy from her future—he would regret breaking his word on releasing her trust fund. No more playing the schoolgirl; it was time to toughen up. She sat on the edge of her bed and punched a telephone number into her cell. A familiar deep male voice answered, and she replied, "It's me. It's time. Move forward with the plan."

The man answered hesitantly. "Nichole, are you sure? We haven't completed the analysis of the trust . . . "

She shook her head, tightening her jaw. "No. I'm done. This is done. We both know he's sucked my trust dry. But thanks. Knowing I can count on you has been a real comfort. It's time to put the plan in motion. Let's talk next week. Bye."

Nichole reflected on the considerable sum of money she had paid to create the plan. It had eaten up most of her annual allowance for two years, but it had been worth every penny. Uncle Guy would soon learn she was not a woman to be toyed with. He would pay for making her grovel and beg for her own money—he would pay for ending her innocence at seven years old.

That taken care of, she turned to thoughts of Marvin Lindon. She wanted to work with Marvin. Marvin represented the future. She would not allow herself to become bogged down in the past.

She punched in another number. Seconds later Marvin's voice came across the line.

"Hello, Marvin? It's Nichole, Nichole Kessler."

"Hey, Nichole. Sure was good meetin' ya. What's up?"

"Thanks for the time you spent with us, it was great!" She took a deep breath and then hurried on. "I wanted to let you know that Andrea needs to go home for the summer, so she won't be part of the Twenty-First-Century Foxes team. But I've got some great ideas for a replacement."

"No problem," said Marvin. "Lookin' forward to meetin' your new truck partner."

"By the way, I didn't have the chance to ask during our meeting. Is Professor Henry Lindon your brother?"

"Guilty as charged. Did you take his class?"

"Sure did. He was my all-time favorite professor. What a small world!"

"Let's get together next week and talk," Marvin said.

Hanging up the phone, her work done, Nichole felt suddenly, terribly lonely. She opened the refrigerator, grabbed the two remaining cans of beer, and headed across the yard to see what Doc Rock was up to.

13

In an early morning taxi from Ezeiza International Airport to downtown Buenos Aires, Henry repeated in his head the exact words he would use with Marylou. During the overnight flight from Dallas, he had thought and rethought every possible variation.

Henry had concluded that Marvin's advice to speak first with Mikel Jiménez would be folly. What possible explanation could he have? Talking with Mikel first would simply postpone the inevitable and potentially make matters worse. Besides, it would be humiliating.

As the taxi pulled off the highway into downtown Buenos Aires, he was relieved that the customary crowd of labor *manifestantes* was not blocking downtown traffic around Avenida 9 de Julio. The cabdriver told him it was a national holiday. The *manifestantes* did not allow labor concerns to interfere with their holiday plans.

As he passed the upscale Patio Bullrich urban shopping mall, he saw the Palacio Duhau hotel on the north side of Avenida Alvear. They stopped in front of the hotel and he paid the driver. One of the many black-clad bellboys took his luggage, promising to deposit it in his room.

Climbing the stairs of the immaculately converted 1930s palace, he veered left at the elevators and went up a set of white marble stairs to the sunny breakfast room. He spotted Marylou sipping coffee and reading the fax version of *The New York Times*. He came to a stop, struck by how beautiful she looked.

She wore a dark blue, pin-striped skirt and white silk blouse. Her reading glasses were perched on her nose. Although she looked ready for the day's business, she also radiated a healthy glow in the morning light.

Maybe the glow is because she was with her lover last night, he thought, clenching his fists.

Looking over the top of her paper, Marylou blinked, tossed the paper on the table, and jumped up from her chair, running to throw her arms around him.

"Henry! You poor thing! You must be exhausted. Want something to eat? How about a *café con leche*?"

He disengaged from her embrace and rubbed the back of his neck, feeling strangely awkward. "I need to hit the sack. I'm beat. Is lunch with Marcello set? Am I supposed to meet him at the Alvear Palace Hotel? My brain's jumbled after that flight."

"I understand," she said, but he saw the disappointment in her eyes. "Lunch is at two and Marcello is looking forward to seeing you. I'm so excited! I didn't sleep a wink last night. Henry, I've had a wonderful string of good fortune these last few days. Good news always comes in threes."

Great. Everything's coming up roses for my cheating wife. "Great," he said without feeling. "What happened?"

"Last night I got the best news of all! While you were on the plane, Laney called from San Francisco." She paused and put her hands on his chest, looking up at him, joyful tears in her eyes. "We're going to be grandparents, Henry!" Marylou threw her arms around his neck again, warm and uninhibited. Henry held her, self-conscious and guarded.

For the next hour, Henry sat quietly at the table while Marylou enthusiastically outlined the plans they would need to make. He was relieved when Marylou finally excused herself to go to a meeting with a retail customer. He desperately needed a few hours of sleep.

As he rode alone in the elevator, his mood darkened. Marylou's news made his pending conversation with her all the more complicated. Once inside the hotel room, Henry shed his clothes and crawled between the covers. But after wrestling with the hotel sheets for two hours, he finally abandoned the idea of sleep.

Thinking some exercise might revive him, he spent an hour on the stationary bicycle in the hotel's opulent spa, watching ESPN Deportes. After showering, he pulled on a pearl-grey sport coat, a sky-blue shirt, and black slacks. He wrapped a royal-blue scarf around his neck and, briefcase in hand, headed out the hotel's rear entrance. He turned his face into the cool winter breeze, grateful for the clarifying energy it brought.

He walked north along Avenida Alvear toward the Alvear Palace Hotel to meet his friend and former colleague, Marcello Cifone. A block from the hotel, he spotted the elegant María José Cifone standing on the corner, in red high-heeled leather boots and matching coat, waiting for the light to change. Standing two feet behind her with a cell phone to his ear was her husband, Marcello. He looked every bit the part of the prototypical *porteño* in a soft, black-leather sport coat and crisp white shirt setting off his salt-and-pepper hair.

They saw Henry and waved their hands above their heads like they were in a religious revival. Wearing wide grins, the two danced across the street to meet him.

"You do not believe I would let you return to Buenos Aires without a welcome hug from me, do you?" María José said as she embraced Henry. "Marcello is not allowed to have all the fun, no indeed!"

"Good to see you, my old friend," said Marcello, when it was his turn to hug Henry. "We have much to talk about."

"Talk, indeed," María José added. "I know you need to make all that serious man talk. I will leave you to it, but Marylou and I will be waiting for you at 7:00 p.m. at my office in Puerto Madero. We have a full night planned. *Hasta la noche, caballeros*."

María José stepped to the curb to signal a taxi. The moment her arm went up, a taxi dangerously jerked across a lane of the avenue's heavy traffic and darted to the curb with screeching tires. The driver jumped out to open the passenger door for María José.

"Beauty has undeniable advantages," said a smiling Henry, after the cab had pulled away with María José waving from the window.

"No doubt, my friend."

"Marcello," Henry began, "would you mind if we went somewhere a bit quieter than the Alvear Hotel?"

"It is no problem. The Café Tranquilo is around the corner. It will be perfect."

Over their poached salmon, the old colleagues reminisced about their days together in Argentina, their families, and the news that Henry and Marylou would soon be grandparents. Henry was growing tired, but he waited for the best time to raise the topic of UNS.

"I was in Mexico City ten days ago and had lunch with Jane Birney and Chester Lawrence," Henry began.

"My sincere regrets," Marcello joked. "How were Queen Jane and her evil little court jester?"

"Lunch did not go well, to say the least." Henry's jet-lagged brain was moving in slow motion, making it harder to find the right words. "Chester made an allegation that there was a bribe paid in connection with the San Miguel Galletas deal, violating the Foreign Corrupt Practices Act. He topped that off with a threat to help the Justice Department prosecute me on felony charges."

"Chester has such a subtle touch," replied Marcello.

"Yeah, a real prince of a man," Henry said with a nod. "When I asked Jane if she had spoken to you about the deal, she intimated that you were no longer acting as their counsel in Argentina because of your role in our Deal from Hell."

"True, but nothing to do with the deal," replied Marcello, sounding surprised. "Five months ago, Nestlé approached us about representing them throughout South America. It was obviously a welcome compliment for our firm, but Nestlé insisted that the retention include our agreement not to represent other food companies. I sent a letter to Jane Birney saying we would, regrettably, have to withdraw from representation. Never heard a word back from her and, obviously, I have done no more work for them."

"Curious," Henry said, rubbing his eye. "The meeting in Mexico City has been weighing on me. There's something I need to ask you."

"Anything," Marcello responded, looking directly into Henry's eyes.

"Month after month we worked on trying to close the San Miguel deal. It looked like that deal would go on forever. We sat together through countless meetings with the government officials and could never finalize the details on the tax breaks and the number of locals who would be employed in the plant."

"I remember all too well," Marcello said with a sad smile. "There were days I thought we should have simply walked away."

"I felt the same," agreed Henry. "Then, after yet another frustrating meeting with the local government folks, I was called back to the States." Just thinking about the endless meetings was exhausting.

"Yes, of course I remember," said Marcello.

Henry felt his heart rate spike as he prepared to ask the question of paramount importance. "Two days later, you telephoned and told me the government agreed to the same amount of the tax break they had absolutely rejected before I left for the States."

"I remember that phone call very well." Marcello put both hands on the table and leaned back in his chair. "It was my great pleasure to tell you the Deal from Hell would finally end!"

"Marcello," Henry said with dead seriousness. "Did something happen after I returned to the States that caused the government officials to change their minds?"

"Henry, there is no room for secrets between us. If it had been important, I would have told you. Have you ever heard the phrase *dando y dando*?"

Henry frowned. He was bone-tired. "As a matter of fact, I recently learned about that phrase in Mexico City. It means give a little, get a little. What are you saying?"

"I arranged a bit of *dando y dando* to bring the Deal from Hell across the finish line," said Marcello. "It is how we resolve matters in South America. One of the government officials asked for my help with his nephew's drug arrest here in Buenos Aires. The judge is my friend and I arranged for a plea bargain with no jail time for the nephew. In return, the grateful official helped bring the negotiation to a close on the terms we proposed before you returned to the States. It was nothing, certainly not something to trouble you with."

Henry heard Marcello's words but his jet lag made it increasingly difficult to weigh their consequence. Was the *dando y dando* Marcello described a bribe in violation of the Foreign Corrupt Practices Act? If so, was he implicated in the violation? He silently cursed his leaden brain.

"Henry, are you all right?" asked Marcello. "All of this can wait—we need to get you back to your hotel for some rest. You look exhausted. Your hotel is on the way to my office. I'll drop you off."

The two friends turned down Avenida Alvear and began walking the three blocks to Henry's hotel. The jet lag, sleep deprivation, and stress from the troubling conversation with Marcello had sapped Henry of the power to think.

With his briefcase dangling limply from his left hand, he blindly followed Marcello down the sycamore-lined avenue. It took all of his concentration to put one foot ahead of the other. Before Henry knew what was happening, Marcello was opening the door at Mikel Jiménez's shirt shop.

"As long as we are right here, let's say hello to Mikel," Marcello said. Marcello's voice sounded like it was coming out of a tunnel.

Walking in a daze, Henry trailed Marcello past the store's neat displays of shirts, trousers, and lines of carefully rolled socks. Then, all at once, Mikel Jiménez pushed through the beaded curtains that separated the store from the tailoring room. Running his left hand through his black wavy hair, Mikel extended his right hand to the men.

"Marcello! What a nice surprise! And Henry, it has been too many days, my friend. This is wonderful timing, Marylou was in here just . . ."

As he heard Mikel say Marylou's name, something in Henry's bone-tired body snapped, releasing a primal instinct. As Mikel approached, Henry reared back and, with all the strength he could muster, threw a haymaker punch at Mikel's face.

At the last second, Mikel feinted to his left. The force of the errant punch swung Henry into the wooden display counter. The last thing he remembered was the sound of his head hitting the counter.

▪▪▪

Henry heard someone calling his name from far away.

"Henry? Wake up! Henry, can you hear me?"

He was in dark water, holding his breath, struggling to swim up to a bright light. As he broke the surface, he opened his eyes, shook his head, and looked up into Marcello's face. Relief flooded his friend's gaze. "Mikel, call an ambulance!"

"No, I don't need an ambulance," Henry protested. "Where am I? What the hell happened?"

"Stay still," Marcello ordered. "Mikel, please bring a wet towel and some ice."

Fifteen minutes later, Henry was sitting on one of the store's black velvet chairs holding a makeshift ice pack to his forehead. Marcello stood close to Henry. Mikel, still leery, hung back. The Argentinians exchanged uneasy looks.

"Henry, we need to get you to the hospital," said Marcello. "I fear you've had some sort of . . . what do you call it in English? A seizure? For no reason, you attacked Mikel!"

"No reason?" Henry pulled the ice pack from his forehead. "This *comemierda* is having an affair with Marylou! For Christ's sake, he even admitted he was with her this morning!"

"There has been a terrible mistake," said a stunned Mikel. "She was here this morning picking out shirts for you!"

"Oh yeah? Marcello, hand me my briefcase."

Reaching into his briefcase with his free hand, Henry pulled out the card and held it up to Mikel, who guardedly stretched his arm toward Henry and took the card. He promptly stepped back to a safe distance and read:

Mikel Jiménez on Avenida Alvear
Avenida Alvear, 3133
Ciudad A. de Buenos Aires
Argentina
Querida Marylou,
¡Déjese envolver por esta muestra de mi afecto para mantener el calor hasta que esté en mis brazos una vez más!
Besos,
MJ

Mikel shook his head. "Señor Henry, this is most certainly my paper," he said. "But this is not my writing. I think our friend Marcello has the answer to all your questions."

Mikel held out the note to an incredulous Marcello. Looking at the card, Marcello broke into a huge grin.

"Henry, I not only recognize the handwriting but know quite well who the MJ is who signed the note. MJ is not Mikel Jiménez, it is my María José!"

Henry's throbbing head made it difficult to process the new information.

"I remember the day María José wrote this note," added Mikel. "She purchased a lovely coat to send to your Marylou in the States and asked me to mail it for her. At the last moment, she asked for a piece of paper so she could write a short note. She said she wanted to help Marylou practice her Spanish. The only paper I had in the store was that card."

"Henry, you know María José is a world-class hugger," Marcello said. "As she says in the note, she can't wait to embrace Marylou."

Henry tried to digest what he had just heard. There was no affair, only his mistaken leap to judgment. The initial gloom at his own stupidity broke at the realization that Marylou had not been unfaithful. Then, realizing he had miraculously avoided a disastrous confrontation with his wife, he felt a huge weight lift from him as if tethered to giant balloons.

Henry felt giddy and, still holding the ice to the side of his head, began to laugh. Marcello and Mikel exchanged cautious glances, waiting to see if the mad American would continue his sprint through the spectrum of human emotions. The cathartic laughter of emotional release proved contagious and soon all three were doubled over with merriment.

Their convulsions were interspersed by fragments of sentences: " . . . you thought . . . I was the MJ . . . what will she . . . it said 'embrace' . . . dodged a bullet . . . this is so crazy . . . you just missed . . ." Finally catching his breath, Henry managed to become coherent again.

"I so regret this comedy of errors, and Mikel, I am grateful that it is my head that aches, and not yours. Please, accept my sincerest apologies for what happened here."

Both men nodded their acceptance.

"My friend, as comical as this has been, it must also be a great relief for you," Marcello said. "Marylou is an extraordinary woman, and your doubts must have weighed on you."

"I feel ten years younger." Henry took the ice pack off his head. "I was dreading what I would say to Marylou, and now I can't wait to see her. This is an afternoon to remember! One request . . . can we keep what happened here to ourselves?"

"But of course," responded Marcello. "Our ability to maintain silence is man's only defense against the dominant sex. In Buenos Aires, we say, *los caballeros no tienen memoria*. It means that in matters involving women a gentleman has no memory."

"Perfect," said Henry. "So we agree to drop a cone of silence over the craziness that happened here today?"

"My friend," Mikel said with a tilt of his head. "All I remember about today is how badly I felt when you tripped on the step and hit your head."

14

Guy Wheeless Jr. had finally fallen asleep on his office couch after being awake for almost forty hours. His sleep was uneasy due to a disquieting dream.

He dreamt he was in the medical office of the blonde physician's assistant, his combative date from two nights past. He was strapped to an operating table and she was explaining the procedure she was going to use to surgically remove his good ear with a rusted kitchen knife.

As he struggled against the sedation mask she was forcing over his face, there was a loud bang next to the operating table, then another. Wheeless jolted into consciousness, realizing someone was knocking at his office door.

"What is it!" Wheeless barked. "I said I didn't want to be disturbed!"

"It's me, Edward."

Coming to his feet, he stalked across the room, swung open the door, and glared at his chief lieutenant. "Goddamn it, O'Brian, this better be good."

"Are you feeling all right?" O'Brian asked, his gaze taking in Wheeless's rumpled appearance.

"No, as a matter of fact I feel like shit. What do you want?"

"I think you might want to sit down for this."

Wheeless reluctantly allowed O'Brian to enter and walked back into his office with the thin man trailing behind like a recalcitrant dog.

Back on the couch, Wheeless gestured to the chair across from him and asked impatiently, "What is it?"

"When we started the surveillance on Henry Lindon . . . "

"This is about Lindon?" Wheeless's interest was piqued.

"Kind of. When we started with Lindon, one of the ex-FBI agents suggested we review the status of the other surveillance activities we have in place. He said some of them might be stale and, to limit unnecessary exposure, we should consider discontinuing them." O'Brian stopped to remove a list of telephone calls from his briefcase. "One of the people whose phone calls we've tracked over the years is your niece, Nikkie."

"I remember," said Wheeless.

"You certainly have an outstanding memory," O'Brian complimented him.

"Get to the point." He hated O'Brian's sycophantic ways.

"Okay." O'Brian held up a sheet of paper. "Nikkie recently made three separate calls to Wichita."

"So what? She called me."

"Correct again," declared O'Brian. "But she also made a call to a separate number."

"I'm not here to play twenty questions with you—what the hell do you want to tell me!"

"The other number she called in Wichita belongs to none other than Dan Moore—Nikkie called Moore." O'Brian basked in his news flash.

"Why? What is that little bitch up to?"

"I'm not positive," answered O'Brian, holding up the telephone call list. "All we have is a list of her calls. We have no way of knowing what was said. But, as you know, Moore is deep into the corporate espionage business. If I was a betting man, I'd bet it has something to do with you, maybe about her trust."

"That little bitch!" Wheeless shouted. He jumped up from the couch and began to pace, rubbing the back of his neck. "Is that what she's been doing with all that money? She walks around in that grimy red Southerland University tee shirt and then spends money to spy on me—and with Dan Moore to boot!"

"Do you want me to get on this?" asked O'Brian.

"This is out of your league," spat Wheeless. "You stick with Henry Lindon and make sure that Department of Justice investigation launches." He pointed to the door. "Get out of here—you've given me a migraine."

■ ■ ■

Well rested after a three-hour nap, Henry was swinging the world by its tail. When he arrived with Marcello by taxi in Buenos Aires's Puerto Madero neighborhood, he playfully closed the taxi door shut with both hands.

The long-abandoned port area shone with urban renewal. Nineteenth-century redbrick warehouses had been converted into trendy restaurants, offices, and modern art galleries. The area's centerpiece was the architect Santiago Calatrava's Puente de la Mujer, the Woman's Bridge.

"Henry, have you seen the bridge open?" Marcello asked, pointing at the bridge. "It rotates on the white concrete pylon to let boats pass. It can open in less than two minutes."

"I have, it's amazing. I read that Calatrava intended the bridge to look like tango dancers, and I can see a dancer's leg in the perpendicular wing. Calatrava has built wonderful bridges and sculptures in Dallas. I need to tell you the story about the student who decided to surf Calatrava's wave sculpture on campus."

As Henry recounted the student's painful fate on the wave sculpture, the men walked south along the Rio de la Plata past busy sidewalk cafés. The cafés bustled with waiters serving drinks to the early evening clientele. They stopped in front of María José's office building.

"Henry, what a story! I bet Calatrava never dreamed his creation could become such a danger. I feel myself bending over in sympathetic pain. I hope the student has all his . . . pieces."

"I was told he's physically in one piece. Do you know what our wives have planned for us tonight?" Henry asked.

"All I know comes from bits I've overheard. They have a new item to replace that crazy red pig, but they've been uncharacteristically quiet about it.

I do know they're very excited about this evening. Henry, before we go in . . . do we need to speak any more about the Deal from Hell?"

Henry put his hand on Marcello's shoulder. "Not tonight, maybe never. I need time to think about my meeting with Jane Birney in Mexico City and what UNS really wants from me. But tonight, I want to give my full attention to Marylou."

The men climbed the palm-tree-shaded stairs of the three-story converted warehouse. Seeing the men at the office's glass door, Marylou pushed the door open with arms outstretched to hug Henry. When she saw the bruise on his forehead, she held him at arm's length.

"What happened?" asked Marylou. "It looks like you've been in a street brawl!"

"I'm totally embarrassed," Henry said with a sheepish look. "I was jet lagged this afternoon and not thinking straight when Marcello and I went into Mikel's shop. I lost control of myself and hauled off and just . . . just tripped and hit my head on the counter. Don't worry. It looks worse than it is. In fact, I feel better tonight than I have in months."

"Well, other than that bruise, you look great," Marylou said tenderly giving him a kiss. "Now, gentlemen, sit on down and relax. We have Champagne to pour and a story to tell."

As he walked to the couch, Henry reflected on the women's ingenuity. María José's office was a duplicate of Marylou's Dallas office. No wonder Marylou seemed so at home.

The excited women moved gracefully around the office in red Louboutin high heels and black cocktail dresses cinched with matching wide white belts. Bajofondo's seductive electronic tango music was playing over an Apple computer and María José poured Champagne.

Marylou stood behind the desk where a dark grey alpaca blanket hid a mystery object. When María José joined Marylou at the desk, the two looked like smiling television talk show hostesses.

"You both know that the porcelain red pig from China has been the backbone of our business," Marylou began. "But, like all good things, the clock ran out on our dear red *puerco*. We searched high and low without success for a new product until we had an epiphany! Why, we asked ourselves, did our customers buy the pigs in the first place?"

Henry smiled at Marylou's excitement. "I'll bite—why?"

"Well," she went on, "our research revealed that the red pig satisfied a fundamental need for women. Let's see if you can guess what that need is. Gentlemen, what are women very good at?"

"Is this a trick question?" asked Marcello. "Women are good at all things!"

"That's sweet, Marcello, but be serious," said María José, with both hands playfully on her hips.

"Let me see . . . perhaps keeping secrets," offered Marcello, triggering a conspiratorial laugh from Henry and sarcastic smiles from the women.

"Before we go any further," Henry said, "why are you two dressed like twins with those retro white belts?"

"As you will soon find out," replied Marylou, "the dresses are an integral part of our presentation. Now, back to our question—what are women especially good at?"

"How about shopping?" Henry suggested from the couch.

"That's getting closer," Marylou replied. "But what about shopping?"

As the men grew more comfortable on the couch, they ventured Champagne-fueled guesses about the strengths of the fairer sex. Eventually, the women grew impatient.

"That's it. You two are indeed useless," said María José. "We will now reveal to you, and only you, the future of our business."

With one hand behind her back and the flair of a cabaret magician, Marylou yanked the alpaca blanket straight up to reveal a porcelain cow. The cow was black, except for a solid white stripe around its middle. It was approximately thirty inches long, slightly larger than the famous red pig.

The men were at a loss for words.

"It's certainly . . . uh . . . unique," said Henry. "I don't think I've ever seen a cow with a circle around its middle like that. It looks like an Oreo cookie."

"Henry, these cows are prized in Argentina's estancias," said Marcello. "They are called Belted Galloways."

"Indeed, these cows are treasured in our country and they are nicknamed Belties. That is why we are wearing these," María José said brightly, as both women playfully pointed their fingers at the white belts cinching their black dresses.

"Women are good at shopping, indeed, but women also love building collections," said María José. "Rich or poor, married or single, happy or sad, every woman has some sort of collection. Sharing their collections is a universal currency of friendship. Our customers who bought the red pig will now want a Beltie to keep it company. Next year we will introduce an adorable yellow duck. Indeed, in the years to come, there will be a lamb, a chicken . . . who knows? Women all over Latin America will collect a barnyard full of our animals on their mantels."

"And, gentlemen, the news gets better," Marylou added. "After many conversations with our manufacturer in Canton, I am confident that, with a touch of luck, we will be able to generate a fifty-two percent margin on each of our Belties. That's ten points better than we ever did on the red pigs! It's time to celebrate and we're taking you out for a night on the town on us. What do you say?"

In high spirits, the couples walked the three blocks from María José's office to the Faena Hotel, home of the Rojo Tango show. Marylou amused the group by tango walking—making her high heels click rhythmically on the sidewalk.

They settled in at a table next to the stage and the conversation, over *carne asada*, was an animated discussion about plans for the Belties, the yellow duck, and the rest of the menagerie to come. Henry could not remember Marylou looking more beautiful, and he was thrilled at the feel of her arm draped across his shoulder.

"Henry, do you know the history of the tango, our national dance?" Marcello asked.

Before Henry could reply, an excited María José interrupted. "The tango was born in the waiting rooms of Buenos Aires's brothels. Men separated from families and loved ones danced together to pass the time. As you will see, indeed, it is a way to tell stories of loss and longing in dances and songs. The show is about to start!"

The first lonesome accordion chord, answered by piano and violin, silenced the room. All eyes were riveted on the stage. Male dancers in dark suits and slouch hats tipped jauntily down on their foreheads turned elegant women in revealing dresses in a flurry of legs bent around backs, ankles kicked over shoulders, and flowing hair bent back brushing the stage floor. As the dancers twirled faster, a wave of intoxicating perfume washed over the audience. But this was all a warm-up for the incomparable Carlos Copello.

A man of indeterminate age, Copello was the acknowledged maestro of Buenos Aires tango. He glided a series of women around the oval stage in quick but unhurried steps. His hips turned sharply, he dipped, he strutted, and he pressed his partners close with a tender ferociousness—all with his eyes shut.

He thrilled the room as he blindly guided his partner inches from the raised stage's edge. The daring of his performance and his partners' raw sensuality delighted the audience.

As one particularly passionate song built to its crescendo, Henry leaned over and gently whispered into his wife's ear, "About time for a private tango in our hotel room?"

She turned her head and smiled. "Si, mi amor."

15

Lying in bed the next morning, Marylou held Henry's face in her hands and gently kissed his bruised forehead. "Last night was the best night of my life," she said.

"The best?" She was beautiful and she was his Marylou. How could he ever have doubted her?

She smiled, bit her lower lip, and then nodded. "Until last night, I felt I was losing you. These last few months have been so sad—I could feel you fading away. The moment you walked into María José's office, your eyes told me you were back. Please, tell me what was driving you away."

"I'm sorry, Marylou. So very sorry, especially for the thing I said right before you left for Buenos Aires. I was an ass."

"Yes, you were," she said, and then smiled. "But I forgive you." She kissed him and then grew serious. "Tell me what was troubling you."

"I felt under attack from all sides." Henry paused to gather his thoughts. "I had a bizarre incident with a student and then trouble with those UNS people—I thought I was losing it."

"Henry, you're the smartest man I know. If we talk it through, I'm sure we can find a solution. Please, darling, let me help you."

"It's kind of a long story," Henry said, trying to extend the magic of the moment. "I need to start from the beginning. How about some breakfast first?"

The couple put on the plush white hotel robes and Henry ordered breakfast. Sitting at the table with a view of the well-manicured hotel courtyard below, Henry basked in the warmth of Marylou's company. Her love was the most important thing in his life. He made a silent vow—he would never, no matter what, put that love at risk again.

Lingering over their coffee, Marylou said, "I'm all ears. Tell me everything."

Henry detailed his troubles in an hour-long soliloquy. He described the incident with Nichole and their chance meeting in the park, the Mexico City meeting with Jane Birney, Ken Maltman's call about the Wein CEO job, and Marvin and John-O's misguided stock trades. Marylou listened intently.

When Henry finished, Marylou covered one of his hands with hers and squeezed. "Let's start with the easiest one. If the Wein job is something you want, if you decide academia is not for you, I'll support you one hundred percent. But who knows whether that will become a reality?"

"Agreed," said Henry. "If I don't resolve the issues with Jane Birney and UNS, there won't be a job to consider."

"Correct. Let's split the other two issues," Marylou said. "Start with Nichole. She's young, smart, and obviously, impetuous. Showing you her tattoo strikes me as nothing more than an impulse—maybe it was nothing more than what she told you in the park, a joke."

Henry shot her a look. "Believe me, it wasn't funny."

Marylou smiled. "Darling, a tattoo on a derriere means a whole lot less to this generation. For all we know, God forbid, our beautiful, pregnant Laney has a tart tat, or whatever it's called. It's a different generation. Getting a tattoo today is a fashion statement not much different from when I was sixteen and got my ears pierced—my Dad was apoplectic for a week."

"Well, Nichole will soon graduate—and she apologized. I'll probably never see her again," said Henry. "More coffee?"

Marylou held out her cup and smiled. "So that problem's not worth fretting over," she said. "The second problem with UNS and Jane Birney is troubling because it doesn't add up. If they had any proof there was a bribe paid in connection with the Deal from Hell and, therefore, a violation of this . . .

Foreign Corrupt . . . whatever it's called, then why not just come flat out with the evidence?"

"It's obvious they were on a fishing expedition," Henry said. "But here's what I'm really worried about—*dando y dando*."

"*Dando* and what?"

"Marcello said it means doing a favor and getting a favor in return," Henry explained. "He says it happened between him and an Argentinian official and is frequently done down here. But what he thinks of as no big deal could be considered a bribe under the Foreign Corrupt Practices Act." He got up and moved to stare out the floor-to-ceiling window at the tiered gardens below.

"Don't get upset, Henry, you don't know that for sure," Marylou said softly, rising and moving next to him. She put her hand on his arm and turned him to face her, then cupped his face in her hands. "It will be all right."

He took her hands and pressed them together and kissed her fingers. "Thank you, my love." He took a deep breath. "Tell me what you think. Should I press Marcello for the details? Hell, if I get details and they're bad, then what? If the Department of Justice decides to institute an investigation, life as we know it will come to a crashing halt."

"An investigation of any sort would have unfortunate consequences," Marylou said.

"Got that right," Henry said. "Given Marvin and John-O's boneheaded stock trades, I can envision a multiple-count indictment dressed up with security fraud counts. The least of my problems is the Wein job—it'll be dust in the wind with even a hint of a Department of Justice investigation."

"Marvin really screwed up on this one," said Marylou. "I hope you won't let it ruin your relationship."

"This time he's stepped over the line. I've had it with him acting like a gigantic fourteen-year-old. I've enabled some of his infantile behavior by always playing the supportive kid brother, but those days are over. When I get back to Dallas—"

"Calm," Marylou interrupted. "Let's not get tied up with Marvin. The subject's way too convoluted."

"Agreed. Back to UNS."

"Here's what I was thinking before that detour—the UNS people are acting strangely," said Marylou with quizzical look. "It's like they're not quite sure what they're looking for. But it's even weirder that Dan Moore has spent so much time investigating Guy Jr. Dan's mysterious client, whoever that is, gives me the creeps. The whole mess makes no sense."

"Maybe that's exactly the point," replied Henry as he sat down on the edge of the bed. "We're sitting here as an accountant and a lawyer trying to make logic out of a problem generated by people with hidden agendas. If we keep digging in that same logic hole, we're going to keep coming up dry."

"I don't disagree, but what else can we do?" Marylou sat down on the bed next to him and closed her eyes.

Henry straightened up and Marylou opened her eyes. She looked hopeful, trusting, and it suddenly struck him—she believed in him. For a long moment he wanted to kick his own ass to Mexico and back. How could he have ever doubted her?

He leaned over and gave her a long, slow kiss that seemed to have been a very long time coming. When he broke the kiss, she was gazing at him, her green eyes gentle.

"What was that for?" she asked softly.

"For being incredible," he said. "For being you. I wish I could say forget all this crap."

Marylou's eyes filled with tears and Henry's throat tightened.

"What? What is it?" he asked.

"Nothing," she whispered. "I just thought—I didn't know if we would ever get back to this—to us."

He tried to take her in his arms again, but she stopped him with both hands against his chest.

"Later, Casanova," she said lightly, her tears gone, a smile on her face. "We need to finish hashing this out."

Henry stood and saluted. "Aye, aye, Captain," he said. "Back to work, but just remember, all work and no play makes Henry a very dull boy."

"Never dull, Henry," she said. "Never dull."

They stared at one another for a long moment, and then Henry clapped his hands together. "All right! I've got an idea—yep—it just might work."

"Let's hear it."

"Okay, first, step back and look at the people playing this game. It's really only Dan, Jane Birney, and Wheeless."

"All right, what do you suggest?"

"If we look at the problem from the perspectives of those three, the answer is pretty simple. To start, I ask Dan for a small favor . . ."

"Henry," Marylou interrupted. "Just—one last thing. Are you sure nothing else was troubling you all these months?"

The moment of truth launched Henry's brain into overdrive. Was this his last chance for total honesty with the wife he adored? Why the hell had he not showed her the card when it arrived? If he was totally forthright now, could Marylou find it in her heart to forgive and forget? But, why tell her about the doubts he had secretly harbored? Would it be to simply assuage his conscience? He needed to keep his vow to never again put Marylou's love at risk.

In a flash of adrenaline-fueled clarity, two of Oscar Wilde's quotes from one of his university lectures flashed in his mind: "The truth is rarely pure and never simple" and "A little sincerity is a dangerous thing, and a great deal of it is absolutely fatal."

It was too late to cross the Rubicon to pure honesty. Surely, the opportunity to secure Marylou's love and the serenity of marital happiness was more important than the dangerously unpredictable prospects of total honesty.

With a reassuring smile, Henry replied, "No, not another thing. Ready to hear how we get out of this mess?"

■ ■ ■

Doc Rock sat at his cottage's kitchen table paying bills online. He was exhausted after his second overnight shift in three days. Looking at his depleted checking account, he realized Nichole and Andrea had not paid their rent for the garage apartment.

Thinking it was out of character for them to be late, he realized he hadn't seen or heard his tenants since the night Nichole knocked on his door with two cans of beer in her hands. Was that three nights ago? Four nights? Then again, why would he see them? He had been working all-night and sleeping all day. Too tired to do anything about it right then, he went to bed.

He woke the next afternoon with the girls on his mind. Throwing on a tee shirt and shorts, he walked barefoot the few steps to the garage apartment and knocked on the door. No one answered. He dismissed the fleeting thought that the two had left town without paying their rent—no way Nichole would leave without saying good-bye.

He walked home, got a piece of paper, wrote a note asking them to give him a call, taped it to their door, and left for the hospital.

A day later, after multiple grueling shifts in the emergency room, Doc Rock was bone-tired. Sitting on the side of his bed, the idea of sleep was intoxicating. Then it dawned on him: He still hadn't heard from Nichole and Andrea.

He grudgingly got off the bed, walked the few steps across the unkempt lawn, and approached their door. His note was untouched. He returned with the spare garage apartment key and opened the door. The first thing to hit him was the repugnant smell. Then he saw her.

Dressed only in running shorts, she was laid out on the couch, arms crossed on her stomach, with a red Southerland tee shirt wrapped around her neck—Nichole was dead. Doc Rock bolted from the apartment to call 911, tears of rage streaming down his face.

PART 3

THE DEALS

16

The American Airlines 777 business cabin was sound asleep—except for Henry. He stared lethargically at the television monitor's image of his plane's icon moving slowly up the South American continent. Two hours out of Buenos Aires, Marylou had kissed him goodnight, pushed in her earplugs, and fallen into a deep sleep. He reached over and carefully pulled the blanket up around her shoulder.

Henry reflected on his extraordinary luck. Thank heaven Marcello had decided to stop by Mikel's shirt store to say hello. But for that stroke of luck, he would have ruined his relationship with his wife by accusing her of having a nonexistent affair. He felt blessed that she was quietly sleeping next to him. He had to deal with the UNS issue immediately, but with Marylou at his side that problem no longer seemed insurmountable. He finally fell asleep, confident his rocky days were behind him.

After the eleven-hour flight, Henry and Marylou, bleary-eyed but happy, proceeded through customs and pushed through the doors to the DFW terminal, pulling their roller bags behind them. "I'm going to grab a newspaper," Henry said, veering to his right. "Want anything?"

"No, I'll wait with the bags." Marylou stifled a yawn.

Henry entered the DFW News Connection kiosk and circled around the candy-laden counter, past the magazines to the newspaper stand. He reached for *The Wall Street Journal* and quickly scanned the headlines. Then, beside it, he saw the screaming *Dallas Morning News* headline: "Southerland University Student Murdered." Henry audibly gasped.

Below the headline was Nichole Kessler's graduation photograph.

Henry tossed a five-dollar bill on the counter and walked toward Marylou with The *Dallas Morning News* held tightly in both hands. "Marylou, we need to sit down."

"What is it?"

"We need to sit down."

They moved to a bench and Henry placed the newspaper on her lap. "This is awful," said Marylou with her hand over her heart. "Did you know her?"

"That's her, Marylou."

"What do you mean, 'her'?"

"It's Nichole, the one who flashed her dragonfly tattoo. That's her!"

The two silently read the story. Details were sparse. Nichole had been murdered in her garage apartment and found there by her landlord, an emergency room physician. The article ended with a statement of condolence from the university and background filler about her stellar Southerland University academic career.

"Poor girl," said Marylou as she folded up the newspaper. "So young, so talented, so beautiful."

"That and much more," said Henry. "Who would do this?"

They sat in silence until Marylou said, "Henry, we can't sit here all day, we need to go home."

Stepping outside, they were blinded by the searing Texas morning sun. Henry shielded his eyes with one hand while he signaled a taxi with the other. As their taxi exited the airport, Henry's phone rang.

"Where are you?" Marvin's voice was uncharacteristically subdued.

"Just landed, we're back in Dallas." Henry was annoyed at his brother's intrusion.

"There's some real bad news from Southerland."

"Just saw the paper, it's terrible."

"Met her. I met Nichole just last week," said Marvin.

"You met Nichole?" Henry asked, looking at Marylou to ensure she understood the gist of his conversation.

"Yeah," said Marvin. "Double D met her at some hair place and introduced her and a friend to us as candidates for the food truck. She had some terrific ideas and I hired her on the spot. She told me you were her favorite professor. What a waste."

Henry tried to process what he just heard. He had discussed the tattoo incident with Marvin in his office. Now, through a strange coincidence, Nichole had been introduced to Marvin. Henry recalled that he hadn't told Marvin the name of the girl who pulled down her shorts. Surely, Nichole hadn't told Marvin about the incident. Given Marvin's increasingly erratic behavior, Henry decided to keep to himself that Marvin's food truck girl, the murdered girl, and the student who had flashed her dragonfly tattoo in his office were one and the same.

"It's all very sad," said Henry. "We're beat and on our way home."

"So, Marylou's with you?"

"Absolutely."

"So . . . everything's all patched up between you lovebirds?"

"Everything's perfect," said Henry, holding the phone tighter to his ear.

"Does that mean you took my advice and spoke with Señor Shirts before you spoke with Marylou? And he straightened you out?"

"In fact . . . I did speak with him first and . . . my initial conclusions I shared with you . . . proved . . . to be in error," Henry replied, trying to talk in code.

"Well, I'm not goin' to say it."

Henry rolled his eyes. "Go ahead, Marvin."

"No, it's not necessary."

"Damn it, Marvin. Just say it."

"Okay . . . I freakin' told you so!"

"Great. Marvin, I don't have time for this . . . I'm exhausted. Maybe we can talk later."

Henry clicked off his phone. He decided there was one more thing he would withhold from Marvin—that he'd knocked himself silly and looked like a total numskull in Mikel's shirt store. If he told Marvin about that debacle, he'd hear about it for the rest of his life.

■ ■ ■

Finally home, Henry carried the bags upstairs while Marylou busied herself with the pile of mail. After a shower and a change of clothes, Henry returned downstairs to his study. Sitting at his desk, he felt immensely relieved that his bottom desk drawer no longer hid the source of his prolonged stress. He reached into his briefcase and removed the card. With a sense of release, he tore the card into bits and piled the pieces on the corner of his desk.

He turned on his computer and saw he had two emails from President Thomas. The first was a university-wide email with the news of Nichole's death, words of sympathy, and details about the funeral to be held in the university chapel. A wave of sadness rolled over him. The second email from Phil Thomas was addressed only to Henry.

> Henry—I regret that you return home to such tragic news.
> Nichole Kessler's murder casts a shadow of sadness and confusion across the university community. We made grief counselors available to all community members and those counselors have been busy. The outpouring of sadness is overwhelming. The counselors reported to me that many of the students they interviewed described you as Nichole's favorite professor. (I cleared sharing this information with you through the university's legal counsel.)
> Because you were Nichole's favorite professor, I am requesting that you represent the university at her funeral with a brief eulogy, following Reverend Brace's sermon. I know this is short notice. But this is a significant moment in the life of the university and I am confident that you are the person who will treat it with the tone and dignity it deserves.
> Thank you.

As Henry finished reading the email, Marylou appeared at his study door in a sleek black-and-green yoga outfit. Henry nonchalantly swept the torn pieces of the card that had tortured him into his left palm and dropped them into the wastebasket.

"Hey you," she said. "I'm stiff as a board after that flight. I'm going to We Yogis to loosen up these bones. Join me?"

"Rain check?" he said, giving her slim body an appreciative look. "Hey, can you take a quick look at something?" Henry swung his computer monitor around so she could read Phil Thomas's email.

"That's some compliment," Marylou said. "In this kind of troubling situation, President Thomas turning to you speaks volumes. I'm impressed. Maybe you should rethink leaving academia?" She signaled good-bye with a playful wiggle of her fingers and was off to her yoga class.

After he heard the garage door close, Henry reread the email. He was ambivalent about the request. Although honored that President Thomas had chosen him to speak, he was uncomfortable with the occasion. He was religiously affiliated, but far from committed. Words of comfort without religious grounding would be difficult. With the funeral two days away, he needed to get to work.

■■■

Detective Esmeralda Ortiz sat at Doc Rock's kitchen table watching him prepare tea. She didn't like tea, but experience had taught her that allowing witnesses to demonstrate hospitality put them at ease and opened their mouths. As Doc Rock busied himself with the tea, he made small talk about the heat and what scorching temperatures meant for an overcrowded emergency room. Although he put on a modest front, Ortiz's instincts told her he was well invested in his self-worth.

"Would you like honey with your tea?" Doc Rock asked.

"That would be nice." She would have preferred a shot of whiskey.

He returned with the tea and settled down in the kitchen chair across from Ortiz. "Sorry we have to sit here, but these are the only chairs in the house."

Ortiz took a sip of her steaming tea. "Very nice, thanks." She set it aside and took out an iPad. "Let's get started with some background. Please give me your full name, date and place of birth, and how you ended up in Dallas."

"Sure, born June 21, 1982, in Wilmette, Illinois, full name is Jack McGowan Rockwood. My parents were Silvia and Michael Rockwood and I have three sisters named—"

"That won't be necessary," Ortiz gently cut him off. "What brought you to Dallas?"

"For a residency. The medical business is like a lottery," he said matter-of-factly. "Newly minted doctors are matched up with hospitals in a national computer system and you get what you get. I got Baylor here in Dallas."

"How long had you known the deceased?" Ortiz asked, typing in her notes.

"About eighteen months," he replied, pulling three fingers through his long grey hair. "She moved in with Andrea last January at the start of the spring semester."

"How would you describe the deceased?" she asked. He was staring at her face. Well aware she was free of the burdens of a pretty face, Ortiz knew he was staring at the angry scar across her chin.

"Same as she's described in the press—beautiful and smart. But she was much more. She was just a lot of fun."

Ortiz feared the interview was proceeding too quickly. She had learned in her criminal investigation course at Sam Houston State University that it was always best to set the table before boring down for important details. But the witness seemed anxious to talk, so she decided to stay with the flow. She asked, "Can you give me an example of what you mean?"

"Okay, for instance, the nickname she gave me—Doc Rock. She loved to stop by and listen to me play piano, especially the boogie-woogie stuff. And," he pulled his hair out to the side, "with this mane, I became Doc Rock. We had fun with it."

Ortiz decided to give him a shot. "And smoking pot with college girls made it all the more fun?"

"Whoa." The laid-back Doc Rock was instantly animated. "What are you talking about? I'm subject to random drug tests at the hospital. No way I'm smoking weed."

Saying nothing, Ortiz reached into her aluminum-sided briefcase, withdrew a document, closed the briefcase, and laid the document on the table. "I interviewed the roommate, Andrea Lucero, at length. She said they visited you frequently because you had the best weed in town. The document in front of you is a search warrant for the garage apartment and this house. Do you really want me to execute it?"

"Come on," Doc Rock implored with grasped hands. "I thought you were here about a murder investigation. What's a little herb got to do with anything?"

Ortiz knew that an interrogation benefits from silence. Silence was like sodium pentothal—it extracted the truth. She stared wordlessly at the rumpled doctor for a long moment and then straightened her back and adjusted the belt around her ample waist. "Let me ask it this way—how comfortable are you with a newspaper headline along the lines of 'Doctor and Coeds in Drug Den'?"

"Really?" He shook his head and his shoulders sagged. "What do you want to know?"

"How often did the roommates come over to smoke and listen to you play piano?"

"They came together about a half a dozen times. Nichole came by herself more frequently." Doc Rock lightly scratched his cheek with the back of his fingers. "She enjoyed the music more than Andrea."

"Did the three of you talk when they came over?" asked Ortiz.

"Of course. Andrea could be glum and quiet, but Nichole carried the conversation for both of them."

"What did Nichole talk about?" asked Ortiz.

"I don't know . . ." answered Doc Rock, who appeared to be becoming frazzled. "Just talk . . . school . . . her plans for the future . . ."

"Did Nichole ever talk about her family?"

"No, basically never. I know both her parents died years ago. She told me she had zero family. She seemed to take some pride in the fact she had to fend for herself."

"Andrea told me that Nichole was complicated, that she could be very different people depending on what she wanted," said Ortiz. "Sometimes she acted like a schoolgirl with ribbons in her hair and at other times she could be uncommonly aggressive. Andrea described her as having a 'cross-eyed personality.' Do you agree with that?"

"I have no idea what Andrea was talking about. Nichole was always the same lively and fun person with me."

"How would you characterize the relationship between Nichole and Andrea?" asked Ortiz, looking down at her iPad.

"Don't know," Doc Rock said with a shrug. "They were roommates, I guess they were close."

"Close in an intimate way?"

"What?" said Doc Rock with a skeptical look on his face. "Sure doubt it."

"Why doubt it?" asked Ortiz as she played with her oversize hoop earring.

"Don't know . . . just do," he answered with certainty.

"Maybe because you were sleeping with Nichole?" Ortiz watched carefully for the usual twitches below the eye that announce a lie.

"Of course not! Really, what the hell is this all about?" he demanded.

The detective fell back once again on the advantages of silence. Witnesses, like nature, abhor a vacuum. Preparing to deliver her next blow, she reached again into her briefcase and extracted another document. Placing the document on the table, she said, "Here's Nichole's autopsy. Take a look at page five."

Ortiz ratcheted up her concentration on Doc Rock's face, waiting for his reaction to her news. She watched his eyes widen and lips separate. She concluded the information was new to him.

"Nichole . . . Nichole . . . she was pregnant? Six weeks? This is all too sad." Doc Rock's face reflected genuine angst.

"I assume," said Ortiz, "you're the father?"

"Why the hell assume that?" asked Doc Rock.

"Number one," she said, "Andrea told me that you and Nichole had 'something going on.' Second, you were awfully sure that the roommates weren't intimate. Maybe because you and Nichole were involved, you couldn't conceive there was someone else."

"This is out-of-control crazy."

"Let's cut the bullshit," Ortiz said with an edge in her voice for the first time. "You know as well as I do that 'Who's Your Daddy' DNA tests are quick and simple. You really want to put me through the effort of ordering the test?"

Doc Rock's gaze was transfixed on the wall behind her. His face fell. He collapsed his head into his hands and openly wept. It was a full five minutes before he could speak.

"You have no idea . . . what she meant to me," he said, still holding his head. "Nichole was perfect in every way. She was the foil my life needed . . . she was the opposite of the horrors of the emergency room. She . . . she completed me. We were in love. Please leave me alone!"

"No can do, doctor. Why don't you take a minute in the bathroom to compose yourself."

Ortiz listened to the water running in the nearby bathroom. She was delighted with her good fortune. In the sleepy confines of College Park, the town surrounding Southerland University, murder cases were rare. Now, she was leading an investigation intertwined with a sex triangle, drugs, and a beautiful dead girl. It was a once-in-a-lifetime case.

She stood up and looked out the kitchen window at the garage apartment. In many ways, Doc Rock looked good for the crime. He had opportunity and access. He lied about the drugs and the sex. Why lie unless there was something to hide? The autopsy said someone strangled Nichole with two hands and the red tee shirt had been draped around her neck after death. Had he strangled her in a jealous rage? Why did he wrap the red tee shirt around her neck when she was already dead?

Doc Rock returned to the kitchen, wan but composed. Ortiz allowed him to collect himself and then asked, "The day you discovered the body, why were you in their apartment?"

"They hadn't paid the rent." He took a deep breath. "I left a note asking them to call and when I didn't hear anything, I feared there might be something wrong, so I used my extra key to open the door."

"Why think something was wrong?" Ortiz asked, pushing her long, thin braid off her shoulder and down her back. "Wasn't it possible they were on vacation, took a trip home?"

"I guess that was possible," he replied. "But Nichole would have told me, I know she would have."

"What did you see when you entered the apartment?"

"She—Nichole—was lying on the couch, topless, her arms crossed over her stomach, and a red Southerland tee shirt was wrapped around her neck. She was obviously dead."

"Did you touch her?"

"Absolutely not."

"Did you wrap the red tee shirt around her neck?"

"Hell no. Why in the world would I do that?"

"I know this has been a tough day for you," Ortiz said, as she stood. "I'll need to speak with you again this week, so don't leave town."

She grabbed her briefcase and headed for the door. But seeing Doc Rock's ashen face, she decided it was an opportune time to probe a bit deeper. With her hand on the doorknob, she turned back. "By the way, was the red tee shirt around her neck a favorite of Nichole's?"

"Don't know. Both Nichole and Andrea wore red Southerland tee shirts from time to time," he answered in a detached voice.

"One more thing," Ortiz said. "The autopsy confirmed Nichole was murdered between 11:00 p.m. and midnight on Thursday. Where were you between those hours?"

"Asleep in bed," he replied, his voice low and tired.

"Alone?"

"Alone. Do I need a lawyer?"

"Suit yourself," Ortiz said. She went out and closed the door behind her.

Walking to her unmarked black Impala, Ortiz wondered if she had her man. The lies, the evasiveness, all pointed to him as the murderer. But there was a softness about him that said no way. His tears were all too real.

She had more leads to chase down. After years of mind-numbing police work, she finally had the salacious case she had always dreamed about—a case she would solve.

17

With Nichole's funeral only a day away, Henry had made precious little progress on the eulogy. He had wasted hours on a Shakespearean theme. In trying to explain Nichole's tragic death, he reasoned that life was more tragic than comedic, which is why only seventeen of Shakespeare's thirty-seven plays were comedies. He concluded that the theme was too academic in tone and would sound disingenuous coming out of his mouth. He trashed it and decided to take a break.

Despite the late June heat, Henry took a walk around the neighborhood to clear his head. The streets were empty; everyone had taken shelter in the air-conditioning.

He walked along, eyes fixed on the pavement, thinking about Nichole. He recalled her explanation for dropping her shorts in his office. She said it was "complicated" and had something to do with a relative. He remembered she had assured him she had some kind of plan to resolve her issues. He thought that beneath her bright smile and drive there must have been a torrent of sadness. He wondered if that sadness and her death were connected.

As he began to sweat, he realized that he had become totally engrossed in Nichole's death. He was so absorbed that he had neglected a problem that would only expand with time. The UNS issue could not wait. He had a strategy to resolve it, but it depended on getting the dirt Dan Moore had uncovered on Guy Wheeless Jr. He turned around abruptly and headed home to make the call.

He sat at his desk thinking through possible ways to get what he needed from Dan. Was there some way around his friend's commitment to keep the information confidential? The call would be uncomfortable, but he had to at least try. Dan answered on the second ring.

"Henry. How are ya?" Dan said.

"Hot as hell down here. Marylou and I just got back from Buenos Aires where it's winter. We should have stayed longer."

"Been thinking about you," Dan said. "When you and Marvin were in Wichita, you asked about the information we've collected on Guy Wheeless. I told you about the confidentiality requirement but, as I'm sure you already know, that confidentiality commitment is gone."

"That's great news . . . but I've got to tell you, I don't have a clue about what you're saying." Henry pressed down on his cowlick.

"Oh, man, sorry, got way ahead of myself," said Dan. "It has been absolute bedlam around here. Let me roll 'er back. The client . . . the one I collected all the information for on Guy Wheeless . . . she was Wheeless's niece. She was murdered while you were in Buenos Aires. She was a student at your school named Nichole Kessler."

An electric jolt of anxiety shot through Henry. *What the hell's going on?* First he learned that Marvin met Nichole. Now Dan's mysterious client turns out to be Nichole! And she's Wheeless's niece! *What's with this girl?*

"Henry, you still there? Did you know her?"

"Yeah, absolutely. She was one of my students, one of my very best students. I've been asked by the university's president to give the eulogy at her funeral."

"This is all way too weird. I'm traveling to Dallas for the funeral, so I'll be there to hear your eulogy," Dan said. "I'm on the first Southwest flight in the morning. I'll be there."

"I'm not getting this. Nichole was your client?"

"That's right," said Dan. "Worked for her for almost two years. In fact, I spoke with her just three days before the murder. She called to ask me to take care of some business with regard to Guy Jr. I set that business in motion the day after she called."

"I don't know what to make of all this . . . can you give me the headlines on what you've uncovered about Wheeless?"

"I'll give you all the details when I'm in Dallas. It's better to talk in person, you never know who's listening. I'll say this . . . Wheeless has a nasty penchant for abusing women."

"Oh, man," Henry said, leaning back in his chair. "We've got a ton to talk about."

"You got that right. See you tomorrow. But man, I regret the circumstances. Bye."

Henry was incredulous. What was going on? Nichole was Wheeless's niece? Why in the world had she paid Dan to collect information on her uncle? Where did she get the money to pay for the surveillance? Did she know her uncle was abusing women? With all the new information swimming around in his head, he was having a hard time holding a thought. *Who the hell was Nichole? Did I know her at all?*

He took a deep breath, willed himself to push away all the distractions, and set to work on the eulogy.

■■■

On Tuesday afternoon, Henry and Marylou walked arm in arm up the slate path to the Southerland University chapel. "My favorite building on campus," Marylou said. "I love the way the steeple and gold cross dominate the western sky."

"It's beautiful," agreed Henry. "It's like a nineteenth-century New England church, but built out of stone and brick rather than wood. Such a beautiful place, such a sad occasion."

The couple arrived early to meet with Reverend William Brace to discuss the funeral's sequencing. The chapel's sanctuary, painted a creamy white, was airy and bright. The four thirty-foot windows along the sides were set with clear, rather than stained, glass. Nothing but two short steps separated the nave from the altar, giving the chapel an egalitarian feel. Henry thought the chapel was elegantly austere and wished he were there for Nichole's wedding.

Reverend Brace came out of a door to the left of the altar with two men. They were all carrying folded chairs. "Remember," Reverend Brace told the men, "only one row of chairs next to each pew. It's the fire code."

Henry introduced himself and Marylou to Reverend Brace, then he glanced around the chapel. "It looks like you can seat around three hundred," he said. "Are you expecting that many?"

"Yes, we anticipate some will need to stand in the back. It seems the poor girl knew a lot of people."

You got that right, Henry thought to himself. "Reverend, can you give me some direction on what's expected of me this afternoon?"

"You and I will start the service sitting in the choir stall," Reverend Brace said, pointing to the slightly raised area past the altar. "When I stand, you stand with me. After the sermon, I'll return to my chair and sit; then it's your turn. When you're done, just come sit next to me."

"I've never given a eulogy—any words of wisdom?" Henry asked with a furrowed brow.

"Being a professor, you'll do just fine. It's always best to keep it short. You may want to avoid reading any long quotes. My experience is, reading quotes at a funeral chokes up the reader. But you, you'll be fine." Reverend Brace gave Henry an avuncular shoulder squeeze.

■■■

Henry sat next to Reverend Brace in the choir stall, trying to appear calm, the funeral program rolled up tightly in his hands. Marylou sat in a pew halfway up the aisle, facing him. From time to time she smiled, conveying her support.

The three-thousand-pipe organ played J. S. Bach's "Air on the G String" as mourners silently filled the pews. Henry recognized a number of students and faculty members sitting solemnly in their seats. Three members of the task force on sexual assault sat together in the back row.

Henry saw Dan Moore enter the chapel and lumber down the aisle in a dark blue suit and dress cowboy boots. With his thumb and forefinger pulling his soul patch, he gave Henry a slight nod and took a seat next to Marylou.

A young, dark-haired woman in the front row cried steadily into her handkerchief. Henry recognized her as Andrea Lucero, Nichole's roommate, the one who had described the dragonfly tattoo in his classroom. A young man with long, prematurely grey hair sat on her right. He appeared oblivious to Andrea's emotional state and did nothing to console her. Henry realized he was the man Nichole had introduced him to at the ice cream truck in the park.

As the service was about to start, Henry watched two men enter the chapel and make their way down the aisle. One was tall and spectrally thin. His companion was impeccably dressed with his black hair slicked back in teamster-boss style. Henry felt a sudden, cold emptiness in his stomach when he saw the man's mangled ear. Henry tried to catch Marylou's eye, but she was reading the program. At that moment, Reverend Brace stood and Henry followed suit.

While Reverend Brace delivered the sermon, Henry could not stop stealing glances at Guy Wheeless Jr. When he heard the reverend quoting John 14:27, "Let not your heart be troubled, neither let it be afraid," he knew the sermon was coming to a close. He could not force his mind back to his eulogy—his brain was shipwrecked on Guy Wheeless Jr. When Reverend Brace said, "Let us pray," Henry knew that after the "Amen," ready or not, he was on.

Walking toward the fixed, freestanding lectern, he worried about the reverend's admonition not to use lengthy quotes. He had written the eulogy with a poem at the end. It was too late to turn back. He gripped both sides of the lectern and surveyed the audience. He told himself it was just like giving a class lecture. It wasn't.

When he made eye contact with Marylou, emotion welled up in him. Knowing the best way to short-circuit soft sentiments was to think negative thoughts, he turned his eyes on Wheeless, whose slicked-back hair reflected the sunlight. That did the trick. Confident and almost steady, he began.

"It is my honor to speak with you today as we remember Nichole. No one is happy to be here this afternoon. We did not have a chance to wish her well, to say good-bye. The passing of someone we know can shake us. The violent death of someone of such potential, so brimming with life as Nichole, can overwhelm us."

Henry hesitated. Andrea Lucero in the front row had begun to wail uncontrollably. A plump woman with a long, thin braid got up from her seat a few rows back and came to Andrea's rescue by gently helping her to the rear of the chapel. The man with the long grey hair sitting next to Andrea remained stoically detached.

Henry waited for the two to settle in the back of the chapel before he began again. "During the semester Nichole was in my class, I came to know her as a lovely, bright, and engaged student. Nichole was among the finest students I have had the honor to teach. Her impressive ability to learn was surpassed only by her desire to do so. The numerous awards the university bestowed on her are testaments to her academic excellence. But that's not even half the story. Nichole's sunny smile could brighten the worst of days. She had a rare intellectual curiosity that went well beyond her studies. For example, I was amazed by her knowledge about the history of tattoos."

At the mention of tattoos, Andrea Lucero let out a loud moan from the rear of the chapel.

Henry waited a moment for Andrea to regain her composure before he began again. "The last time I saw Nichole was in a city park where she and a friend were enjoying the beautiful day and ice cream cones. We had a short but meaningful conversation. As we parted, she gave me a wonderful smile and a warm hug that lifted my spirits. That was typical of Nichole. She had a priceless gift—she could make each of us feel good about ourselves."

It appeared to Henry that half the audience had Kleenex in their hands. He took a deep breath, retrieved a handkerchief from his pocket, and pressed it under his nose.

"It is said that a person is at peace with death when he has lived a good life and his life's work has been completed. Today, we can take comfort in the quality of Nichole's short life and the depth of her engagement. Nichole's shooting star brightened our winter sky.

"At times like this, faith, family, and friends are needed—in fact, at times like this, our relationship with them is defined. We can all take comfort that Nichole's spirit, bright and true, lives on in each and every one of us.

"While we try to cope with the unfathomable reality that she has been taken from us in an act of violence, we must hold tight to the belief that we will come to know the reason she was taken from us, and that the person responsible will be brought to answer."

Henry looked out into the audience and took a breath, this one sharp and short. Guy Wheeless Jr. was looking directly at him. His eyes, cold and dark, matched the smirk on his face.

"I will . . . " Henry stumbled over his words but caught himself. "I will end today with a poem by Mary Elizabeth Frye. The author wrote this poem on a plain brown paper bag. I'm confident Nichole would have appreciated its simplicity and grace. These words capture how I hope we can all remember Nichole.

> Do not stand at my grave and weep,
> I am not there; I do not sleep.
> I am a thousand winds that blow,
> I am the softly falling snow.
> I am the gentle showers of rain,
> I am the fields of ripening grain.
> I am in the morning hush,
> I am in the graceful rush
> Of beautiful birds in circling flight,
> I am the starshine of the night.
> I am in the flowers that bloom,
> I am in a quiet room.
> I am in the birds that sing,
> I am in each lovely thing.
> Do not stand at my grave bereft
> I am not there. I have not left."

Henry's voice caught on the final stanza, forcing him to read it a second time. He had stopped breathing and felt faint. Forcing air into his lungs, he returned to his chair, emotionally drained. Without moving his head or lips, Reverend Brace whispered, "Well done, Professor."

■■■

The reception in the chapel cafeteria was a sad, simple affair. Without a receiving line, the gathering lacked a central focus. Attendees milled around in mostly homogeneous peer groups, sipping iced tea and conversing in hushed tones. A peer's funeral rendered the students quiet and self-conscious. Faculty members stopped to shake Henry's hand and thank him for his words.

Henry and Marylou stood with Dan Moore making small talk and avoiding the troubling questions flying around in their minds. A portly woman in her early forties with a long, thin braid approached the trio. Henry recognized her as the woman who had escorted Andrea Lucero to the chapel's rear.

She looked him directly in the eye, stuck out her hand, and said, "Those were righteous words, Professor. I'm Detective Esmeralda Ortiz. I've been assigned to investigate Nichole Kessler's murder."

Henry waited for her to continue, but there was only awkward silence as Ortiz stared at Henry's face. Finally, she said, "Seems you knew the deceased pretty well."

"Nichole was my student. I was fond of her. By the way," Henry said, holding out his arm, "this is my wife, Marylou, and our friend Dan Moore."

After businesslike handshakes, Ortiz asked, "Professor, can I have a word?"

Without answering, Henry took a few steps away from Marylou and Dan. Ortiz joined him.

"I'd like to speak with you about the deceased as soon as possible," she said. "Would tomorrow morning at ten o'clock work? I'm happy to come to your house."

"Sure. I'd like to assist in any way possible. So . . . I'll see you then. Do you know the address?"

Ortiz stuck out her hand again and said, "Sure do."

Henry frowned as he left Ortiz, unsettled that the detective wanted to talk to him. After rejoining Marylou and Dan, he looked around to see if anyone was in hearing range and then said to them in a quiet voice, "That's the detective investigating the murder. She wants to talk to me. Dan, I saw Wheeless come into the chapel. What kind of relationship did he have with Nichole?"

"It's called mutual loathing," said Dan.

"Heads up, gents," Marylou interrupted. "Speak of the devil."

Looking at Marylou's eyes for direction, Henry turned to his left to see Wheeless approaching. Lagging just behind him was the thin man Henry had seen come down the aisle with him. Wheeless walked up to the three in a charcoal grey, double-breasted suit and black shoes buffed to a Marine-quality shine.

"Henry, it's been a long time," Wheeless said, showing first one and then the other French cuff to display his gold, monogrammed cuff links. "And Marylou, time has been kind to you."

Marylou gave a slight nod of her head.

"What do you want, asshole?" Dan said.

Wheeless made a loud tsk-tsk sound in response. "And nice seeing you, Dan. Thanks for the kind words about my niece, Henry. Or should I call you professor? I bet you like being called professor."

Henry knew Wheeless was trying to antagonize him. The church in the aftermath of a funeral was the wrong time to rise to the bait. "I didn't know until recently that Nichole was your niece," said Henry.

"Of course. We were very close," Wheeless said, readjusting his necktie.

"Sorry for your loss," said Marylou.

"She was my only sibling's only child. Now they're both gone," Wheeless replied placidly. "Please excuse me, but I must see to the burial details. And Dan, you should know something. It seems a terribly unattractive insect has crawled up under your lip."

The poke at Dan apparently amused the thin man standing behind Wheeless and he began to snicker. Dan started toward Wheeless, but Marylou, with a quick movement, entwined both her arms around the big man's left arm and whispered, "This is a church."

Dan seemed to recover his composure, and he patted Marylou's arm to release him. As he moved to leave, he pivoted sharply to his right and ground his cowboy boot onto Wheeless's highly polished shoe. Wheeless tried to jerk his foot away but lost his balance, and with flailing arms he fell backward, landing hard on the floor.

Dan kept walking and never looked back. Henry took Marylou by the elbow and guided her to the other side of the chapel. Neither of them looked back at Wheeless.

After the commotion of Wheeless's fall, the crowd in the chapel thinned out quickly. With Marylou and Dan in his Tahoe, Henry headed the short distance home. Dan broke the silence in the car, exclaiming, "What an asshole! Guess I scraped the shine right off his shoe!"

"Yeah," Henry said sarcastically. "Real smooth move—stomp on a foot at a funeral. Nice."

"I kind of enjoyed it," Marylou said, turning around to smile at Dan in the backseat. "Marvin will love hearing about it. Wheeless said he was close to Nichole. Is that true?"

"What a crock of shit," Dan said, too loudly. "Nichole couldn't stand to be in the same room with the miserable son of a bitch. It's something Nichole and I had in common. It's rich to think that, with my help, she'll reach out of her grave for her revenge."

Henry wondered what Dan meant by revenge from the grave, but he didn't ask. Dan was worked up and Henry needed a calm conversation. There were many moving parts to the Nichole Kessler enigma that did not compute. He was relieved to finally pull into his driveway.

There were no objections when Marylou suggested they could all use a drink. Henry opened a bottle of tart French Vouvray and poured three glasses. They each took seats on the living room couches under two large abstract canvases Marylou had purchased in Buenos Aires.

"Nice job with the eulogy," Dan said to Henry.

"It was beautiful, darling," added Marylou, tipping her glass in his direction.

"Thanks." Henry shook his head. "I hope I never have to do it again. Dan, this soap opera starring you, Nichole, and Wheeless is confusing as hell. Can you take us through this mess, soup to nuts?"

"Before I head down that long highway," said Dan, draining his white wine in a single swallow, "chance of a taste of something stronger?"

Henry went to the bar and returned with two healthy pours of Maker's Mark on the rocks. One for Dan, one for himself.

"Okay," said Dan, after taking a long draught. "It all started with Guy Jr.'s sister. She grew up in Wichita, but was older, I never knew her. Did you?"

Henry shook his head and glanced at Marylou, who added, "I think she graduated a few years before us."

"She died, in Kansas City, of a drug overdose." Dan took off his necktie. "Her father, Guy Sr., had set up a trust for his granddaughter, Nichole. When his sister died, Guy Jr. became the trustee of a very healthy trust."

"How much are we talking about?" asked Marylou.

"At the start, north of twenty million," replied Dan. "But not now. We discovered that Wheeless methodically siphoned off most of the money."

Henry leaned forward. "How much is there now?"

Dan took an appreciative sip of his bourbon. "Somewhere south of a million."

"Good grief!" said Henry. "Did Nichole know this?"

"Yep, we kept her informed about what we learned," Dan said. "She repeatedly asked Wheeless for an accounting but he refused. He paid her an annual allowance, but that was it. She was looking for leverage to force him to give her an accounting. That's when we got hired."

"From what you told me on the phone, I take it your investigation didn't come up empty-handed," said Henry.

"Not a pretty picture. Henry, remember I told you about the warehouse he converted? Called the Bunker? Wheeless stays hunkered down in there for days on end."

"Yeah, you said he was like Howard Hughes."

"Like Howard, with one very important difference."

"What difference?" Marylou asked.

"First, I'll need some more talking fuel," Dan said, lifting his empty glass.

With a fresh glass of bourbon in hand, he continued. "Old Howard liked women—Wheeless likes to use them as punching bags."

"What? Are you sure?" asked Marylou.

"One hundred percent," said Dan. "Think back on the crap he pulled in high school. He's always had an appetite for violence. There were also rumors that his father used to beat up Jr.'s mom. There's perverse logic to all of it. Just like the way Guy Jr. elevated the bank to a whole new level; he did the same with his dad's taste for abusing women."

"What exactly do you mean?" Marylou asked, clutching her wineglass with both hands.

"He's in cahoots with his chauffeur, an ex-middleweight boxer from Louisiana named Larry. Old Larry's no sweetheart. He did a five-year stint in Leavenworth for assault with a deadly weapon. When he got out of the joint, Guy Jr. hired him. Larry drives around town scouting for potential victims. Once Wheeless decides on a target, he romances his victim with lavish gifts." Dan placed his half-empty glass on the coffee table. "For weeks at a time, he showers them with flowers twice a day, every day.

"These women all fit the same profile—lonely working women, slightly past their prime, and desperate for love." Dan picked up his glass and finished his drink. "Once Wheeless has them thinking they've died and gone to heaven, he gives them his parting gift. After a gin-fired evening in the Bunker, he forces them into whatever sadistic sex act is on his warped mind and then, because in his sick head the woman must have led him to the debauchery, he beats the livin' bejesus out of her. One of the women told us that his weapon of choice is a white sock filed with soap bars."

"Soap bars?" asked Henry with raised eyebrows.

"He probably thinks it's a way to avoid leaving bruises," replied Dan. "But with Wheeless, who knows?"

"This is incredible," said Marylou, putting her hands on the top of her head. "Piece of garbage. To think we grew up with him!"

"My investigators interviewed five of his victims. Ugly stuff. Most of 'em were too shell-shocked to provide much detail. But two of 'em mentioned dogs."

"Dogs?" Henry said. "What about dogs?"

"I don't have details," Dan said with a shrug. "Hey, we're not the police, and when the women didn't want to elaborate about the dogs, there was nothing we could do. With that sicko you can bet it wasn't pretty."

"I understand, go on," said Henry.

"So where was I? Oh yeah. After Wheeless finishes with them, Larry drives the woman home and, without a word, opens the car door for them, hands over an envelope with $10,000 cash inside, and tells them if they say a word, he'll kill them. They're too terrified and traumatized to go to the police."

"Did Nichole know about all of this?" asked Henry.

"Sure did. She got biweekly reports from me," said Dan.

"Got to admit it," said Henry, "I hoped you had some dirt on Guy Jr., but this is over the top."

"As awful as this is, it's perfect for Henry's plan," Marylou said.

"What plan's that?" Dan asked, holding up his empty glass.

Henry went to the bar, brought the bottle to the table, and filled Dan's glass. It looked like Dan was going to tie one on, so he set the bottle down on the coffee table.

Henry, returning to his seat, said, "I was hoping to use your information on Wheeless as leverage with those folks at UNS I told you about—the ones who want the Department of Justice to investigate me. I assume at some point you intend to take the information to the police?"

"You bet . . ."

"If you can hold off a week or two," Marylou said, sitting forward on her chair's edge, "Henry has an idea to put the information on Wheeless to excellent use."

Dan grimaced. "Well, that's a problem. I mentioned to you that Nichole called three days before she was murdered and asked me to take care of some business with Wheeless. The business she asked me to take care of was reporting his crimes to the police."

"You already gave the information to the police?" asked Marylou.

"Not exactly," said Dan, starting to slur his words.

"What's 'not exactly' mean?" asked Henry.

"Guy Jr. casts a mighty long shadow in Wichita," Dan said, with more than a touch of animosity in his voice. "To make sure the police didn't just sit on their hands, I previewed what I had with the police chief. Told him a prominent citizen was involved but didn't name Wheeless."

"Great. Can you wait a week or two to give him the complete report?" Henry asked.

"Got good news and bad." Dan drained another glass. "Good news, the chief is hell-bent for leather to make the arrest. The bad news is the chief is hell-bent for leather to make the arrest." Dan chuckled at what he alone thought was funny.

"What are you saying, Dan?" asked Marylou.

"What I'm saying is the chief is raring to go and I've got to give him the info pronto." Dan chortled at his rhyme.

"Surely it can wait a week, can't it?" Henry gripped his hands together tightly. "This is important, Dan."

"No way I can wait a week. The fuse is lit. If I delay beyond Friday, I'm looking at obstruction of justice charges. No way I can deal with another legal issue."

"That gives you three days, Henry." Marylou turned to their friend, smiling hopefully. "Come on, Dan, help us out?"

"Marylou," he said, listing to the right, "if it's important to you, I'll make it work . . . but only till Friday," replied Dan, reaching for the bourbon bottle.

"How about this," Marylou said, giving Henry an anxious glance. "I'm going to get dinner on the table and you two can talk over Henry's plan. Back in a bit."

Dan splashed more bourbon in his glass and, clinging to the bottle, said, "What's the plan, Stan?"

Hoping Dan wasn't too drunk to comprehend, Henry began. "It all revolves around the issues I'm having with UNS, and their threat to go to the Department of Justice. They say they have information that I violated the

Foreign Corrupt Practices Act. Before I get into the details, what do you say about a cup of coffee?"

"I'm jest fine . . . " Dan mumbled, lifting his glass in a toast.

Henry hurried into the kitchen. Marylou had put on an apron and, with a large paring knife in her right hand, she was busy chopping fresh vegetables.

"We need to get some coffee into Dan," he said, "or he's going to pass out."

"Some food, too. Dinner won't be ready for thirty minutes. I thought you said he's been through detox?"

"He has," said Henry. "Guess bourbon was an exception to the treatment. I'll bring out some cheese and crackers and go over the plan with him."

She wiped her hands on the apron around her waist. "I'll bring out some coffee," she said firmly.

He returned to the living room with a tray of crackers and cheese. Dan was slumped back on the couch, his cowboy boots crossed at his ankles in front of him. With his mouth wide open, he was gently snoring.

Henry sighed. The clock on his plan with UNS would run out Friday when Dan went to the police with all the facts. It promised to be a long night.

18

The Southerland University campus was a different place on Wednesday morning in late June. The college students were replaced by legions of high school students shipped to Southerland to learn mathematics, geology, or archaeology. Each week of the summer focused on a different discipline.

This week in June was devoted to a particularly ephemeral teenage dream: Texas high school cheerleaders. Groups from different schools huddled together in their matching phosphorescent shirts, with pom-poms dangling from one arm and a cell phone held in the other. The cheerleaders did not talk among themselves; cell phone conversation was clearly the preferred medium of communication.

Marvin stood out as he walked across campus in a light green Tommy Bahama shirt, a straw fedora, and dark, round sunglasses. The cheerleaders could have mistaken him for a Cuban cigar roller. By the time he pushed through the wall of summer heat to reach the administration building, he felt like his entire body had sprung a leak.

Southerland's president, Phil Thomas, had been insistent Tuesday night over the phone; he needed to see Marvin first thing Wednesday morning. As Marvin swept past the sentinel receptionist without breaking stride, she stood and nervously called out, "Mr. Marvin Lindon?"

"The one and only," he answered, without slowing. He sprang up the long staircase, not even glancing at the oil paintings of past Southerland presidents hanging on the wall.

In his second-floor office, from behind his ornate desk, Thomas stood and extended his hand. "Marvelous, thanks for coming on short notice."

"My pleasure, Phil. Always good to be on campus."

"Please, sit down." He gestured toward the chair in front of the desk and retook his own seat. "I've got a problem on my hands and I need your counsel. It's Henry."

"What about Henry? I'm sure his students think he walks on water."

"They do," said Thomas. "His student evaluations are spectacular. He works hard on everything he does for his class and it shows. Classroom performance is not the problem."

"So what's the issue?"

"I received an anonymous email, presumably from a female student, complaining that Henry had condoned antigay rhetoric in his classroom." Thomas tipped his head back and looked down his long nose at Marvin. "The email is now three weeks old. I didn't see it until last night because it originally went to spam. I called you as soon as I saw it."

"Phil, you don't know Henry," Marvin said, dismissing any issue. "There's no way he would condone gay bashin' in his classroom. Hell, Henry's 'bout the only man I know who's never even told a gay joke."

"All right. But the email raised another issue."

"Which was?"

"The student, again presumably female, but I can't be sure," Thomas said with a shrug, "alleged she has a tattoo on her butt and said that Henry has seen it. She was very specific about the tattoo, described it as a bright purple dragonfly."

Thomas's mention of the dragonfly tattoo struck Marvin like a sudden summer storm. This must be the same girl Henry had told Marvin about. *Who is this sociopath? Dropping her shorts in Henry's office and then complaining to the university's president!*

In a defensive reaction, Marvin locked in his poker face, waited a beat, and asked, "Is there something more? Is there an allegation that Henry acted inappropriately?"

"The email said this 'showing' occurred in Henry's campus office," Thomas answered calmly.

Thinking through his next move, Marvin fleetingly wondered what Thomas thought about his own tattoo and wished he had worn a long-sleeved shirt. Sensing Thomas was not fully committed to a specific course of action, Marvin went on the offense.

"Phil, I'm not sure where you're goin' with this. Hell, you don't know who sent the email or even if we're talkin' 'bout a male or female student. This whole thing could be a complete fiction comin' from a student who didn't like their grade; hell, it could be from some frat boy who mooned Henry on a dare. There's no allegation Henry did anything wrong." Marvin sat back in his chair with open hands.

"Marvin, no need to raise your voice," Thomas scolded. "I asked you here to get your counsel. Just yesterday, at my request, Henry represented the university at a murdered student's funeral. A very sad affair. Henry's been great for the university. He's even put up with those incompetents running the task force on sexual assault. Believe me, I wish the damn email had stayed in spam."

"So," said Marvin, "why not just let 'er slide?"

"I can't pretend I didn't receive an email alleging an impropriety by someone so visible in our community." Thomas sat back in his chair. "I think the best course of action is to take the issue to the university's board of directors."

"Whoa, what the hell are they gonna do, conduct an investigation that'll trash Henry, no matter what the outcome? Phil, effective leadership sometimes means simply stayin' quiet."

"What's your point, Marvin?"

"Remember a few years back when you went with us to Vegas on the annual Final Four trip?" Marvin stood and walked to the side of Thomas's desk, put his knuckles on it, and leaned over.

"What about it?" Thomas said, looking up at Marvin.

"Recall how you somehow got locked out of your room without a key and nothin' on but your tighty whities?" Marvin leaned in closer to Thomas. "Remember we went to my room and called security? And when security let us back into your room we discovered a certain someone else in there? And you proceeded to toss cookies all over the rug? And 'til this very moment, I never said boo about any of it? Well, that's an example of sometimes sayin' nothin' is the best course of action."

"Marvin," Thomas said with darkening eyes, "are you blackmailing me?"

"Heavens, no!" Marvin leaned away from Thomas with a feigned look of hurt on his face. "You asked for my counsel and I'm just tryin' to make a point 'bout effective leadership. Just drawin' an analogy."

Marvin sat back down as the two contemplated their positions. He had been feeling guilty about the predicament he had placed Henry in with the stock trades in the Bahamas. This was his chance to make amends. After a few tense minutes, Marvin broke the standoff.

"While you think over my advice, Phil, let me give you somethin' to chew on. I've been thinkin' about that request you made a couple of months back for a ten-million-dollar namin' grant for the new basketball arena—I think I'm ready to make the commitment."

"That's fantastic, Marvin! Incredibly generous!" replied Thomas, with a 180-degree change in tone. "We'll schedule a press conference immediately to announce the gift! We'll do it Friday, the day after tomorrow!"

"It's my pleasure. We just need to chat a bit about Henry's situation. Don't ya think silence might be the best option?"

■ ■ ■

Dan had quietly left the Lindons' house at the crack of dawn, long before Henry and Marylou were up. The couple sat reading the morning papers. "What do you think the detective wants from you?" Marylou asked from behind her paper.

"Don't know," Henry responded offhandedly from across the living room. His concentration was on the sports section.

"With everything on your plate the next couple of days, the timing's not good," Marylou said, lowering her newspaper section.

"Uh-huh."

"Maybe you could call her, tell her you're sick."

"Uh-huh."

"Maybe tell her I've put you in chains and locked you in the basement."

"Uh-huh."

"Henry! Please put down the paper and talk to me!"

"Sorry," he said, lowering the paper and smiling sheepishly at his wife. "What did you say?"

"I'm just concerned that with the little time left before Dan goes to the police with his information on Guy Wheeless, and your need to catch up with Jane Birney, well, having to meet with the detective just seems like an ill-timed distraction."

"I agree, but how do I say no?" Henry said, folding up the sports section and placing it on the table. "Who knows, maybe I can be of some help finding Nichole's killer."

"Do you think she'll ask you about Nichole showing you her dragonfly tattoo?"

"How could the detective possibly know about that?" Henry got up from his chair. "I need to get ready for her. Want to sit in with us?"

"I'll pass. If I'm involved it might prolong the interview." Marylou stood and leaned over Henry, giving him a soft kiss on top of his head. "Good luck."

Thirty minutes later, Henry, escorted Detective Ortiz to his study, the obligatory coffee mug in her hand.

"When was the last time you saw the deceased?" asked Ortiz, as her eyes ran up and down the crammed, floor-to-ceiling bookshelves in Henry's study.

"Saw her in her cap and gown at the commencement procession," he said from behind his desk. "Before that, I ran into her briefly in a city park. We were both getting ice cream."

"Do you recall the time you saw her before that?" she asked.

"Yes, she came to my office, wanted to finalize a recommendation for a summer job, in DC, I think."

"Y'all talk about anything other than the recommendation?" asked Ortiz, sitting up straighter.

"Believe it or not, we talked about tattoos," Henry said. "Nichole seemed very interested in tattoos and their history. I remember she told me about a tattoo Winston Churchill's mother had on her wrist."

"Remember anything else about the meeting?" Ortiz asked, her eyes burrowing into Henry.

Henry wondered why Ortiz was so interested in the meeting in his office. Was it possible she knew about Nichole flashing her tattoo? How could she know? He realized this was the moment of truth. If he tried to fudge any facts, it could lead to significant problems.

"Well . . . yes. This is sort of embarrassing." Henry's gaze dropped to his desktop, then back up to meet hers. "She . . . Nichole, showed me a dragonfly tattoo on her butt."

Ortiz arched one brow. "Any idea why she did that?"

"Thought about it a fair amount," said Henry. "Talked it over with my wife, Marylou. We think it was just Nichole's idea of a joke. Sometimes it's a bit hard to tell with this generation."

"Professor Lindon, can you tell me where you were last Thursday night?"

"Yes," he said, nodding. "I was in Buenos Aires with my wife. We took a flight home Friday night and landed Saturday morning."

As Ortiz tapped on her tablet, Henry wondered who else she had interviewed. "Professor, do you know any students who had a conflict with the deceased?"

"Not that I know of. She had a lot of friends," Henry said, with sadness in his voice. "You were at her funeral. It was an impressive turnout." He shook his head. "So tragic. So pointless. She was a wonderful, complicated girl."

Ortiz shifted in her chair, making her silver hoop earrings bounce. "Is there anything else you can think of that might help me get the full picture of Nichole?"

Henry stared back into the eyes drilling into him. He remembered Guy

Wheeless's maleficent stare at the end of Nichole's funeral. The detective's question provided the perfect platform to ensure scrutiny on whether Wheeless was involved in Nichole's death. He remembered his father's admonition, echoed by Marvin, that in the vengeance game, no one is satisfied with a single helping. He hesitated about jumping into the game but decided to take the plunge. "Maybe . . . I recently learned she had an uncle," he said. "Guy Wheeless Jr. out of Wichita. I understand they weren't on the best of terms. I was told Nichole went so far as to hire a firm to investigate Wheeless, but that's secondhand information."

"Who told you about the Wheeless investigation?" Ortiz pressed on, with two fingers gently touching the scar on her chin.

"My friend Dan Moore. He lives in Wichita too. He's the big man I introduced to you at the funeral."

"Do you know Mr. Wheeless?"

"Knew him in high school," Henry replied. "Haven't seen him since—except he was also at the funeral."

"So the three of you grew up together in Wichita?" Ortiz asked. Henry did not appreciate her quizzical look.

"Yep, my wife, Marylou, too."

"Anything else you think I should know?" asked Ortiz.

Henry shrugged. "Not that I can think of."

Ortiz stood and shook his hand. "Thank you Mr. Lindon, I appreciate your time."

"Of course." He led her to the front door and softly shut it behind her.

■■■

Ortiz walked down the sidewalk and got into her car, confident it had been a productive morning. But there were still many pieces of the puzzle missing. In her interview with Nichole's roommate, Andrea Lucero, the girl had gone out of her way to negatively paint Henry as a cold academic. Ortiz didn't see it. Andrea also described the tattoo incident in Henry's office as a sexual peccadillo. But, if that was the case, would Henry have told his wife about the incident? *Did he actually tell her?*

Henry seemed to have a bulletproof alibi for the night of the murder. The alibi was almost too perfect. Could he have hired someone to murder Nichole? But why? And why had Henry gratuitously steered her toward Nichole's uncle, Guy Wheeless Jr., in Wichita? There was no mention of Wheeless's name in any of the reports. Both Andrea and Doc Rock had been adamant that Nichole had no family. Was Henry telling the truth, or trying to divert suspicion to Wheeless? Who was this Dan Moore in Wichita? Was there some connection to Wichita she needed to look into?

Ortiz started her car and turned toward police headquarters—she needed clearance for a trip to Wichita to visit Guy Wheeless Jr.

19

Late Thursday morning, Jane Birney was in her New Brunswick office packing her briefcase. She looked up and saw Chester Lawrence standing in her doorway. "Chester, please come in," she said. "I'm tying up a few loose ends before I head to Paris tonight."

The man walked in and Jane motioned for him to take a seat. "We haven't talked in a while. Anything new about the situation at San Miguel Galletas or Henry Lindon?"

"The situation at San Miguel is an unmitigated mess," Chester said, the usual pout on his face. "The business is in a death spiral and the union has been staging daily work slowdowns. I hear nothing about Professor Smart-Ass. Remember, you told me to back off."

"Yes, I remember. I got an unexpected call from Henry last night. He asked for an urgent meeting—said it had to be today. He's flying into JFK for the meeting before I catch my flight."

"Did he say why he's so anxious to meet?" asked Chester with an intent look.

"All he said was that he had a 'deal' to discuss."

"There! You see!" Chester cried, punching a fist into his hand. "He's had second thoughts. He's obviously ready to come clean about the San Miguel Galletas situation and make a deal with us on that Foreign Corrupt Practices Act violation."

"No need to jump to conclusions," said Jane. "He gave no details of what he has in mind."

"Why else would he call? This is great news!" Chester rose, grinning from ear to ear. "Why don't I tag along to make sure the great professor fully understands the strength of our case?"

"Thanks, but he was very clear that the meeting has to be one-on-one." She distractedly shook her head. "It's hard for me to believe that Henry is ready to change his position, but we'll see. Thanks, Chester. At some point I'll fill you in on the meeting."

■■■

Chester Lawrence forced himself to walk, not run, to his office. He shut the door and pulled out his personal cell phone. He hit the buttons excitedly.

"Hey, it's Chester. Man, do I have big news! Henry Lindon called Jane at home last night and wants to have an urgent meeting this afternoon. He's flying in from Dallas to pitch a deal. I knew that spineless academic would fold like a cheap suit. I'm sure it's a deal to settle the Foreign Corrupt Practices Act violation. I told you keeping pressure on Henry would work! How do you like that?"

Guy Wheeless's voice echoed over the cell. Chester could tell he was pleased. For once.

"Nice work," Wheeless said. "Call me as soon as you hear from Birney. We have Henry on the ropes. When this comes together, there will be a nice bonus for you. And Chester—there will be no settlement, no deal with Henry. Just get the information we need to make a case for the Department of Justice to start an investigation."

Wheeless hung up, elated. The pursuit of Henry was proving to be more delicious than his cleverly orchestrated disbarment of Dan Moore. Thinking of Dan, he unconsciously looked down at his shoe as he methodically pushed down and released the vintage chrome Swingline stapler on his desktop. His desk phone rang and he picked up.

"Edward O'Brian is here, sir," his assistant said.

"It's about time. Send him in." Wheeless folded his arms across his chest and a second later O'Brian hurried through the door.

"Edward, where the hell have you been?" Wheeless asked, in an ill temper.

"Sorry to keep you waiting." O'Brian looked nervously at the corner of Wheeless's curled-up mouth. "I was down on the trading floor trying to unwind our position on the wrong side of a Brazilian real trade. It should save us almost a million."

"All right, sit down. Give me an update on Henry Lindon and the Foreign Corrupt Practices Act investigation you were supposed to make sure Birney is launching with the Department of Justice. What do you hear?"

O'Brian gave Wheeless an apologetic look and scratched his head. "Last I heard, Birney's unwilling to do anything with the Department of Justice, and Henry's stonewalling."

Wheeless drummed his fingertips in front of him. "So, as far as you know, there's nothing going on, no progress?" asked Wheeless.

"I'm afraid that's right," O'Brian said, swallowing hard.

"What if I told you," Wheeless said, with a scowl on his face, "that Henry called Birney last night to offer a deal?"

Sweat beaded up across O'Brian's forehead as he answered. "Why, I'd—I'd be surprised . . . I'd be very surprised."

"I'll tell you what you ought to be!" barked Wheeless. "You ought to be wondering why I don't fire your sorry ass! Am I the only one around here that gets anything done?" He stood, picked up one of his antique Swingline staplers, carefully weighed it in his hand, and violently hurled it against the wall. "Get the hell out of here!" he bellowed. O'Brian scurried away like a terrified mouse.

Sitting back down at his desk, Wheeless calmed himself by smoothing his perfectly pressed lapels. O'Brian had to go. He was smart as hell and his uncanny grasp of financial markets had made Wheeless a fortune. But the skinny bastard had no understanding of priorities. However, this was a banner day, and he would not allow O'Brian's ineptitude to ruin it. He would deal with O'Brian next week.

Wheeless straightened his shoulders, opened the red folder on his desk, and slowly thumbed through the photographs of the museum guide. His special date with the woman who looked so much like that stone bitch Jane Birney was scheduled for the following night.

The coincidence of Chester's call about Birney and his date with Birney's look-alike was tantalizing. With the great professor about to take a precipitous fall from grace, Nichole out of his hair, and tomorrow evening's activities ready to go—nothing, but nothing, would be allowed to dampen his mood.

20

Henry arrived at the Ambassador Club conference room on Thursday morning, two hours early for his one o'clock meeting with Birney. He sent an email to the conference-room copier and printed out two copies of a single-page agreement. Looking again at his watch, he realized that in less than twenty-four hours, Dan Moore would make his report to the Wichita police. Soon, any chance to make a deal with Jane Birney would evaporate.

Henry's phone rang. It was Ken Maltman. He let it go to voicemail. Predictably, Maltman's message asked whether Henry was ready to start the vetting process for the Wein CEO job. Henry smiled sadly at the irony. If his meeting with Birney was unsuccessful, there would be no need to go through the vetting process—the whole world would soon know he was under investigation by the Department of Justice.

His phone rang again. This time it was Marvin.

"Yo, where are you?"

"I'm sitting in a conference room at JFK," Henry said.

"What the hell?" Marvin snorted. "You need to get your fanny back in Dallas by 3 p.m. tomorrow afternoon. I got one big-ass surprise!"

Henry sighed. "Look, Marvin, I've got some important business here. What's so pressing?"

"Henry, it's a surprise. I'm tellin' you this is mighty important. Have I ever misled you?"

Yes, you've misled me and screwed things up any number of times, he thought. "Marvin, I'll do my best. Bye."

As he clicked off the phone, Henry spotted Jane Birney through the conference room's glass wall. She was making her way through the crowded lounge area with her briefcase hanging from her shoulder by a long strap and dragging her roller bag behind her. As always, she wore a fixed Botox mask.

Henry left the conference room to meet her. As they awkwardly shook hands, her briefcase slipped from her shoulder, landed on their joined hands, and Henry caught it before it hit the floor.

"Nice catch, Henry," Jane said, breaking the tension.

Settling into the conference room, Henry reminded himself that Jane was all business, all the time. Small talk would get him nowhere. His best chance of success was to get to the point, quickly.

"Jane, I appreciate you rearranging your schedule." Henry took the pen out of his shirt pocket and placed it on the table. "I've thought about our discussion in Mexico City, and I did some research on UNS. I have a proposal that I believe will solve both our problems. Before we start, I have a Rule 408 agreement for us to sign. It's real simple: This meeting and everything we say is a compromise negotiation and nothing about it will be admissible in evidence if there's ever litigation."

Jane quickly read the one-page agreement and, without asking a single question, signed it and requested a signed copy back from Henry.

"After our lunch in Mexico City, I was struck by a couple of things," Henry began. "The accusations Chester made about the San Miguel Galletas transaction in Argentina made no sense. I looked at it from every possible angle and I can see no feasible violation of the Foreign Corrupt Practices Act. I got to thinking that something else must be in play."

"Are you looking for me to comment?" Jane asked with a wave of her hand.

"No, it's best if you hear me out," Henry said with an assuring smile. "You said a Midwest hedge fund is making your life very difficult. I lived in the corporate world for a long time and I know what it's like when an activist investor has a company in his sights."

Jane sighed. "Please tell me you didn't ask me to turn my schedule upside down to talk about activist investors?"

"Just hear me out," said Henry, putting up his hand. "My research revealed that a hedge fund run by a man named Guy Wheeless Jr. out of Wichita has a huge position in UNS and he's the one making life miserable for you folks."

Henry saw a flicker of recognition in the woman's eyes, but her face remained locked in stillness. "How do you know your information is correct?" she asked.

"Let's just say I have a friend who makes it his business to know this kind of thing," Henry said with a tilt of his head. "Here's what I'm thinking—Wheeless is all over UNS and pressured you to investigate the San Miguel deal and my role in the deal."

"Assuming you're correct, for the sake of argument, where does all this conjecture get us?" Jane asked.

"Here's where it gets us," Henry said, slightly cocking his head. "I'm in a unique position to solve your problem. I can get Wheeless out of your hair, permanently. I'm willing to make that happen if you agree to drop your Foreign Corrupt Practices Act investigation."

"Let's review the bidding here," Jane said, slowly tapping a clear-lacquered nail on the conference table. "Are you telling me you have some magic trick up your sleeve to make Guy Wheeless Jr. drop his attacks on UNS? And all you want in exchange for your wizardry is for me to drop an investigation that you have just finished arguing, yet again, is baseless?"

"About sums it up," Henry said with a grin. "You have an enormous upside and nothing to lose."

"Why would you make that deal?" Jane said, leaning back from the conference table. "Why use your mysterious power over Wheeless to get him off our backs and ask for nothing more than dropping an investigation? An investigation you say is baseless? This all sounds too good to be true."

"It's real straightforward," Henry said with a shrug. "I now have a far simpler life as a professor, and I want to tie up the loose ends from my former life. We both know that litigation has nothing to do with fairness and everything to do with who has the deepest pockets. After watching Chester get all lathered up, I bet he's willing to do just about anything to prove his point. I want to move down the line without looking over my shoulder."

"Can you assure me that no illegal action will be taken?" asked Jane.

"No illegal action will be taken by me or anyone working with me. In the end, Wheeless will no longer be a problem for you."

"Then we have a deal," Jane said as she stood. "Care to tell me what kind of spell you're conjuring up for Mr. Wheeless?"

"I think it's best for everyone if I keep the details to myself."

"I thought you might say that. You're a curious man, Henry. People don't see you coming, do they?"

"I have no idea what you mean."

"I think you know exactly what I mean," she said, trying to force a smile. "When can I expect delivery from your end?"

"No point in delay," Henry said, clipping the pen into his shirt pocket. "If we're done here, I'll make a call and set things in motion. Once I make the call, you can consider Wheeless gone."

Jane walked around the table, and stuck out her hand to shake. With an inquisitive look in her eyes, she said, "Henry, your gift is that people underestimate you. I'd love to think we'll be in touch, but it's probably not in the cards. Safe flight home."

Henry waited until she gathered her bags and left the conference room, then he broke into a self-satisfied grin. Jane believed she had negotiated a great deal. She would receive the windfall of getting Guy Wheeless Jr. out of her hair for nothing more than dropping a worthless investigation. But Henry knew he was the one who had hit the jackpot. He dialed Dan Moore's number.

"Dan? We're ready to roll. Sure appreciate you giving me the time to resolve things on my end. The meeting with Jane Birney went precisely according to the plan we discussed at my place."

"My pleasure. I wonder what Jane will think when she learns exactly how you got Guy Jr. off her back! Tomorrow's Black Friday for old dickface."

"Hey, Dan, one more thing," Henry said. "The other night we stayed up awfully late, drank far more than our share, and maybe said some things we shouldn't have."

"My aching head the next morning confirmed that. Please tell me you didn't open a second bottle of bourbon," said Dan.

"Afraid I did. Well, we covered a fair amount of territory, but one thing you said has been weighing on me . . . Dan, did you say you were the one who put the cherry bomb in the chapel candlesnuffer?"

"Said it, did it," replied Dan.

"Why keep it under your hat all these years?" Henry's hand was firmly on his cowlick. "We've talked about the cherry bomb incident about a hundred times and you never even hinted you were responsible."

"Sheer embarrassment," admitted Dan. "Henry, you and Marvin planned and executed that whole deal with the gal going heels over head in Wheeless's car. That prank lit up the high-school phone lines for weeks. It was the biggest thing that had ever happened. Let's face it, I just tagged along.

"So, I wanted to get a leg up on you boys. Thought you two would think the cherry bomb gag was hysterical. You know, with Guy Jr. so proud of that stupid tattoo and having a cherry bomb blow up in his face. But then . . . half his ear got blown off—all of a sudden it wasn't funny. I was scared shitless. So, I decided to keep it to myself for a bit—before I knew it, that bit became decades."

Henry could visualize Dan pulling on his soul patch. "But after all these years, all the times we've talked about that day in the chapel and speculated endlessly about who did the deed. How could you keep it to yourself?"

"At first I was afraid to say anything and then, as time passed, fear transformed into embarrassment. That embarrassment about keeping it to myself grew into a mighty powerful force. You probably don't know what I mean."

Henry laughed. "But I do," he said. "Take care, Dan. Marylou and I owe you a visit." He disconnected and thought about what Dan had said as he packed up his briefcase to catch the next flight back to Dallas.

He understood Dan's reasons for staying silent. For Henry, keeping a secret for too long had almost cost him his marriage.

■ ■ ■

Walking up the stairs of Southerland University's Hunt Hall at a quarter to three on Friday afternoon, Henry leaned into Marylou and asked his question for the tenth time that day.

"Come on, tell me what Marvin's cooked up."

"You never give up, do you?" Marylou said, giving him a playful shove with her shoulder. "And no, I'm not going to tell you. Marvin swore me to secrecy."

"I bet I know what he's up to," Henry mused. "He's corralled some hot-shot high school basketball prospect for Southerland, and they're going to announce the signing."

Marylou laughed and took his hand, squeezing his fingers lightly. "I'm not saying another word other than you're working in the wrong hemisphere."

"Do you realize," said Henry, "that at this very moment Dan Moore and his investigators are with the Wichita police detailing Guy Jr.'s crimes?"

"That misogynist sicko deserves whatever he gets," Marylou replied. "Darling, your plan was genius in its simplicity. Now it's time to shut the door on Wheeless and toss away the key. Leave everything that's happened in Wichita, in Wichita. Please, just enjoy the here and now."

"I will," he promised, squeezing her hand in return. "I promise."

As they reached the top of the stairs of Hunt Hall and passed the six huge Corinthian pillars guarding the entry, they got their first glimpse of the crowd gathering inside. Pushing through the door, Henry spotted a camera crew.

"Look over there. That's an NBC film crew. Whatever Marvin is up to must be a big deal."

Henry saw Marvin, standing, as usual, a conspicuous head taller than the rest of the crowd. Uncharacteristically, he was wearing a well-pressed, light-grey summer Zegna suit with a powder-blue shirt and a blazing-red

Southerland University tie. Marvin caught Henry's eye and signaled them to join him as he moved to the left of the press-conference podium.

As they wound through the crowded Hunt Hall rotunda, Henry spotted John-O leaning against one of the room's concave walls and chatting with Marvin's ex-wife, Susan.

"I'm delighted you two jet-setters could make it," Marvin said, when they finally reached his side. "You won't be disappointed. Henry, today's fixin' to be a banner day for the Lindon family."

As Marvin wrapped his arm around Marylou's shoulder and gave her a warm hug, Henry was about to ask Marvin what was happening, when the crowd began to politely applaud. President Phil Thomas strode to the podium, acknowledging the applause with his right hand while he buttoned his blazer's middle button with his left.

"Welcome, friends of Southerland," he shouted, as he turned his better side to the television cameras. "Today marks a game-changing chapter in the storied history of Southerland athletics. Today will be remembered as the first step to reclaim the past success—with all due modesty, I think it is fair to say—past glory, of our men's basketball program. And it is fitting that this day is made possible by one of the greatest and certainly the most exciting basketball player in Southerland's history! I am proud to call this man not only a Southerland teammate, but a lifelong friend. That man is, of course, Marvelous Marvin Lindon!"

A grinning Marvin took a step forward to give the crowd a wave. The room erupted in applause that echoed off the rotunda's ornate ceiling as John-O led a good-natured "Mar-vel-ous, Mar-vel-ous!" chant.

"Through Marvin Lindon's remarkable generosity," President Thomas continued, "we are now able to break ground on a new basketball arena that will be the very finest in collegiate America. The home of Southerland basketball will be second to none. Our new facility will help attract the caliber of student athlete this great university and this world-class city justly deserve!" He paused and gazed out at the gathered crowd. Henry smiled, realizing the pompous man seemed to be sincerely excited.

"And now," he continued, "I have the privilege to announce that our new facility will bear this proud name—the Lindon Brothers Arena!"

Henry's mouth dropped open as Marylou squeezed his arm and leaned her head against his shoulder. He looked down at her and she beamed up at him.

As Marvin moved toward the podium to accept President Thomas's extended hand and pose for photographs, he gave Henry and Marylou a stage wink. Henry shook his head and smiled.

"Marvin," he whispered to Marylou, "you gotta love him."

Henry saw Marvin signaling him to come to the podium. He kissed Marylou and then she pushed him forward, to the sound of further applause. Henry walked over to the podium and was pulled forward by President Thomas's vigorous handshake. Thomas then expertly maneuvered the brothers to either side of him to pose for the press.

"Now it's time to hear from the man who made all of this possible," President Thomas announced. "Marvelous Marvin Lindon!"

"I'll try not to embarrass you," Marvin whispered to Henry as he moved to the podium and began to speak.

"Thank you, President Thomas, for your kind words, and also a heartfelt thanks to all of you who braved the heat to be here this afternoon. Today is a big day for my brother, Henry, and me. We were raised on a wheat farm in a tiny town called McPherson, Kansas. We were, in the truest sense of the words, farm boys. That farm taught us the values of hard work, self-reliance, and brotherhood. We've lived in Dallas for most of our years, but that farm's dirt flows through our veins and is probably still under our nails."

The crowd laughed and Marvin laughed with them. As Marvin described Southerland's pivotal role in his life, Henry's mind drifted to the meeting going on inside the Wichita police station. It was ironic that while he and Marvin stood basking in their good fortune, Dan Moore was turning Guy Wheeless Jr.'s life upside down. Were Dan's actions just another skirmish in the decades-long cycle of revenge? Had his disclosure to Detective Ortiz about Guy Jr.'s relationship with Nichole reinserted himself into that endless loop?

Henry was jolted back into the moment by the crowd's burst of laughter in response to Marvin's story about his student days at Southerland.

"I could stand here all afternoon tellin' stories 'bout Southerland, but I believe livin' in the present is life's best course. Since I'm havin' a celebration at my place as soon as we finish here, and heaven knows I do love a good party, the time is right to say thanks y'all . . . good afternoon . . . and GO SOUTHERLAND!"

■■■

By the time Henry and Marylou had returned home, changed clothes, and driven to Marvin's apartment, the celebration was at a full roar. The apartment was jammed with many more people than had attended the campus ceremony. An invitation to one of Marvin's parties was rarely declined.

Slender waitresses dressed in bright green, yellow, and black Jamaican-flag dresses sashayed around the noisy room offering a variety of Caribbean dishes, including jerk chicken, salt fish, and fried plantains.

At the bar, Marylou ordered a glass of orange-colored rum punch with a matching umbrella. Henry opted for a Red Stripe beer.

"I can hear music up on the party roof," said Henry. "Want to take a look?"

"Way too hot, I'll just mingle down here in the air-conditioning," replied Marylou while fanning her face with her hand.

Henry opened the glass doors to the terrace and climbed the stairs to the Caribbean sounds of a four-piece steel band. Blinded by the dazzling light reflecting off Dallas's downtown glass towers, he slipped on his sunglasses. On the roof, he found the enthusiastic musicians playing with huge smiles despite the shine of sweat on their faces and arms.

A group of intrepid partygoers stood slowly swaying to the island sounds while cooling themselves in the clouds of mist spraying from the rooftop's pergolas. Henry made small talk with the group, but he soon surrendered to the heat and headed for the air-conditioned apartment below.

As Henry was about to start down, he saw Marvin climbing up the stairs.

Marvin stepped onto the rooftop with both hands shielding his eyes from the sun.

"Been lookin' high and low for you. Whaddaya think about the Lindon Brothers Arena?"

"It's terrific and you're mighty generous to include me in the name," Henry said, clapping his brother on the back.

Henry noticed Marvin was wearing long sleeves, despite the heat, and wondered if he was having second thoughts about his tattoo.

"My pleasure," Marvin said, moving to get the sun out of his eyes. "Hey, we haven't really talked since the night we got back from the farm. I know that by definition brothers fight, but let's bury the hatchet. I'm feelin' real bad that John-O and me . . . kinda made a tougher road for you with the Department of Justice. What can I do to help?"

"Not a thing."

"Come on, don't be that way. Let me help."

"The problem's gone," said Henry, with arms playfully raised to the sky. "Vanished into thin air."

"Hot damn! There ya go. I knew all along you could handle it, never a doubt! How'd you make it disappear?"

Henry waited a beat before answering. "Since a woman was involved, I think this falls within your definition of the Code of the West."

"So?"

"So, I'm keeping all details to myself." Henry had finally learned that loving his brother and not trusting him were not mutually exclusive.

"The Code doesn't apply to brothers. Now why are you smilin' like that?"

"Because you're my brother, I love you, and there's not a damn thing I can do about it."

"Not sure what the hell that means. So, you're not going to tell me?"

"Nope, I'm not going to tell you."

"Well if that's the way it is, might as well go back down to the party."

"I saw Susan at the announcement," Henry said as they headed down the stairs. "It's good to see her again, and Marylou loves her company."

"Yep, she's workin' her way back into the startin' lineup."

Reentering the apartment through the terrace's glass doors, the brothers ran into well-wishers excited about the coming Lindon Brothers Arena. Henry turned to get another Red Stripe and Marvin headed for the kitchen, where he leaned against the polished steel counter and began regaling a group of friends.

In the living room, Henry saw Marylou in a conspiratorial conversation with a woman in a short, lemon-yellow dress with an oversize silver zipper running down the length of the back—it was Susan, Marvin's ex-wife and current date. Henry watched as Marylou bent forward at the waist, put one hand on Susan's arm, and cupped her other hand over her mouth.

He made his way through the crowd to the two women and asked, "Hey, you two, what's so funny?"

Henry's innocent question ignited giggles. "Just talking . . . men," a laughing Marylou responded, triggering greater hilarity from Susan.

He furrowed his brow, giving a look of fake disapproval, and then laughed, shaking his head. Marvin appeared at his side and asked, "What's so funny?"

"You two," said Marylou, eliciting a giggle from Susan. "Look at the two of you. You've been acting like this for as long as I can remember."

"Acting like what?" Henry asked.

"You're as mean as a couple of rattlesnakes to each other," Susan said. "And in the next breath, loving beyond reason. Men!"

At that moment, an inebriated John-O came up behind Marvin and put him in a tight bear hug, lifting Marvin high off the ground. Marvin howled in delight and joyfully kicked his legs in the air. Susan turned to Marylou and said, "Yup, men!"

John-O let Marvin loose and said, "This is a photo op. The four of you scrunch together and give me your best smiles."

As John-O moved into position with his iPhone, Marylou whispered to Henry, "Still thinking about leaving the university?"

"Still thinking. Smile."

21

As the island-themed party in Marvin's apartment caromed into the night, Wichita police lieutenant Will Klepper banged on the door to Guy Wheeless's private residence on top of the Bunker.

"Mr. Wheeless," Klepper shouted at the door, "we know you're in there. Don't make us break down the damn door."

As two patrolmen prepared to do exactly that, Wheeless opened the door, dressed in a black silk kimono. He looked over the three officers with narrowed eyes.

"What can I do for you?" he asked, pulling the robe's sash tighter.

"Mr. Guy Wheeless Jr., you are under arrest for criminal assault and battery." Taking a laminated card out of his coat pocket, Klepper began to read the Miranda warning:

"You have the right to remain silent when questioned. Anything you say or do may be used against you in a court of law. You have the right to consult an attorney before speaking to the police and to have an attorney present during questioning now or in the future . . ."

"Cut the bullshit, I know my rights!" Wheeless snapped. "What the hell do you want?"

"Cuff him and put him in the car," ordered the lieutenant. "I'll be down in a minute."

As Wheeless was being cuffed, Klepper heard him mumble, "Little bitch, that little bitch."

"You talking to me, Mr. Wheeless?" Klepper said in a no-nonsense voice.

Wheeless said nothing and turned his head away.

Lieutenant Klepper had heard rumors about the plush living quarters atop the Bunker and had read the witness statements about the alleged assaults that took place there. He decided to take a look for himself. He reached into his coat for his tin, inserted a pinch of Copenhagen under his lip, and headed into the apartment.

The apartment's living room decor confused him . . . it was entirely Victorian. Dainty side tables were covered with white lace doilies and the room's only lights were dark, stained-glass Tiffany lamps next to the tables. Over the carved chestnut fireplace mantelpiece was an ornate oil painting of a Cavalier King Charles spaniel.

A tall silver vase filled with peacock feathers sat next to the fireplace. The walls were covered with dozens of oil paintings of various sizes and shapes. All the paintings were of different breeds of dogs. Klepper picked up the only photograph in the room. It was a small photograph in a silver frame of a young Wheeless, his mother, and the family collie. If Klepper had not known better, he would have assumed an aging dowager lived in the apartment.

When he opened the door to the bedroom, the contrast was jarring. The enormous bed, against the rear wall, was anchored on each corner by square posters of highly polished steel. The cold hardwood floor had no carpet. In the middle of the fifteen-foot-high ceiling was an eight-inch hook holding a steel chain. Hanging from the chain, two feet off the floor, was a chrome cage large enough for a kneeling human. Klepper gave the cage a slight turn. In one corner of the cage was what appeared to be human hair.

On the floor beside the bed were two small bowls, one filled with water, the other with dry dog food. There were no other signs of dogs. Klepper walked around the bed and saw on the floor a large, lumpy, white athletic sock. He picked it up and toyed with the contents. He put the sock to his nose to confirm what he suspected—it was filled with soap bars. He concluded it was the "weapon" described in one of the assault reports.

He walked across the bedroom to the closet door. As he opened the door, lights came on, exposing a vast illuminated space. He walked into the closet past scores of perfectly pressed suits on one side and shirts of every imaginable color on the other. At the end of the shirt racks was a tie carousel. He could not resist pushing the on button. As the ties cycled past, he guessed there were easily a thousand.

The closet ended in a T shape. Down the right corridor were enough shoes to make Imelda Marcos green with envy. The left side was empty except for a door at the end. Klepper walked down the twenty-foot hallway and tried the door. It was locked. He knew it was against regulations to open a locked door at a crime scene without a witness. He tried the door again and then called out to see if anyone else was in the apartment. Satisfied he was alone, he reached into his back pocket for his sheath of SouthOrd lock picks. He chose a pick with the correct gauge, opened the door in less than a minute, and stepped into another closet.

On the right side of the closet were a series of chrome Shaker hooks. Above each hook was a number between one and twenty engraved on a bronze oval. Hanging from each hook was a dog costume. Some of the costumes were indistinguishable, but the Dalmatian, poodle, and Great Dane were obvious.

He moved up and down the closet, examining the costumes. He stopped in front of the poodle costume and touched the hair. It was soft to the touch and felt human. Klepper remembered his sixteen-year-old had wanted hair extensions for her birthday. Klepper had been surprised at the cost of the extensions and that they were made from human hair from Brazil or Malaysia. He wondered if all the costumes had been made from human hair.

He took the collie costume off the hook to examine its construction. It was no Halloween costume. There were holes for arms and legs and a hat with ears that came over the wearer's head, leaving the face exposed. Under the tail was a flap with snaps. Klepper recalled the photograph of Wheeless, his mother, and the pet collie. A shudder of disgust ran through him and he dropped the collie costume on the floor. Dropping the costume was a rookie error but he was not about to touch it again.

On a stand-up desk at the end of the costumes was a black leather-bound notebook. A silver pen was inserted between two pages to mark a spot. Klepper paged through the book. Each page contained the name of a woman, a date, and a number between one and twenty next to the name. At least three names had the number nine next to them—he looked over at the rack of costumes and realized the number nine was assigned to the collie costume.

In all, there were thirty-four women's names written in neat print. The last page had a name and that day's date written on it, but no corresponding number. The name without a number was Jennifer Sessel. Klepper took out the notepad from his shirt pocket and wrote down her name.

Back in the bedroom, he again surveyed the room and shook his head—*and I thought I'd seen everything*. He called the police station and ordered a team of technicians to the scene, immediately. After placing yellow police barricade tape across the door to cordon off the apartment, he crossed the hall and entered the elevator to go downstairs and join the other officers.

As Klepper exited the building he saw a commotion on the street. An attractive woman with flowing brunette hair, dressed in a green dress for a night on the town, was trying to communicate with Guy Wheeless Jr. He was sitting handcuffed in the back of the police car. The woman was rapping her knuckles on the car windows and calling to Wheeless, but he remained silent and stared straight ahead. To his right, Klepper saw a muscular man in a chauffeur suit standing with folded arms next to a gunmetal-grey Bentley parked well behind the police car.

Lieutenant Klepper approached the distraught woman. "Ma'am, everything all right?"

"No, everything is not all right, officer," she answered, turning to face him. "There's been a terrible mistake. I have a date with this gentleman tonight," she said, pointing at Wheeless, "and for no reason, he's been arrested. Do you have any idea who this man is and what he means to this city?"

"Ma'am, I know his name. He's Guy Wheeless Jr." Klepper took the notepad out of his shirt pocket and after glancing at his note asked, "By any chance, is your name Jennifer Sessel?"

"That's correct. How did you know that?"

"Well, I know one more thing, ma'am," Klepper said as he moved his gaze to Wheeless. "You are one lucky woman."

■■■

Henry was up Saturday morning at dawn, despite getting home late from Marvin's Caribbean soiree. In his bathrobe, he retrieved *The Dallas Morning News* from his front stoop.

Turning to the sports section, he was pleased to see the headline:

LINDON BROTHERS ARENA TO BE SOUTHERLAND BASKETBALL'S NEW HOME

A very different news story had drifted in and out of his head all night. He turned on his computer, took a deep breath, and googled *The Wichita Eagle*. There was no missing Saturday's lead story.

PROMINENT WICHITA BUSINESSMAN ARRESTED ON CRIMINAL ASSAULT CHARGES

A task force of local and state authorities took into custody well-known business and civic leader Guy Wheeless Jr. on multiple charges of criminal assault and battery. The arrest was made Friday evening at Mr. Wheeless's private residence at the Wheeless Strategic Fund offices on First Street.

In the only official comment about the arrest, Police Commissioner Robert Craine released the following statement: "After months of intensive and coordinated investigation by local and state law enforcement, Guy Wheeless Jr. was taken into custody and charged with multiple counts of criminal assault and battery. He is currently being held in the Sedgwick County jail. There will be no further public statements about the arrest until after the bail hearing scheduled for Monday afternoon."

> An anonymous source disclosed that five women have provided police with sworn statements detailing alleged assaults by Mr. Wheeless. Mr. Wheeless's spokesman, Edward P. O'Brian, was unavailable for comment.

Henry turned off his computer. It was over. Just weeks earlier he had been besieged by intractable problems, and now, with a bit of creativity and a touch of luck, it was over. He tucked *The Dallas Morning News* under his arm, poured two mugs of coffee, and, with a hop in his step, headed up the stairs to share his good news.

He bent over a sleeping Marylou and gently waved a mug of coffee under her nose. In a few seconds, her eyes fluttered open. She sat up and giggled. "I do love my morning coffee," she said. Henry handed her the coffee mug and hoisted himself onto the bed. They clinked the mugs in a toast.

"What are we celebrating?" she asked.

"I've made a decision," Henry said.

"Well glory be, a decision from you is always a momentous occasion. Cue the royal trumpets!" she teased. "What have you decided?"

"With the turmoil of the last few months, I didn't give teaching a real chance. I'm staying at Southerland to see if I can make a go of it. With the pandemonium behind us, it's time to focus on things that really count. We've got a lot on our plate, with a grandchild to welcome into the world and a wheat farm to sell."

Marylou smiled and raised her coffee mug. "I'll drink to all of it! It's a brand-new day for us, literally and figuratively. All that craziness is in the rearview mirror."

"Yep, a brand-new day," Henry agreed, not entirely confident of his words.

22

A week later, Esmeralda Ortiz sat in the waiting room of Wheeless's former office. Reviewing her iPad notes of her useless interview with Wheeless, she feared her trip to Wichita would be a bust.

Wheeless, on the advice of his attorney, had cited the Fifth Amendment right against self-incrimination in response to her questions. With each refusal to answer, Wheeless had given her a needling look that had gotten under her skin. To avoid the trip being a total waste, she decided to interview the interim head of the Wheeless Strategic Fund, Edward O'Brian.

O'Brian had kept her waiting for forty-five minutes. She decided to run word searches on her notes to evaluate any commonality among the witness statements. When she ran "Wichita," she was surprised at the numerous mentions of the city. As she contemplated the significance of the repetition, the door to the waiting room opened.

"Detective Ortiz," the secretary said, "Mr. O'Brian will see you now."

As the terribly thin O'Brian came around the glass-topped desk to greet her, Ortiz wondered if he had some kind of parasite.

"Thanks for seeing me," Ortiz said. "This must be a difficult time for you."

O'Brian's smile faded into a somber grimace. "Yes, well, we have work to do, but we'll get it under control. Please, let's sit over here at the conference table. Can we get you some coffee, tea?"

"I'd love a cup of tea, thanks." She was grateful to avoid another cup of coffee. From her seat at the conference table she looked around the office. There was not a single photo or other memorabilia.

With the fine china saucer in one hand and his coffee cup in the other, O'Brian looked very much at ease. "I assume you're here to discuss the tragic death of Nichole Kessler, Guy's niece?" he said.

"Correct. Mr. Wheeless was unwilling to provide any information, so I hope you can fill in some of the background. Since you're sitting in his office, is it fair to assume you're now running the business?"

"Yes," replied O'Brian. "The bylaws of the Wheeless Strategic Fund provide that if the chairman is indisposed and unable to fulfill the obligations of his office, the chief operating officer assumes all those powers for the period the chairman is indisposed. I was the chief operating officer, so here I sit."

"Mr. O'Brian, did you know the deceased, Nichole Kessler?"

"Never met her."

"Have you and Mr. Wheeless talked about her?"

"Oh yes," O'Brian said, with a knowing nod.

"What do you remember hearing?"

"Guy and his niece had a . . . let's call it, a contentious relationship."

"Why?"

"Guy's father set up a trust for Nikkie," explained O'Brian, placing his cup on the saucer. "When Nikkie's mother, Guy's sister, unexpectedly passed away, Guy became the trustee. That relationship led to friction."

"Do you know why there was friction?" Ortiz pulled her long braid over her shoulder. She wished O'Brian would stop sneaking looks at the scar on her chin.

"As I understand the situation, Nikkie asked Guy to provide her an accounting of the assets in the trust. For obvious reasons, he refused."

"What obvious reasons?"

"The trust was materially depleted. We are doing an internal investigation to determine how that happened. As you might imagine, we're not in the habit of losing money."

"That would be a good reason for friction," Ortiz said, as she made notes on her tablet. "Do you know any other basis for the poor state of their relationship?"

O'Brian waited a moment before responding. "Nikkie was paid an annual allowance to cover school and living expenses. It was a generous amount. Guy learned she was using that money to have him investigated by a man named Dan Moore. He was understandably upset."

"How did Wheeless know he was being investigated?" Ortiz looked searchingly at O'Brian. He was straddling the borderline between cooperative and manipulative.

"No idea," he said.

His left eyelid was twitching. O'Brian was lying. She was confident O'Brian knew how Wheeless learned of Dan Moore's investigation. She wondered what was on the thin man's agenda. "Okay, any other reason they didn't get along?"

"This will sound silly," O'Brian said, removing his glasses. "But Guy is a very meticulous dresser and it offended him that Nikkie was a jeans-and-tee-shirt kind of girl."

"So, he didn't like the way she dressed?"

"Yeah," O'Brian said, cleaning his glasses with a handkerchief. "I remember a couple of times he complained about a particular tee shirt she wore."

Ortiz watched O'Brian intently as he held his glasses up to the ceiling lights. "Was there anything special about the tee shirt?"

"As I recall," O'Brian said, putting his glasses back on, "Guy said it was a red Southerland University tee shirt."

Ortiz said nothing for an uncomfortable moment. Information about the red tee shirt around Nichole's neck had been withheld from the press. She debated whether O'Brian was playing her, giving his honest recollection, or both. "Mr. O'Brian, have you been in Dallas in the past two weeks?"

"Yes, I attended Nichole's funeral with Guy. A sad affair. I may be mistaken, but I think I saw you there."

"That's correct, I was there. Just that one trip?"

"Yes, Guy and I flew down on the corporate jet."

"Do you know if Mr. Wheeless visited Dallas another time before the funeral?"

"He may have." O'Brian cocked his head in a look of nonchalance. "There's an easy way to find out. Guy never flies anywhere without using the corporate jet. The jet has a very specific log that the FAA requires we keep. It documents who has flown where. If you think the log might help in your investigation, my assistant can provide you with a copy."

"Thanks for your time, Mr. O'Brian," Ortiz said, standing to leave. "I wish you luck in your new position. Looks like you might be running the show here for the foreseeable future."

"Quite possibly, Detective," O'Brian said, shaking Ortiz's hand with an earnest look on his face.

Ortiz stopped at the secretary's desk on her way out. "Mr. O'Brian is certainly a nice young man," she said.

"Oh yes," said the young assistant. "To tell you the truth, lots of folks around here are happy to see him in charge."

"I don't want to make work for you," said Ortiz, "but Mr. O'Brian said I could get a copy of the corporate jet log."

"No trouble at all," the assistant replied, reaching for a folder on the corner of her desk. "Mr. O'Brian asked me to make a copy of it after you called. He thought you might want to review it, especially last Thursday's flights. I clipped the spot. Mr. O'Brian is very diligent; he thinks of everything. Have a nice day."

Ortiz left the Wheeless Strategic Fund building, confident Guy Wheeless was her man. Everything about Wheeless made him good for the murder. The fact that he was already incarcerated for crimes against women was frosting on the cake. But . . . there was a vague, nagging voice in the back of her head damping down her excitement. As she thought through each step of her investigation, the source of the nagging voice gradually appeared out of the shadows.

How had Wheeless become a person of interest? Witnesses had told her that Nichole had no family. It was like Wheeless appeared out of a vacuum. But he hadn't come out of nowhere. Henry Lindon and Henry Lindon alone had pointed her in Guy Wheeless's direction. Without Henry's suggestion, she might have chased her tail for months and maybe never focused on Wheeless.

Had Henry Lindon fingered Wheeless simply in the interest of being forthright? After all, he had been truthful about the tattoo incident in his office. Or did Lindon have some ulterior motive? Was there some significance to the fact that so many of the people involved were from Wichita? Did something happen in Wichita that she needed to track down?

She dismissed her doubts. In the end, Lindon's motives were of no consequence. All that mattered was that she had her man; she would solve her case.

23

One year later. Cell B-208, Leavenworth Penitentiary, Leavenworth, Kansas

Today's session with that pathetic, so-called psychiatrist bitch ended like all the others. I supposedly need to forgive those bimbos who testified against me at the trial before I can get on the road to rehabilitation. Rehabilitation, my ass. I'll be out of here before I step one foot in that direction.

My lawyers tell me the police have zero physical evidence tying me to Nikkie's murder. That's exactly right—do they think I'm stupid? The red tee shirt was a brilliant touch. It will drive them nuts. And the little doggie misunderstanding Nikkie couldn't stop harping on? That's all safely buried now. Buried. Just like Nikkie.

I can smell it, hear it on the wind, feel it between my teeth. Somehow, someway Henry is responsible for me being inside. That prick thinks he shines like the sun. He thought he was so smug, so professorial, giving that eulogy. He's clueless about what Nikkie was really like. Hiring Dan Moore to spy on me and constantly complaining about her trust fund—she was a perpetual pain in the ass.

Someday real soon I'll get something to stick to Henry from that Argentina deal, and when I do, I'll cloud up and rain all over him. Up next, Marvin will taste the crescendo of my retribution. Perfect.

Nothing and no one in Henry's life is safe. His little wife is already teed up. My people assure me that her new trinket, all those thousands of stupid yellow ducks, will arrive from China adorned with a most unfortunate lead paint. When we leak that little product-design flaw, there'll be hell to pay. And that will be just the start of their problems. What that good-looking woman sees in that putz is beyond me.

Thank God for Larry and his stint here in Club Fed. With him taking care of the guards from the outside, I just relax and take care of business from the inside. The privacy of solitary confinement and a smuggled Samsung Chromebook are not too shabby. Not too shabby at all. Larry assures me he and the others are making solid progress on getting the bimbos to recant their testimony. Money talks and someday real soon I'll walk right out of here.

I have no intention of evening the score with Henry—I'm going to run it up. Like my father said, "Kill my cat, better watch your dog." Revenge is never cheap or quick. I've always had the money and now I have the time.

THANKS

First, thanks to Sally and Tess at Greenleaf; without them, there would not have been a book. And thanks to so many friends and family members who patiently read along the way through various drafts—Chad, Lyn, Nat, Mike and Christine, Hubo and Doris, Steve and Molly, Hank and Nancy, Mark, Ryan and Allison, Will and Molly, Leah, Jessica, Katrin, Mary, Michael, Linda, Ellen, and Rob. Finally, thanks to Phyllis and Hubo, who pushed me along.

ABOUT THE AUTHOR

Clay G. Small is the former Senior Vice President and Managing Attorney for PepsiCo, Inc. He lives in Dallas, Texas, with his wife, Ellen, and teaches at Southern Methodist University.